HOLLYWOOD
IS NOT
HOME

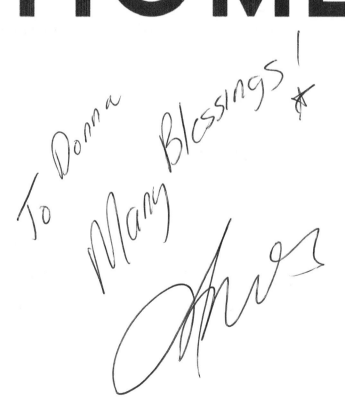

To Donna
Many Blessings! *

ENDORSEMENTS

I have long believed that if you can tell a great story, you earn the right to share your message, and the best life-lessons come from the best stories. Within these pages, you are going to take a journey with Annmarie and discover a lot about her, but even more, you are going to discover who you are and who you are meant to be.

JIM STOVALL
Best-selling author, *The Ultimate Gift*

Hollywood Is Not Home is a gift. The ease of digesting the content is remarkable. I haven't felt so close to a story's characters. Their developing is so subtle and down to earth, I begged for more.

Projecting the outcome of this story was impossible . . . waiting for the surprises, of which there are many.

Annmarie's approach to "Southernism" rings soft and true. One can hear the gentile South and feel the dynamics of a family and community who love each other.

A story well written. I look forward to the sequel.

GALE B. CRAWFORD
Award-Winning Woman Leader in Business,
Keynote Speaker and Seminar Leader for Women's Issues,
Retired Board Member of Financial and Educational Institutions

It is easy to say that we would never be Maggie, but how can we know if our Christian roots are deep enough until something begins to tear us from them? Roberts gives us plenty of reason to ponder on what it means to be true to oneself, to one's values—and most importantly, to one's Lord.

DR. TOM LEGRAND
University Chaplain and Professor

HOLLYWOOD IS NOT HOME

A NOVEL

ANNMARIE M. ROBERTS

Ambassador International
GREENVILLE, SOUTH CAROLINA & BELFAST, NORTHERN IRELAND

www.ambassador-international.com

HOLLYWOOD IS NOT HOME: A NOVEL

ISBN: 978-1-64960-074-5
eISBN: 978-1-64960-077-6
Library of Congress Control Number: 2021939886

Editing by Daphne Self
Cover design by Hannah Linder Designs
Interior typesetting by Dentelle Design
Digital Edition by Anna Riebe Raats

Scripture taken from the King James Version. Public domain.

AMBASSADOR INTERNATIONAL
Emerald House
411 University Ridge, Suite B14
Greenville, SC 29601, USA
www.ambassador-international.com

AMBASSADOR BOOKS
The Mount
2 Woodstock Link
Belfast, BT6 8DD, Northern Ireland, UK
www.ambassadormedia.co.uk

The colophon is a trademark of Ambassador, a Christian publishing company.

"We are all rich and famous in His eyes."

Annmarie M. Roberts

ACKNOWLEDGMENTS

I DEDICATE MY BOOK TO the Lord. He has shown me great strength amongst great strife.

He has guided my heart and hands to create a story about how we are all celebrities in His eyes. No matter your financial status, or public stature, you're worth millions to Him. He can work through you no matter the size of your wallet. Everyone has a God given gift, realizing your gift can make a better world.

To my family, Brad, Lena, and Hailey, you give me the smiles, encouragement, and love that I need every day to see how God works through others. I love you so. Thank you.

To Rosemarie, my sweet mother, who is in Heaven with the Lord. You are the reason I have my faith. You always said two things that meant so much to me:

"I have given you faith, not just religion, and that's what you'll need most in life."

"God will always be with you when you need Him. You just do all that you can to help yourself, and He will do the rest."

Mom and Dad raised nine kids. We never had much, but we had the two things that mattered most: faith and love.

To all the churches in the south, full of sweet old ladies, holding close families, blessed music, and amazing fellowship and worship, you fill my heart and confidence with faith and hope.

To two sweet ladies, Virginia and Kathy, for providing me with inspirational feedback. Your kindness touched my heart.

CHAPTER ONE

TOP O' THE MORNIN' TO YA, MAGGIE!

IT HAD BEEN SO LONG since she could just relax. Maggie treasured a slow sip of her green iced tea while the cool breeze coming off the ocean kissed her face. She heard only the peaceful sound of the waves sneaking up to bump the beach.

Maggie Malone, renowned Hollywood movie star, was a stunning twenty-seven-year-young lady with a fit body, shiny gorgeous blonde hair, and an inviting, youthful face. She plainly referred to herself as an actress.

Today she was enjoying a much-needed reprieve in her schedule as she lay pondering on a chaise lounge by the pool of her back deck.

She had a meeting tonight for a script review. That afternoon, she would possibly do some work in the greenhouse and read the paper. The thought of treating herself to playing video bowling or listening to some new Christian music was a consideration. Hmm, what to dare for lunch today—chicken salad on whole wheat or salad with grilled chicken? Having so much light fare, it was a wonder she wasn't floating. Dreaming of the chance to sneak off and have a greasy, cheesy, Chicago-style pizza and fries loaded with ranch dressing—yeah, that would not happen.

If she ordered in, it wouldn't be the same. Why was it that ordered-in food always tasted like the to-go box? Not to mention that everyone would know her order by the five o'clock news.

Maggie took a deep breath, shook off the bad thoughts, and tried to clear her mind.

It's a beautiful day outside; I should enjoy it.

Maggie sipped more of her tea then settled herself in the lounge chair as the tranquility quieted her.

Suddenly, two helicopters appeared out of nowhere. A man hung out of one of the choppers, camera aimed to take her picture. Another man yelled from a speaker in the other chopper. "Come on, Maggie, show us how you wear that swimsuit! Take a jump in the pool; do a pose! You know you love it! Give us something!"

Maggie jumped up, causing the glass of tea to fly out of her hand and spill all over her sky-blue swimsuit before smashing to the deck. She grabbed her towel and sprinted for the back door. The short distance to the door seemed like a mile. Maggie snatched open the door and slammed it behind her. Finally, the choppers soared beyond the perimeter of her property.

Retreating to a corner in the living room, sobbing, anxiety mixed with adrenaline made her feel overwhelmingly lightheaded. She leaned her back against the wall, sliding her whole body down to sit on the carpet.

Tormented persistently, why did they do this to her? They monopolized so much of her time. She only wanted a minute with no one around to judge. Why couldn't they give her that?

The feeling of violation raged on in her head as she hugged her towel close for support.

Maybe thousands of women were out today enjoying a day by the pool. Why should she be any different? Tolerant of their simple curiosities, it was clear that they ignored her unending small requests for a moment of privacy. She lost sight of what it meant to be a normal person, like the ability to stroll out the door for a walk.

Maggie stood up, wiped her face, and took a deep breath. She grabbed for her phone and called her manager, Susan.

"Susan, the choppers were back! I am standing here in the living room shaking. They came out of nowhere!" Maggie continued talking over the sound of Susan's responses.

"No, I did nothing to provoke it. I was enjoying the sun. No, they didn't see me nude; I was wearing a swimsuit." Maggie paused, feeling insulted by Susan's line of questioning.

"Hold on Maggie, now let's calm down. What swimsuit were you wearing? Did you look good, hair and makeup?"

"What difference does it make what swimsuit I was wearing? No, I didn't do my hair; it was up in a bun. Listen, I didn't call you to get an inquisition. Find out what magazine or TV show or whatever those choppers represent. I won't be granting any interviews with those people for a while. I'll call you later." Maggie slammed down the phone.

"Ridiculous!" She belted out with aggravation as she headed to the bathroom to clean up.

"Not a great start to the day!"

Maggie settled into a bubble bath desperate to relax while watching TV and enjoying a new glass of green iced tea. The *Celebrity Scoop* news show was running. Names and scandals flashed across the screen.

She lifted her glass, toasting the television sarcastically. "Nothing on me yet today, huh guys? Well, you're slacking! Where are the pool

photos? I hope you dropped those cameras in the ocean. Cheers!"
Taking another sip, Maggie shook her head in disagreement.

Putting her drink down, she shut off the television and tossed
the television remote across the room onto an armchair.

"Nice landing," Maggie commended herself on the throw. If only
she could find the peace that was lost by the pool. Her thoughts began
to wander as she leaned back and closed her eyes.

How long could she sit in this bathtub before anyone would notice she was missing?

Maggie deeply appreciated the feeling of time standing still.
Everything in her life was rush and hurry. Her eyes hesitated to peek
up at the clock. To her despair, bath time was over. She pulled on a
robe, grabbed her tea, and walked down the hall. Looking down at
the shriveled skin on her hands, she remembered the time when, as a
little girl, her dad told her that if she stayed in the bath too long, she'd
turn from a cucumber to a pickle.

It was the thought of her dad that caused her to stop at the entrance to another room. She retrieved a key from her robe pocket
and unlocked the door. She stepped into a place of solitude, grinning
with happiness.

This was a place where she felt at home being herself. The walls
were decorated with a memory lane of pictures and mementos from
her childhood: 4H club, high school proms, and family pictures with
her brother, her mother, and her father. The word "Faith" and the
influential poem "Footprints in the Sand" hung next to each other
on the wall.

Maggie looked around the room as memories flooded her mind.
Setting down her tea, she moved closer to the pictures. Immediately

she was drawn to a picture of Michael seated beside a much younger Maggie as they fished by a creek.

She picked up the picture, running her hand along the frame envisioning the memory.

Michael caught the biggest fish that day. He was so excited.

Smiling broadly at the thought of her brother, looking fondly at the photo, Maggie reminisced. "That was the big one, Mike. Good job. You made us all so proud."

Maggie stepped over to a picture of her mom and dad and picked up the picture, whispering words of endearment. "I miss you both so much; wish I was home with you more."

The longing for her family began to encourage the anxiety pecking away at her since the helicopters. Maggie turned to look at several bottles of medication resting on a table.

"Eeny, meeny, miny, moe. Which one today?" Her hand shook finally choosing a bottle, and then suddenly she slammed it back on the table. She tilted her head back, closing her eyes tightly attempting to black out tortured feelings about taking medication.

A bath wasn't calming enough. She'd never had to take this stuff when she first started acting. Paparazzi had pushed her here. No peace. Unmanageable anxiety. They were smothering her, and she couldn't breathe. She struggled; she just couldn't become another drug-loaded Hollywood burnout victim.

Maggie stared again at the photos, finding solace in being surrounded by visions of her life before stardom. However, today it was not enough. Taking a deep breath, she picked up the bottle and then popped a pill in her mouth. Washing it down with a swig of iced tea, she left the room, gently closing and locking the solitude behind her.

CHAPTER TWO
MOM'S PEP TALK

THE NEXT MORNING, MAGGIE CALLED Susan to assure that there was not a repeat of the advanced breach of privacy from the preceding day.

"Good morning, Maggie. What is the plan for the limo today?" Susan seemed ready to get it done.

"Let's try the two limos half an hour apart. Then bring the black SUV, sunroof open, with the mannequin in it. I will be in the second limo. I made it to the studio that way before without too much fuss." Maggie had it all mapped out.

"Will do." Susan agreed.

"Thanks. Oh yeah, also please call my mother and have her reach me on Syl's cell. Don't forget to remind her of the newest number; we changed it again last week."

"Sure thing, bye for now." Susan was off to take care of things.

Maggie put the phone down and headed into the bathroom. She looked at herself in the mirror, smiling at the image of a young woman dressed in a jogging suit and sporting very little makeup. "Hey there, stranger, fancy meeting you here. Do you remember me? The real me? The plain, normal Mags?"

She stared blankly into the mirror brushing her hair, overcome by a feeling of abandonment. "I miss you," she mouthed to her reflection. Then she set her brush down and walked out of the room to face reality.

Grabbing a bag, a coat, and a hat, and covering her eyes with a pair of huge sunglasses, she headed out the door. Her house was a medium sized contemporary beach home, gated with a private drive and security cameras. She had always felt that large mansions were created to bring attention to the owner, face it she had enough of that. *If you don't need the space, why waste it anyway?*

Maggie was greeted at the end of the stairs by her bodyguard, Syl, short for Sylvester. Syl was a tall, well-built black man with a bald head, a kind smile, and a soothing voice.

"Good Morning, Sunshine," Syl followed his greeting with an apology. "I am really sorry about the helicopters. Some creep down the street sold out, and the copters took off from his yard. I had no warning of their coming at all."

"It's okay, Syl. I know you would've warned me if you knew. Keep on your toes, please. They are getting more clever and devious each day," Maggie reminded him.

"Yes, Ma'am. Will do."

He held the limo door open for Maggie as she scanned the area, still uneasy.

Noticing her continued worry, Syl put his hand on her shoulder to reassure her. "Perimeter is clear. I double checked it all." Syl walked around to the driver's side. "Oh yeah, by the way, your trash is now protected. I hired a service that takes it clear across town to an incinerator there. They gave a hundred percent assurance that it will be secure." Sylvester sounded proud of himself.

"Sorry, Syl, that's not good enough. I want an incinerator installed in my home somehow. I want to burn my own trash," Maggie snapped. She had lost all patience with the world today.

Sylvester spoke up hesitantly, yet deliberately. "I know, Maggie, but remember that the city won't allow an incinerator in a private home here, something about the environment and dangers to surrounding houses."

Maggie could always sense when he was trying to approach her cautiously. Truly, Syl meant *It's not happening, lady!* So, she replied with more patience.

"Yes Syl, I remember now. Sorry." Maggie spoke to the back of Sylvester's head as he drove the limo down the driveway. "Honestly, I agree with them. I am surprised we all aren't covered in some toxic layer in one way or another." Maggie paused. "Well, let's do this. I will use the service for now, but I want my trash split up into two parts, delivered to two sides of town, and incinerated separately in case we do get a privacy leak somewhere. Thank you, Syl, for always trying to watch out for me."

Syl stopped just before the end of the driveway and turned back to Maggie with a reassuring grin on his face.

"You know I have your back, girl. Protecting you from them is the easy part." He became more serious as he continued. "You know what the hard part is?"

Maggie, a bit curious, sat back against the leather seat, smiling at him. "Yeah, what is that?"

Syl slowly winked. "Protecting them from you." Then he continued to drive.

They both laughed, but the humor was short-lived. The noise of loud voices accompanied by blinding flashes of light met them at the end of the driveway. A group of twenty members of the paparazzi, frantically waving cameras, crowded the limo. Demanding words spoken at a fast pace filled the air, "Put the window down, Maggie. Come on, show us that look! Come on Maggie; give us one for the covers!" The demands persisted. "Hey, Maggie, how's the script going? Are you requesting that they change it again?" Another of the relentless voices asked, "Who's the new man in your life? Or are you switching sides?"

Maggie put her hat on, pulling it down taunt. She hoped the dark limo windows would shadow not only her face, but her disagreeable attitude. She pleaded with Syl in exhausted frustration, "Not today, Syl. Just go."

Syl made sweeping hand gestures to the paparazzi to motion them away from the car. He rolled his window down slightly to remark, "All right, not today, guys. Move on."

As Syl maneuvered the car down the road, his cell phone rang, and he answered it.

"Hello, sweetie. How's my favorite lady today?" he greeted the caller. "Yeah, rough morning. Already two choppers and the usual mess at the gate. You know Maggie, though; she's a trooper. I'll get her." Syl spoke out to Maggie in the back. "Maggie, it's Mom."

Maggie accepted his phone. A maternal pep talk right now was much needed, mom always had a way of putting everything in perspective.

"Hello, Honey, tough start today? Are you okay? Did you try your breathing exercises in your quiet room?" Concern sounded in her mom's voice.

"Hi Mom, it is so good to hear your voice. Yes, I did go settle down in my quiet room," Maggie answered reassuringly.

Her mom was the sweetest of old ladies. She kept her hair styled in gray tidy waves of curls close to her face. Not much of a fancy dresser, her style consisted of casual mixed with sensible-meets-old-fashioned. She carried a kind face which she touched with light bits of makeup, but never too much. Her favorite pastimes were talking on the phone and drinking hot tea which sat on a doily placed on the table next to her. Maggie couldn't believe she still had doilies in her house. It was so Mom.

"Maggie, please remember you're our Mags! No matter what, you are still the same sweet girl we love. You can be anything you want to be. You can change your life if you want to. I worry so much about you. People always pressuring and demanding so much from you just because they think they have the right to."

Maggie listened while she peered out the window of the limo as the vehicle came to a stop. Her eyes were drawn to a mother with her little girl, around six years old, talking to a floral vendor. The lady bought a tulip and handed it to the little girl, hugging and kissing her as they smiled and laughed together.

Maggie finally responded to her mom, who had continued to talk while Maggie's thoughts had wandered.

"I know Mom, I know. I would love a chance to make it all go away, but I can make a difference. If my acting brings a story that inspires people's hearts, giving them some kind of comfort, bringing them hope and help, then it is worth it to me. I am lucky to have landed some roles that have done this already." Maggie reassured her mom.

"Okay, honey, but your family is here for you. We understand the public pressure you feel. The paparazzi show up here, too, on most days. No paparazzi around today," her mom reported. "It's a good thing we live in the desert, most of them simply start to melt and go away. Your father gets the lawn hose out once in a while and starts spraying them. Funny thing, I don't think he is trying to comfort their heat exhaustion. That hose can be strong if wheeled right." Mom and Maggie enjoyed a good laugh at the thought of Maggie's dad "accidentally" spraying the persistent paparazzi.

"Mom," Maggie said, "I am so sorry for what my job puts on you and Dad. I know it hasn't been easy for you both. I worry about Michael, too. He's so busy trying to save lives at the hospital. I can't believe he has to screen his patients for stalkers faking illnesses trying to ask questions about me. He should be healing people, not dealing with that!"

"Don't worry about your brother," Mom responded after taking another sip from her tea. "He is tough like you. You know, he gave the last weirdo a shot that gave him diarrhea for the whole day," Mom giggled to Maggie. "Now remember, that didn't happen; you didn't hear that from me. Michael would be so upset if he knew I told you. He stands up for you Maggie. He is so proud of his baby sister and loves you very much."

Maggie wrapped up the conversation with Mom as her limo was about to enter the studio gates. "Hey, Mom, thanks for the talk. You always know what to say to make me feel better. I've got to go now; we are at the studio. Take care of Dad. I love you both."

Maggie hung up the phone and shouted to Syl, "Bring it on; let's go get them!"

Syl sounded out with cheer. "That's the spirit, Maggie. You go, girl!"

CHAPTER THREE

GETTING YOUR GOOD SIDE

IT WAS ANOTHER LONG GRUELING day at the studio, and Maggie was on the thirteenth take of a short scene. Technical difficulties were parading on her nerves, which weren't yet fully recovered from the shenanigans of the morning.

Maggie yelled out to her director across the room. "Jimmy, come on! What is with this today? We should be halfway done with five scenes by now!"

"Sorry, Luv, bit of a computer freeze or fry or something. We will have it squared away in no time," Jimmy answered, trying to smooth over Maggie's temperament.

Jimmy had a strong British accent that identified his citizenship instantly. He was quirky and loved chewing gum. Although young and handsome, he could be terribly annoying. Maggie tolerated him; he was likable for some reason.

He walked over, putting his arm around her shoulder. The other arm held a clipboard of papers. He peered at her with a cheeky grin. "You know the catering trolley has that pasta salad you adore."

Changing the subject to food had been a smart move on Jimmy's part. Maggie loved food; it was a comfort to her. Unfortunately, having to look a size zero but fitting a size five wasn't easy, so she had to work out at least three to four times a week to keep up. Self-indulgence in comfort food was dangerous, so for Maggie, refraining was key.

Maggie shrugged her shoulders and let out a sigh, shooting Jimmy a playful look. "Why Jimmy, you're the devil!" Then she finished in jest turning her head away, "But I love you anyways." They both laughed as Maggie headed towards the catering truck.

She noticed Stan, the cameraman, deep in conversation on a cell phone. He was clearly upset, throwing his arms around wildly while talking loudly. He hung up the call in anger. Maggie approached him to see if he was okay.

"Sorry to be nosy, Stan, is something wrong?"

Stan turned his head away slightly, as if not to worry her, but Maggie touched his shoulder. "It's okay, really."

"We have been at it for weeks with Grace's doctors. They can't seem to get it right. Now they aren't sure if the medicine is working, and they want to run more tests. They want her to go somewhere in Minnesota to a special clinic," Stan pleaded with the situation. "I can't leave now. I almost lost my seniority last time. I need my job, Maggie. The medical bills are piling up."

Maggie spoke without hesitation. "You will always have a job as long as I do. You go, and I will make a call to my friend at the union. Your job will be here. Also, I insist you fly out in my private jet to the clinic. See my man, Syl, while we are on break. He will take care of the details." Maggie nodded at Syl, who had been watching the entire time.

Stan began to tear up, and he put his arms around Maggie, giving her a squeeze. "Maggie, you're an angel; I don't know how to thank you for this."

Maggie didn't let go of the hug. Stan gently pulled away, taking a deep breath, he tried to get a hold of himself. He looked over to Maggie with a concerned look on his face, locking eyes with hers and saying softly, "She is my little girl, Maggie. She's my world."

Maggie scooped up his hands in hers to reassure him. "I know, sweetie, and you go take good care of her and love her with all your might. Have faith and be strong for her."

Stan settled with newfound hope, started to walk away. Maggie called to him once more.

"Hey, Stan?" Stan turned back to Maggie as he tried wiping his tears. "You could do something for me." Maggie comedically crunched her face and crossed her eyes. "Always film my good side, okay?"

Stan smiled and nodded. "Maggie, you only have a good side!" Now with the mood lightened, Maggie continued her mission to the food truck.

☆☆☆

Later that night as the limo headed home Syl was driving while singing old jazz songs with the radio. Maggie watched the lights of the city going by. She sat slumped against the seat, her mind on going.

Ugh! It was an awfully long day. A four-hour scheduled shoot turned into eight hours on account of technical issues. Feeling exhausted, she wished she could get out of the premiere tonight. The bright side was without that break, she might have missed helping Stan. It was a great privilege to do her part for him. It must be devastating to have such a sick child. She was just a little girl with the world at her feet. Today Maggie kept counting her problems until she talked to Stan. Unexpected prospective revealed; her problems were nothing in comparison.

Soon they arrived home. Syl got out of the limo and walked around to let Maggie out.

"Not much action at the gate tonight; maybe they lost us on the ride home," Maggie mused as she exited the limo.

"Mags, why don't you let me open the door for you?" Syl asked as he shook his head in wonder.

"Some things a girl has got to do for herself, at least once in a while. Besides, Syl, you are always there for me when I need you. Sometimes you deserve a break."

"A break? Really, Mags, you know that I love working for you. There's nothing I'd rather be doing."

Maggie headed up the stairs to the house while Syl stood at the bottom.. "Geez, Louise! Syl, come on really? You know that playing pool and dining your lady are your favorite things to do. You can't pull the wool over these eyes." Maggie then stopped suddenly half-way up the stairs, all joking aside, the realization of how her career demands personally affected Syl set in.

Syl's smile faded, and he queried with concern in his voice. "Everything okay, Mags?"

She looked down at him with a worried expression. "Please don't let this life of mine make you miss yours. Stay true to yourself and don't change."

Syl smirked and winked to ward off the seriousness in her voice, but Maggie wasn't biting. Respecting her directness, he nodded in agreement and replied. "Mags, I won't, and thanks for reminding me."

Maggie traveled slowly the rest of the way up the stairs. The day had worn her out. She had barely opened the door to the house when Syl shot out one last message to her. "Ready at nine then, Mags?"

Without looking back to Syl, she answered flatly, "Nine it is then, looking fine at nine." She closed the door behind her.

CHAPTER FOUR
RUNNING SCARED

PREMIERE TIME CAME FAST.

"Wow, looking fabulous tonight, Maggie!"

"It's great to see you!"

The red-carpet reporters were in a frenzy. Maggie was nervous on the inside but didn't let it show on the outside. Her smile fought off drowning by an overcoming dizzy feeling as camera flashes went off inches from her face. She just kept waving to the crowd while balancing her clutch purse, impatient thoughts streaming through her mind with each flash.

Smiling on, she let them shoot away, tempted to hit the pushy ones with her clutch but she kept her composure instead.

Maggie was stopped by John Lane, reporter from *Celebrity Lane*, the hottest celebrity talk show in prime time. He coaxed her into a quick red-carpet interview, so they stepped aside receiving a cue from his camera man.

"We are here with Maggie Malone on the premiere of her new movie. Thank you, Maggie; you play a remarkably convincing character in this movie. Where did you draw your emotion from?"

Maggie replied kindly, focused on the certainty of her words. "Thank you, John. I developed the will of this character after spending time with some amazing women struggling with breast cancer. What would it feel like to be in their shoes? These women are tremendously courageous. Learning about their daily struggles and powerful strength to survive gave me unending admiration for them. Each one of them represent personal inspiration to fill my performance, I am blessed to have met them."

John was taken back by Maggie's response—not the standard fluff reply. "Okay then . . . wonderful to hear how you connected with your character and hats off to you for your performance."

Maggie thanked him and excused herself, continuing down the red carpet. As she headed to her seat, she felt a tug on her arm.

Syl looked at the arm puller, Susan, Maggie's manager. "Susan, chill; what's going on?"

Susan was clearly upset, saying under her breath to Maggie, "I need a word with you, little lady!" She ushered Maggie aside discreetly. "Let's stop in the ladies' room for a minute." Maggie was confused, but she complied.

They both shuffled into the ladies' room. Susan made sure the room was empty by checking the stalls. They were alone.

Maggie's patience began to wear thin. "Susan, what is all this about?"

Susan cut her off. "Are you crazy saying what you said to that reporter?"

Maggie still didn't understand. "What do you mean? I thought I handled it well?"

"Really, Maggie, you were laying it on a pile thick suggesting you are **blessed** and all that! Too close to the cause. Do you have any idea of what religious references, even in the slightest context, can do to a star's career? Why didn't you stick to their cancer struggle and care? You had them eating out of your hands!" yelled Susan infuriated, pacing hard, throwing her hands about.

Maggie scowled at being lectured; she turned away and rubbed her forehead, angry and frustrated. Finally, she had enough of Susan's berating. She slammed her hand down on the counter. Targeting her angry eyes, wildly shaking her head in disagreement, she let Susan have it.

"Susan, I am tired of trying to hide my faith in God, especially how I reference or not reference being blessed—worrying about how it sounds. I refuse to hide the reason I am here today. Without my faith, I wouldn't be here, and you wouldn't have a job!"

Susan composed herself. She tried to calm Maggie, reaching to touch her hand. They were getting loud, she had to quiet the situation before they drew attention. "Calm down, someone will hear you."

Maggie jerked away her hand from Susan. "No, that is exactly what I am talking about. Why is it that Oscar winners, Noble prize winners, and presidents can thank God for their success in front of millions of people, but I can't say I am blessed?"

Susan put her hands on Maggie's shoulders focused on getting her point across. "Because you are not any of those people today or yesterday, and you want to be one tomorrow."

Maggie pulled away and began to walk out. She grabbed the door handle, still angry, and turned back to Susan. "Susan, I know you are top-shelf smart about this business. I wouldn't have hired you otherwise. You and I have accomplished a tremendous amount together. You have made a fortune off me. I have never questioned you about your beliefs. Stop and think. Perhaps it's time you count your own blessings."

Maggie stormed out. She didn't witness how Susan behaved after her abrupt exit, but she probably already knew. Susan wouldn't bother batting an eye at Maggie's behavior but instead would have turned her attention to her dress and lipstick. As a true player, Susan was known to keep her head in the game no matter the fuss.

The rest of the evening took off like a jet. The premiere was a hit, and the critics raved about Maggie's performance.

In the morning, the responses flooded in even before Maggie's teatime. She basked in pride. Phone rings and text messages chimed melodiously in by the dozen. All her producers, writers, directors, and fellow stars were trying to reach her to congratulate her.

Maggie sat in her robe and slippers with her feet up. Hearing all the rings and notification sounds, she didn't rush to answer a one of them. Instead, she sat smiling, whistling to herself and bobbing her toes up and down. It was a pinch of glory under enjoyment.

No shooting on the set tonight meant time in her quiet room reading the reviews. The movie critics credited her portrayal of the daily struggles many women face fighting breast cancer. Maggie concentrated on only one thing: they took notice, which brought attention to the cause.

She began to think about all the women that shared their fight with her. Hopefully, their personal battle stories had reached the world. Praying for the success of the movie, Maggie arranged with the studio for part of the proceeds to go directly to these women for their medical bills. She allocated another portion to breast cancer research.

Maggie was truly proud to know these women. She started to cry, touched by the memories of time spent with them. As tears of happiness slowly ran down her cheeks, she said out loud. "They are the stars, not me!" Before she left the room, she looked towards the ceiling in gratitude. "Thank You, Lord."

In between filming, Maggie cherished personal down time. She hoped to go for a run on the beach and maybe do some shopping. Syl was already working out all the details. An uneventful excursion seemed reasonable after a ton of strategic planning. Nevertheless, the spotlight of her great review now made the planning more delicate.

Maggie began to stretch out. She started pacing, ready to run. She made a quick call to Syl. "Syl, is the coast clear? How is the beachfront?" Maggie shaded her eyes against the light of the sun, and she caught a glimpse of Syl on the beach.

Like developing a spy mission, Syl found an out of the view corner near the beach showers. He had binoculars at the ready and kept his motions low key.

"All is clear; I am getting the men in position. Be ready."

Maggie held the phone, awaiting instruction. Finally, Syl cued.

"Secured, come on down."

Maggie took off down the back stairs toward the beach. She put in her earphones just as she hit the sand. Her stride matched the beating of her heart. Her breathing was off, but she kept running. Anxiety caused by leaping out into public awakened in her.

Suddenly, she felt as if she were being watched. She focused her eyes for a better look, thinking she had seen something from a house up on the hill. Could it be a cameraman? She looked again and again, but she couldn't be sure. She started to panic, pulled out her earphones and called Syl.

"Syl, do you see him? The house up there on the hill—big black camera shooting away at me! Can you please handle this? Don't you see him?" Maggie yelled, clearly out of breath.

"Mags, I don't see anyone; it's clear. There is no one."

Maggie begged, "Please, Syl, go up there—last house on the hill, please!"

Syl proceeded without hesitation. "Okay, Mags, I am on it."

Maggie stopped running. She turned away from the homes and looked out over the ocean. Her breathing was erratic, and she started to feel faint. She couldn't seem to shake the anxiety. As the waves slammed violently against the shore, she bent forward and grabbed her knees, desperately wheezing for a breath. Nothing was helping; everything she tried seemed useless.

She slowly stood up and walked back to her house, pulling her hat down taunt over her face. As she got closer to the house, she anxiously ran the last few feet slamming the door behind her. She leaned her back against the wall, sliding down slowly to the floor. Her arms folded over her knees, her head tucked down on her arms, she began to sob angrily, screaming, "Why, Why?"

A knock at the back door interrupted her. She jumped up and wiped her face with her sleeve. It was Syl.

"Mags, there was no one there. I promise we checked everywhere. The only one there was an old lady and her dog watching game shows. I don't know what you saw."

Maggie took a short hug from Syl. She rubbed her eyes, pushed the sweat-damped hair from her face, and looked up to Syl. "Sorry,

Syl, I don't know what I saw." Maggie admitted feeling doubtful as she shook her head.

Syl put his hands on her shoulders expressing his concern. "Mags, you don't look good. Are you okay? Do you need a doctor?"

She walked to the fridge, grabbed a bottle of water, and took a seat in her kitchen. "No, I am okay. It was just a little panic attack. It's the added pressure with the review and interviews coming up. Anyway, you can go, Syl. I will be fine. I just need to get some rest and shake it off."

Syl, not convinced, replied, "Okay, but if you need me, I will be just a second away. Just call, okay?"

Maggie smiled. "Will do, thank you again, Syl."

Syl left, and Maggie retreated into the shower. Anxiety battered. She stood still, hot water running over her. Exhausted and overcome with emotional numbness, she barely felt the warmth. Finishing her shower, Maggie lay down in bed. Seconds passed—she was asleep.

CHAPTER FIVE

SAVING FACE–FAN MAIL AND FAITH

THE PHONE RANG, INTERRUPTING MAGGIE'S peaceful nap.

"Hey, Susan, three interviews lined up in two weeks? Wow, that's great," Maggie mumbled still half asleep.

"Yes, girl you are ready to go! How about the overall equipment refresh we discussed?"

"Wait, what do you want me to do? Didn't we talk about this already? Yes, I thought about it, but I decided against it." Maggie was firm.

"Oh, dear, for once, don't be so dramatic. It's just a nip here and a tuck there. Lasers keep it clean and neat"

"I know, I know. Anyway, how is it possible that plastic surgery would heal in time for the interviews? Lasers?" Maggie couldn't even think of this now, "Susan, I need to call you back."

Maggie hung up the phone imagining that Susan was probably still talking.

Susan could never understand Maggie's side of the argument. Maggie knew that surgery could make her look new, younger, and fresher. However, she would be same person on the inside. Looking in the mirror each day at someone else's face, who would she really be? What was hers was hers! She had to hang on to what she could. Susan would recycle every part of her if it meant Maggie would never be out of the spotlight.

Tears began to roll down Maggie's face; a suggestion of plastic surgery was the last straw to a difficult day.

Maggie lay still. "Am I losing me? I promised not to lose me."

She closed her eyes, pushing out all the tears she had left. Her exhausted mind forced her to sleep; she drifted off just as the last tear rolled to the pillow.

The day off was harder on her than she had planned. The much-needed sleep was welcoming. That night went smoothly, just a signing with Susan at a private event. No issues, thank goodness.

The next morning came along quickly; it had been a late night. Maggie sat at her computer, clicking away on the mouse. Her hair was in a messy, shambled ponytail. She sported a flannel shirt thrown over a tank top, black leggings, and her black-rimmed glasses hung off her nose. Dressed in comfortable grunge, she sat less than impressed by her junk emails.

"Wow, look at this trash." She squinted and moved closer to the computer screen. "Is this me? Or is that my head on someone else's body? Yeah right, I wish that was my body!" She laughed out loud. "I can't believe how much time people have on their hands. What's next? Alien antennas?"

Maggie shook her head, still looking at her computer with wonder.

She always felt strongly about one thing. The amazing positive change that could be made in the world if obsessed celebrity minions would instead focus their creative efforts on helping others in need.

Maggie moved her mouse to her fan website email inbox. She was always happy to answer any and all fan mail. She read the first email out loud.

"Dear Maggie, do you really believe in God? Thanks for the reply. Mitchell Cassidy, NYC, NY Age 11."

Maggie moved her hands to her computer keyboard slowly. She paused, looked up to the ceiling, cracked a smile, and then looked down again to type.

"Dear Mitchell, Yes, with all my heart! Sincerely, Maggie Malone."

Hitting send on the keyboard, she sat back in her chair pondering what Susan would say.

Maggie spent hours typing reply letters to fans, mostly by email. She always gave special attention to letters from children and the elderly; those were answered with handwritten letters by postal mail. In Mitchell's case the reply couldn't wait by postal mail; she sensed urgency and had to respond immediately.

After hours at the computer, Maggie was just about finished. She tossed herself backward onto her couch plopping down with the last letter in hand. She smiled and raised the letter above her head, turning her pen round and round, as she read her response out loud. "In closing, Marie, I wish you a fast and speedy recovery from your hip replacement surgery. I am sure you and Bernie will be dancing again in no time. Many blessings, Maggie Malone."

Maggie hoped that sweet handwritten messages would touch Marie's heart. As a child, she loved how special she felt when someone would send her a handwritten letter. The time put into handwritten letters was worth the effort. It felt like the senders embedded their feelings into the pen strokes, the care curved up and down in letters of cursive.

Maggie smiled, sat up, and finished signing the letter. She folded it into an envelope and placed it in a basket. The basket already held about fifty letters.

Putting down the pen, she began rubbing her hands to work out the cramps. She should have been resting before her busy schedule, but her words might provide the lift a fan really needed the day her letter arrived.

Looking at the clock, Maggie jumped up. "Shoot, late again. I've got to get ready for that interview." She hurried towards her bedroom door.

An hour later, Syl brought the limo around, and Maggie headed out of her house and down the stairway.

"Hey there, handsome. How's the horde by the front—on a scale of one being unusually tame to ten being super annoying?" Maggie smiled with a little laugh following.

Syl replied, remarking on her tone. "Well hello, it looks like someone is feeling peppy."

Maggie smiled in response to Syl as she got closer to the limo. "Yes, I actually feel pretty good. I answered some letters earlier today. I have the basket upstairs, as a matter of fact. Can you make sure they get to the mail please?"

Syl readily complied. "Okay, little lady, I will. By the way, in answer to your first question, I don't believe our audience up front has had their afternoon coffee. They are a little slow tonight. We might have a smooth exit." Syl chuckled a bit while opening the car door for Maggie.

Soon the limo proceeded down the drive and out the gate without too much trouble. Halfway to the TV studio, Maggie picked up her phone.

Syl was up front singing along to a fifties hit; his musical interests varied widely. Regardless of the genre, Maggie found his singing so uplifting. She laughed quietly to herself at Syl rocking back and forth, singing away.

Syl you're quite a guy; you make me laugh!

Maggie looked down to the phone and dialed. "Hey, Mom. Today is the first interview. It's been awhile since a request for one. I just want to be myself. Of course, Susan is trying to get me to be more politically correct, more Hollywood, more star, blah, blah, you know."

Mom finally got the chance to reply. "Mags, you can't lose yourself in all this. Remember when you got your first role. The producer cast you because he saw how passionate you were for the role, how much you felt for the woman who was burned. He told you that you had a natural way of connecting with the character. You know that this is you, the real you, that accomplished this—not someone they made you into for more money and stardom. You will do fine, honey. I have faith in you."

Maggie gave in to agreement. "Yes, Mom, you're right; you're always right." She appreciated her mom's guidance, finding reassurance in her voice. Now only if her nerves could be convinced.

"Mom, are you there? Mom?" Maggie called out as the line went dead. The phone had dropped the call. She hung up the phone, yelling at it. "Ah, the coverage in this area stinks; my carrier always drops calls here." Asking up to Syl, "Hey, Syl, do you have any service on your phone?"

ANNMARIE M. ROBERTS   37

Syl checked his phone. "Sorry Mags, no can do. I don't know what's up with the coverage in this area. Supposedly it's being worked on."

The rest of the ride to the studio turned boring. Of course, once phone reception was live, Susan called to make sure Maggie was en route. Her wardrobe instructions were followed by a Maggie "pump up" speech delicately layered with yet another list of do's and don'ts. Would Susan ever stop talking? Not a chance! She even had the nerve to start on the surgery spiel again.

"Maggie, plastic surgery is so common. All the stars start nipping and tucking even in their teen years. To them, you are already an old woman because you haven't freshened up a bit. You should reconsider this, honey, because it is dog eat dog out there. You don't want to be the old droopy-faced poodle."

Maggie replied in a snappish manner. "No, Susan. I don't need it. I was reminded today that who I am got me here. If I give in to all the changes, I won't be me. I refuse to play someone other than myself in my own life."

The conversation ended quickly again with disagreement. Maggie rode the rest of the way to the studio, just staring out the window. She enjoyed the sight of a beautiful old church. The sun reflected through the stain glass windows projecting a rainbow across the sidewalk. Rainbows always felt like hope to Maggie, hope and inspiration. A block later she saw a dad with his toddler son on his shoulders. They were pretending to be airplanes soaring along, arms out gliding through the wind, both of their smiles lifting their flight. It reminded her of her father and her brother in his youth.

Syl stopped the limo at a red light, allowing the observation of a family in a restaurant bowing to pray before their meal. Prayer at meals—Maggie was delighted that people still practiced this in public. Again, the limo slowed for traffic, she admired two young people who appeared to be in love. They were seated on a bench, conversing with each other in sign language. They kissed softly and embraced one another. Maggie sat in awe with a grin on her face matching the same feeling in her heart.

She rested her head against the window, contemplating what she had seen. Were the everyday magical wonders of life out of her reach because of her fame?

Peering out of the windows was so important to Maggie. However, she was always so afraid someone would recognize her. The old catch twenty-two again. The darkened windows that kept her protected from the world were the same ones that shaded her vision to it. How she longed to walk through a park or take a bike ride like a normal, non-famous person. The pressure of publicity conjured invisibility jealousy.

Maggie loved her job as an actress, but stardom was a different beast. There was a price to pay for fame. *Does the loss of my freedom weigh heavier than the rewards of stardom?* She struggled with this question daily, never answering it. She swore to put it out of her mind, such thoughts were non-productive. Someday the stubborn question would demand an answer, fear of her reply; she kept it at bay for now.

Arriving at the studio, Syl opened the limo door for Maggie, she sat still in daydream.

"Mags?" Syl extended his hand to her. She looked up, startled from her reverie.

"Oh, sorry, Syl. My mind was distracted. That was a great drive by the way." Maggie slowly became alert, grabbing her bag and getting out of the limo.

"Really, Mags?" Syl puzzled with her reply, shot an odd look her way. "All that traffic and slowly squeaking through that last intersection? Okay. I am glad you had fun."

Maggie was just about to get out of the car when her phone rang. Guessing it was her mom, she smiled as she looked down to confirm the number.

"Hi, Mom, sorry I lost signal back there."

"Mags, I was just going to tell you that we love you no matter what. Honey, where is your faith? Let your faith guide your heart and your heart guide your words. You will be great!"

Maggie didn't answer her mom's question. It was the hardest question anyone had ever asked her. Where was her faith? Why had she put it aside—especially when she needed it most?

CHAPTER SIX
PROUD OF YOU

MAGGIE WAS ABOUT TO FACE her most critical interviewer. Could any of the questions be as hard to answer as Mom's? She had to be ready. This interview would reach thousands of viewers. Game on.

"Maggie, are you there? Did I lose you again?" Mom called out to Maggie from the phone.

"No, Mom, I am still here. We've arrived at the studio. I have to go. Love you, Mom. Thank you."

"Oh, okay dear; love you, too. Let's talk again soon, please."

Maggie hung up the phone but continued staring at it. The conversation with her mom was whirling around in her head. Again, Mom had a way of making a person think.

She rushed out of the car and into the back door of the studio. Syl followed, escorting her directly to makeup. It was a chance to calm her anxiety down and build her gumption up.

Soon it was time for the interview with Carly Carlotta, TV's most demanding interrogator. This lady had mighty word whipping power. She made grown men cry, distinguished women storm off the set, and even presidents refuse to answer. An interview with her was like playing chess with a master, never knowing what move was next. On the upside, if a person played her cards right, Carly's interview could set her career up for life. It was all about being a smooth smart talker with conviction. However a person came out of the ring, fighting or being dragged, decided whether she ever had a decent interview again. Carly drew the lines of challenge, and then she crossed them.

Maggie was sitting on a couch in the green room preparing for her interview. She reviewed some of the prearranged questions, all standard stuff: How do you pick your roles? Have you turned down roles? How do you prepare for a role?

Maggie knew that Carly had left out the meat on this shopping list. For instance, the questions that she would snake bite Maggie with. The spot-on personal hits about Maggie's faith, family, and lack of husband and children. Not to mention deluging on her constant role choice involving characters who struggle with illness, loss, and despair. Will she answer them with Susan's preconditioned replies? Dare she use free will or fall to the industry standard—telling them what they want to hear.

Beginning to perspire as her nerves twitched, Maggie thought of facing Carly. This interview could make or break her future. Shaking some, she sipped from her water bottle. Grabbing her purse, she rattled around in it for her pills. Finding the bottle, she read the label, and stopped. Closing her eyes and taking a deep breath, she threw the pill bottle back in her purse. She stood up, turned toward the couch, and knelt, leaning her elbows on it. Folding her hands to her face, she began to pray.

"Dear Lord, please give me the strength to remember who I am and not to forget You and what You have done for me."

Maggie remained still. Her eyes were closed, and her hands were calm when a knock sounded at the door. She ignored it.

The door opened softly as the stage attendant peered in then quickly looked away out of respect for Maggie's prayer. "Five minutes, Ms. Malone." Then he slowly closed the door again. Maggie stood up, looking at herself as she walked towards the mirror. She dusted off her clothes, fluffed her hair, and stated confidently, "My faith is right here, Mom, where it has always been."

Hot lights and nervous sweating didn't mix; Maggie's makeup was already starting to run. The makeup attendant was called to dust Maggie's face.

"Geez, just getting started, and I'm already melting," Maggie teased nervously, attempting to break the ice.

"It's perfectly normal, Maggie; just relax. We will get along fine," Carly encouraged, as she sat still while her hair and makeup people freshened her up.

Maggie wanted to believe Carly's reassuring kindness, impressed with how she conducted herself. She was cool, like a breeze flowing off the ocean. Appropriately refined, dressed immaculately in a navy blue suit with a tan camisole. She wasn't a bit overdone, nor the slightest bit old-fashioned. A striking kind face with small beady eyes. At first glance, one might think she was sweet, but Maggie wasn't fooled.

Her angelic appearance was all for show—don't be fooled. Every actor knew she could tear down even the classiest of them in less than a minute flat. Hitting them where it hurts with an approach as sly as a fox with a strike like a cobra. Maggie's interview was scheduled to last fifteen minutes. An exceedingly long fifteen minutes. How would she survive?

Maggie turned her attention to her water bottle. Dry mouth had already set in. She took a drink, set the bottle down, and folded her hands in her lap. After a few seconds, she unfolded her hands forcing them to rest to either side. So much for trying to shake off the nerve twisters!

Finally, she found fun distraction in finger tapping a rhythm erratically forming in her mind. The words to the piece were, *"I hate interviews with mean ladies in navy and tan. I hope making me cry is not her plan!"* Aligning them to rhyme brought Maggie's eyebrows up as she was amused by her drummed up talent.

Finally, she noticed that Carly was staring right at her, watching her jittery physical twitching the whole time. Maggie's tapping stopped immediately, and she smirked at Carly before placing her hands back in her lap very still.

Maggie grimaced. Nice, now she looked like a nervous Nelly. Carly must be convinced she already had Maggie right where she wanted her.

Carly winked at Maggie as the camera turned on, introduction time for her viewers.

"Well, hello and welcome. We have a great treat in store for you today. We are sitting here with Maggie Malone, star of the recently acclaimed blockbuster hit, *A Choice?* Welcome, Maggie."

Maggie, sounding calm, responded, "Thank you for having me. It's great to be here."

"Well, little lady, you have certainly been busy. Great new movie, top reviews, rumors of awards, and choice movie deals headed your way. Things seem golden for you. How are you feeling about all this?"

"Carly, I feel great. I have been working hard for a long time, so it's great to have the opportunities . . . "

As Maggie was speaking, Carly leaned forward, straightening her suit coat. Maggie knew what was coming. *Here she goes!* she thought right before Carly cut her off abruptly. "That's great. So nice, dear."

Tone set, start with a childlike approach with a flair of condescending manner. Maggie geared up.

Carly continued to beat her drum like a one-woman show. "What do you think about the women you have portrayed? How do they keep fighting? Do you think it's entirely physical, or is there a spiritual fight they are handling as well?"

Carly sat back, squinting her eyes as she plastered an intrigued look on her face.

Maggie had to think quickly. *Here we go. No more than five minutes into the interview, and she's going spiritual. Okay, ways to handle this . . .* She could suddenly leave. No, that would look bad. She could avoid the question or give a false answer like Susan told her to. Try to change the subject? What to do?

Maggie started to rethink her decision not to take that pill in the green room. No, she had this. She wasn't going to bow out. Finally, she was ready to reply. It had only been seconds, but it seemed like forever. Carly waited with a puzzled expression on her face, her head cocked to one side with daggers of impatience emanating from her eyes.

Maggie approached steadily, fighting off the sting of Carly's verbally whipped beginning.

"Well, first let me finish what I started to say. It was such a great opportunity to make a difference. I am very touched by how we completed this movie with such great respect and honor for the women represented. Their stories continue to reach more than just the audiences."

She continued without hesitation. "And yes, to your question. I believe even you would turn to your spirituality, Carly, if you needed it to fight breast cancer. To endure such a fight, one has to have strength way beyond physical endurance."

Maggie had just made the last tag. You're it, you're it! Like two kids on a playground. She took a deep breath sitting back slowly, waiting for Carly's next move.

Carly was clearly taken back by the power of Maggie's words. She straightened her glasses, cocked her head back straight up sternly, and crossed her legs. Finally, after swallowing hard, she spoke up.

"Yes, well, it would seem that you know a bit about spirituality these days, Maggie. You did mention faith in a past interview as I recall. Are you presently expressing faith and religion, and can you tell us more about your personal beliefs? We are all very curious to hear more about what you believe."

Carly smiled confidently now, looking like she had won this round. She set Maggie up for the ultimate cliffhanger.

Maggie very seriously replied, "Yes, Carly. I would love to discuss my faith."

Carly dropped her jaw.

Maggie knew what she was doing. She plunged right in, "It's time to realize that people draw strength from things we cannot always see. That's faith."

Carly, still in shock, didn't interrupt.

"Carly, I have faith in you. Faith that you will come out to see the movie, along with all of today's viewers. I have faith you will be moved to ask about how all the women in the film are doing today with their fight against breast cancer. Let's talk about how you and the viewers can help them with donations. After all, this is the point of the movie."

After Maggie's confident reply, Carly ran out of tough question ammo. The rest of the interview went off without a hitch. As a matter of fact, the interview finished before the fifteen-minute time slot was filled.

Carly had purposely avoided the daggering questions about Maggie's love life and kids, having lost her footing to force on. Better for her to retreat with integrity.

Maggie sat in the green room once again. This time, filled with strength, no longer scared or nervous. Applauding inside her path to keep it real, a perfect execution of personable and reasonable answers. Furthermore, and more importantly, she did it without sounding like a dingbat and without waiver.

Susan had already called saying, "Good job, girl! You really showed that tough old trout how to take one in the trousers." Susan had a bit of the South in her, but her Southern vernacular rarely showed. It came out only when the occasion suited. Maggie laughed. It was always a stress reliever when Susan said something funny. A refreshing instance from a woman was always too serious. If Susan was joking, then she was cool with Maggie's answers in the interview.

Next call was from Syl, the limo was ready. A stage helper was there to escort Maggie out the back door. He was the same guy who had knocked on the green room door earlier to alert her of show time. When they reached the door, he held it for Maggie. They shared a smile, and he then softly spoke. "Ms. Malone, can I tell you a quick something?"

Maggie stopped and answered, "Sure. I'm sorry. What is your name?"

"George Williams, ma'am." The stagehand put out his hand. His old worn dark face smiled sweetly. "Pleasure to meet you." His soft soothing voice was pleasant to the ear.

Shaking his hand, she responded, "Thank you, George. What did you want to tell me?"

"Thanks for what you said tonight. My wife just passed of breast cancer. I think it was very nice how you directed the viewers to the fight. Most stars would have talked it up all about themselves. You made it about the fighters. If my wife was still alive, she would have been . . . "

George stopped himself. Seeing the pain of his loss bringing up wells of tears in his eyes, Maggie put her hand on his shoulder..

"George," Maggie encouraged him. "It's okay. Go on. She would have been . . . ?"

George replied politely, looking up again at Maggie, tears escaping from the corners of his eyes, "Well, Ms. Malone, pardon me, but she would have been very proud of you today."

Maggie looked at George, really seeing him now. She could feel his love for his wife flowing out with his tears. "She must have been a special lady," she encouraged. George looked at Maggie fondly. One little act of kindness from her today had made such a difference to him, and it clearly showed. Maggie held open her arms. George hesitated for a minute, still shaken up; then smiling, he leaned in to receive Maggie's hug.

"Thank you, George. I appreciate your words more than you know. I hope the movie brings forth the donations for the education that I pray will end this disease, so others don't have to be taken like your wife. You take good care now. Have a good night, sir."

George smiled gratefully, "Night, Ms. Malone. Thank you kindly. Take care of yourself as well."

As she reached the limo, Syl let her in. As they drove away from the studio, Syl looked back encouraged by Maggie. "Mags, you really touched that man's heart, didn't you? I could see by the look on his face."

Maggie didn't reply right away. She sat thinking about what Syl had asked.

"I guess I did, Syl, but you know what?"

"What's that, Mags?"

"I think he touched mine more."

Looking in the rearview mirror at Maggie, Syl shook his head in agreement.

CHAPTER SEVEN

DEATH THREAT

AN EARLY MORNING BROUGHT A kick-start to the next day. Maggie was headed to a script reading, but first she wanted a quick walk around the studio, so she arrived early.

She meandered past the different sets taking in all the graphic color ordinations and visual wonders of set décor and props. She walked onto an outside scene set for a rain forest. Everywhere the flowers and trees were on rolling carts. Maggie stopped to run her hand down the intertwining rope-like plant vines. She looked up to the tops of the trees, bright yellow and red flowers adorned them. The sun kissed the flowers with a glow, bringing a warm smile to her face. She looked away, drawn by the delightful sounds of chirping. Cages of multi-colored tropical forest birds were nearby.

"Hello, guys," Maggie greeted the birds. They continued to chirp as if in answer to her. "I am sure you would much rather be flying in the rain forest, but thanks for singing for me today." Maggie was happily amused.

Touching one cage, running her hands around the edges. A perfectly kept safe place, yet no freedom to fly. Imagery of the whole idea played with Maggie's thoughts. She truly connected with the feeling of being trapped. Her smile staled, her face turned concerned.

"I know what it is like to be stuck," she said to the birds somberly.

Maggie continued in a trance-like state—watching and listening to the birds. She didn't notice that Syl had dropped back in the distance after stopping to chat with a friend. Suddenly, she felt an eerie feeling come over her like she was not alone. She turned her head to see a strange man dressed in green camouflage with dark makeup on his face standing within breathing distance just behind her. He grabbed Maggie by her left arm and in a deep threatening voice whispered, "How do you want to die, Maggie Malone?"

Maggie gasped and pulled away from the man. She put her hand to her mouth in terror and stumbled back in shock, nearly falling over. Her heart was racing, and she could feel the rush of adrenaline and tears surging. Before the man could blink an eye, Syl tackled him to the ground and cuffed his hands behind his back.

"Security! Now! Security!" Syl screamed through the radio to the studio office.

Security came to take the man away as Syl escorted Maggie to a private dressing room. Maggie fell down to the couch breathing erratically, shaking as tears poured over her cheeks.

"Why, Syl? Why?" Maggie yelled as she held him tightly, her head pushed against his chest. Syl could feel her heart pounding against him.

"It's okay; it's okay. He's gone. He isn't going to hurt you." Syl got out his phone to call Susan, semi-reluctant to free a hand from holding Maggie. "Suz, we have a problem. We had a weirdo here. He threatened Maggie, and she is really shaken up. I am not sure how well the read will go."

Maggie continued to cry as she moved her head to the arm of the couch.

"No!" she said to herself under her breath. Then her words became louder and clearer as she cleared her throat. "No! No!" She pulled her head up angry, wiping away her tears. Stubbornly stood up, taking a deep breath. She walked to the mirror, immediately trying to fix her makeup. Then she turned to Syl.

"Syl, is she okay, do we need to reschedule? Should I come there, does she need me?" Susan was anxiously waiting to hear news. Syl didn't reply, he was looking at a direct stare from Maggie.

"Tell Susan I am going to do the read. I just need a few minutes to get it together." Maggie spoke outwardly but still in a shaky voice.

Syl shook his head and said to Susan, "You know our girl; she is tough. She wants to do the read. She just needs a few minutes to breathe and get cleaned up." Then Syl answered a question Susan had posed, "You better bet I will be all over that guy. I will have a restraining order drawn up ASAP. It will go public as you know, so you will have to deal with the clean up on that."

Maggie shook her head and looked down in disbelief when he mentioned the restraining order. Another media surge of negativity to deal with but she needed to stay safe. Syl hung up and turned to Maggie. "Mags, are you okay? Are you sure about going ahead with this right now?" He walked over consoling her again by putting a hand on her shoulder.

"Yeah, I'm okay; thanks for being right on it, Syl." She put her arms around Syl's shoulders and gave him a hug of thanks.

Syl finally pulled away slowly and instructed Maggie. "I will get the hair and makeup people in here for you. Take a minute to breathe. I will let them know you will be a bit late getting down there. They will be more than accommodating after I give them a piece of my

mind about that jerk that threatened you. If someone dropped the
ball on security clearance, they will be sorry!" Syl wasn't having it; he
was fit to be tied. No one scared Maggie like that, ever.

"Okay thanks, Syl." Maggie coaxed the words out in between wiping her tears. Syl left Maggie alone to compose herself.

She went to the fridge and pulled out a water bottle. After she
screwed off the top and took a drink, she scanned the room for her
purse. Where was it? Frantically she searched the room—on the couch,
by the door, on the chair, by the pillows. Finally, Maggie found the
purse right where she left it, in a corner. She sat down, grasping hard
onto it. She took out the bottle of pills, opened it, and swallowed
one down with a swish of water. She closed her eyes, hung her head
forward and threw her purse back near the couch without looking.
Feeling defeated, falling to the quick cure, Maggie gave in.

The knock at the door startled her. Every nerve on edge, rattled
within her. Slowly she made her way to the door, still on guard after
her scare.

The lady at the door announced herself as Annie from hair and
makeup. Maggie stared at the door handle. Fear had not left her. After
stalling for a few minutes, she unlocked and opened the door just
enough to peek out. Maggie recognized Annie, so she let her in.

The reading of the script went surprisingly well. Maggie harnessed the adrenaline energy surging via the threat, spinning it directly to her advantage.

☆☆☆

The next few days to unwind were definitely in need. At home,
she lay on her couch listening to soft jazz, wearing pajamas, staring

at the ceiling, and contemplating her mysterious life. From one day of instilling a kind impression on an old widowed man to the next day facing a death threat. Having the power to send a friend with his sick daughter off in her private jet, while losing the sense of personal freedom. At times she felt like a prisoner in her own home.

All these situations were made possible because of star status. With any good comes some bad, and it is often impossible to separate the two. God gives the hardest tasks to those He thinks can handle them. Was this the case? She could have been a doctor like her brother certainly still making a difference, but could she reach as many people as she does through the movies, bringing the focused attention to worthy causes?

Maggie sat up and began walking down the hall to her quiet room. She unlocked the door, went inside, picked up a book from a coffee table, and sat down, speaking her thoughts out loud, "Let's see what today's date is. Oh, yeah, today is the twenty-third."

She went to the page in her journal designated for the twenty-third of the month reading aloud the Bible verse written for that day. "And be not conformed to this world: but be ye transformed by the renewing of your mind, that ye may prove what is that good, and acceptable, and perfect, will of God" (Romans 12:2).

Maggie looked up to the ceiling and back down again before closing the journal. She brought the book up to her mouth to rest on her lips and closed her eyes. After Maggie finished praying, she opened her eyes and hugged the book to her chest.

"Okay, God, I get what You're trying to say. I will stay true to You and true to myself. I will find a way to make it work and keep doing the good while surviving the rest. Thanks for the strength You give me every day. Thanks for the opportunity to help people because of the fame. Make my stardom work for You. This is what is good and perfect."

Maggie placed the daily journal back on the table and left the room, closing and locking the door behind her. She went directly to the phone and called Syl.

"Hey there, can you arrange for me to get a facial and a massage. Please ask for Danielle at the usual place. She is so pleasant—and private. She always makes sure I have total secrecy."

Maggie giggled a bit in the middle of her next thought. "And?" Syl questioned, his curiosity getting the best of him.

Maggie fessed up. "And she always has my favorite cookies. I feel like a cookie day today."

Syl laughed. "Color me surprised. You know you deserve one, too, lady." They laughed together to lighten the nightmare of previous days then hung up so Syl could go make the arrangements.

☆☆☆

Another adventure? Yes, time for the cat and mouse game of entering a public place of business: drive around back, service entrance, private corridors reserved for the staff. Syl had backup, plain clothes guards hanging around other entrances, administering extra precaution this time due to the recent events.

All the staff at the spa referred to Maggie as Jennifer Black. That was her code name for now. It changed regularly to avoid the possibility of staff leaking it to the paparazzi.

Maggie worked with one person at the spa: Danielle. Danielle had Maggie's back when it came to privacy. Danielle had grown up in a small town in Georgia where she had been taught proper respect.

She made Maggie feel like a normal human being who needed a massage and some relaxation, not like a star. A short little blonde with a twisty curl trademark ponytail and red lipstick, Danielle was a peppy young woman still in her mid-twenties. Her chipper personality accompanied with a subtle Southern accent, displayed her charm.

Syl and Maggie finished making their way down the corridor to meet her. Danielle walked up with a quick wink and a smile to Syl, then took Maggie by the arm like a true escort.

"Hello, Mr. Sylvester, I will gladly escort Ms. Black to her tranquility room. Why don't you have a seat right outside here? I will have Annette bring you a fresh cappuccino and some of my grandmama's homemade lemon butter cookies."

Syl smiled broadly, "Why thank you, Danielle. Don't mind if I do. You know I can't pass up those cookies, girl."

Maggie chuckled at their cheerful bantering as Danielle opened the door to the tranquility room a few steps away, and welcomed her in.

"Come on in, Ms. Black, so great to see you again. It's just fixin' to be a lovely day out there today, isn't it?" Maggie enjoyed Danielle's positive attitude.

"Yes, it seems to be quite nice out today. I can really use this massage, Danielle. Please knead away the knots; I have got to relax," Maggie pleaded.

"Sure thing. Yes ma'am. We will have you all fixed up in a jiffy. I will be right back with your favorite music, and you can just get relaxed and put on your robe. Okey dokey? Oh yeah, silly me, the goods are there next to ya." Danielle nodded her head up once in jest referring to the cookies on the chair next to Maggie. Then she stepped out of the room and closed the door behind her.

CHAPTER EIGHT
MEET MS. A

MAGGIE SAT PERFECTLY STILL, JUST eyeing the cookies. She was a bit jealous that Syl was already enjoying his. She reached over to pick up a cookie but was interrupted by a knock at the door. Maggie giggled, assuming that it was Danielle forgetting something. "Danielle, come in. What did you forget?"

The door opened, and a mysterious woman entered quickly and closed the door behind her in the same fashion. She was dressed all in a black, wearing a pantsuit and dark sunglasses, with a black scarf draped around her head. She was carrying a black briefcase, very much like a secret agent.

Maggie, terrified, stood straight up and was about to yell for Syl when the lady motioned to her with a shush finger to her mouth. Maggie still spoke out in a controlled angry tone. "Who are you? What are you doing in here? Get out!"

The unidentified woman sat down in an open chair and began to speak calmly as she crossed her legs and brushed off her black pantsuit.

"Calm down, Maggie. Let's be civil. I am not here to scare you or hurt you, least of all to photograph you. I would like just a moment of your time. I promise it is all on the level and only between the two of us. Syl is still out there watching over you. He doesn't know I am here, but don't be concerned. Again, I am not here to harm you. Take a deep breath, Maggie, please sit down."

Maggie inhaled a deep breath and tried to calmly take a seat. She didn't know why, but she seemed to believe her. It could have been the smooth relaxed way the lady in black kept her voice steady and her movements gentle.

"Okay." Maggie lowered her voice. "Who are you and what is it you wanted to talk to me about?"

The mysterious lady sat up, folded her hands in her lap, and slowly moved about getting comfortable in her chair. Then she spoke directly. "Consumed, Maggie? Has fame consumed you?"

Maggie looked puzzled and seemed a bit angry. "You said you weren't a reporter. I suspect by your get-up that you're undercover for some tabloid. What is it then?"

The woman obviously didn't care for Maggie's tone. She spoke sternly, "This is not a game, Ms. Malone! I take my job very seriously!"

Maggie was having a hard time reading this woman who still had not removed her dark eyeglasses.

The woman continued resetting back to a calm voice. "Now understand, Maggie. I was just trying to establish how much you are in need of our services. My name is Ms. A, for all intents and purposes; this is how you will address me. I am not here to gather dirt on you, nor am I interested in making a dime by asking you a lot of personal questions that certainly are none of my business. In fact, you can count yourself blessed, Maggie, that you have been chosen today."

Maggie began to get a bit queasy. She felt a chill when the lady said blessed. She was remembering the Bible verse she had read earlier in her daily journal, "renewing of your mind." *Was this a renewal?* Compelled to know more, she encouraged Ms. A to go on.

"I'm listening," Maggie offered.

Ms. A stood up, picked up her chair, and set it down directly in front of Maggie. She leaned forward, grabbing the arms of Maggie's chair. Her body stance and voice were stern and clear but not intended to frighten.

"Maggie, I am here to offer you an opportunity for an escape, to see what it's like to live a normal life, as an average today's lady—without the fame. This is a one-time offer, offered to a limited few people and only to those deemed worthy. The opportunity will cost you one million dollars, but the value you will gain will be priceless.

"Also, just so you know, all of the money you pay will go to help several families who are in need due to the economic fall of the U.S. industry. Before I continue, I need your word that you will listen very carefully to what I am about to say. You also will need to sign this document.

"All of the information that I have shared since I walked through this door, including my very existence, must be kept completely confidential. You will not tell a soul, not your family, not Syl, not even your house plants. Do you completely understand what I have just said?"

Maggie was nervous, considering such an unbelievable offer, yet still extremely interested. Her mind buzzed, hurry in wonder. *A chance to be me,* she thought. *Just to be me, with no fame. How is that possible? Is this all a crazy joke? Is someone trying to play a prank on me?* Finally, her mouth let out an answer, regardless, "Yes, I understand. Please continue."

Ms. A let go of the arms of Maggie's chair, sitting back comfortably again. "Okay, great. Let's move forward. First, obviously, you will have to reschedule your facial and massage," Ms. A stated with a bit of a humor. "The previous schedule simply doesn't work anymore," Ms. A continued. "For the next hour or so, I will be going over the details of our contract. To get this done, Danielle was told that you were going to be using the room for an important studio call. She has already moved on to her next client. Syl was told that you would be opting for a more intense treatment. He is expecting you to be longer than usual. Neither Danielle nor Syl nor this facility knows anything about my being here. All is well outside these doors. Everyone is cool. I expect you to be the same now that we are on speaking terms." Ms. A smirked bringing her briefcase to her lap continuing, "So let's move on."

She took one piece of paper out of her briefcase. Maggie was a bit leery of signing anything at this point. After all, who the heck is this lady? Why would she sign anything without her attorney looking over it? Nervous to mention this, she blurted out, "I am not sure I should be signing anything."

Ms. A interrupted with, "Relax"; then she continued. "Maggie, this is a legal, binding contract that only I will possess—only one copy exists—besides, you have not read it yet. It is very short and to the point. We don't like confusion, and we don't waste money on attorneys. Take a look."

She handed Maggie the paper which read: "I, Maggie Malone, a.k.a Maggie Marie Malone, a.k.a Maggie Marie Jackson, do hereby swear to uphold the secrecy surrounding Ms. A and the Anonymity Project and all that it entails, from this day throughout all the days of my life. So help me God."

There it was, her real name: Maggie Marie Jackson, printed on ordinary white paper with this simple statement and a place for her to sign, nothing more. It didn't even look legal.

Maggie ventured a question. "This is it? That whole build up, and this is your big contract?"

Ms. A, looking serious, drew closer to Maggie and reached for her hand. "May I?"

Slowly and nervously, Maggie extended her hand to Ms. A. Grasping her hand gently, Ms. A set out to reassure Maggie's ill at ease with a personal touch, she took her free hand and pushed her sunglasses down slightly, revealing her dark smoldering eyes.

"Maggie, the contract is binding legally, but it does say 'So help me, God.' Our trust in you is our protection. So long as we keep our end of the bargain, you will find no difficulty in doing the same. Your faith and honesty, if we have you figured out, will cause you to keep your contract with us. Will it not?" Ms. A delivered consideration with this accordance.

"Yes, yes" was all that Maggie could squeak out. She said it twice, still not sure exactly what her answer would mean.

Ms. A stood up as she pushed her glasses back up to her eyes. "Okay then, sign the contract, and I will tell you the best part, the news you really want to hear. I will keep it simple for now. However, I will be available by secure line for questions later. But please, make the questions count. My time is limited. My focus is on the project."

Ms. A handed Maggie a pen, and Maggie signed the document with still-shaking hands.

"Great!" Ms. A seemed glad to get that over. Once she put the document back inside her briefcase, a weird flash of light and a strange noise, resembling the sound of a copy machine, escaped from within. The unusual sound was followed by the slightest spray of smoke, seeping out the edges. Maggie's worried expression revealed her thoughts concerning the spy technology in use.

Ms. A noticed and she spoke reassuringly. "It's okay, sweetie. That's just an auto-scan feature. If something were to happen to me or to the case, a copy of what you just signed is held in a secure server. The original document was destroyed, and no trace of it will be left on paper."

Left speechless, Maggie nodded her head yes in amazement. How cool was that? Auto-scan? Technology advanced so fast that one literally flashed right by her.

"Okay, then," Ms. A continued. She paced the floor as she explained the steps. "This whole project lasts one month. Now, I know it is impossible for a famous star like you to take a holiday for a month without anyone noticing, so that is where your doppelganger will come in. See, we find a girl of your height, weight, and proportions; adjust her eye, hair, and skin color with makeup, and cosmetic technology. We will also teach her some of your mannerisms, habits, and movements.

"I think you of all people would really appreciate how we choose our doppelgangers. They are chosen from the several thousands of small-town girls who come to the big city trying to make it as an inspiring actress but instead spend their time waiting tables. We look for girls of good character and faith.

"They have the chance to test out their dream of becoming famous. In the big scheme of things, they also see what the down sides of their dream would be: all the paparazzi, the loss of privacy, and pretty much the prison of being a star. We are not trying to rain on their parade. We just provide them insight into what it's really like for stars like you and what you go have to go through outside of the money, glitz and glamour. Believe you me; they all thank us when it's over. Honestly, most choose different career paths. Occasionally, they still choose acting, but stage instead of film. Hmm, go figure."

Ms. A shrugged her shoulders a bit sarcastically after the last statement, then continued to explain, "See, Maggie, you are truly blessed, job well done so far in your career. You handle the stress, although we know about the meds."

Maggie felt somewhat violated; they knew about her medications? She took a hard swallow, revealing her ill at ease. Ms. A didn't give her a break. She kept drilling out the details.

"Oh, yeah, I forgot to tell you. We know everything about you. Don't worry. No one close to you ratted you out. We got most of our information by doing a bit of intricate cyber searching. Also, we have friends in high places and low places."

Just then, Ms. A looked directly up. Maggie wondered if she was looking at the clock on the wall, or at the ceiling. Friends in high places—was she referencing heaven? Or was this just a form of Maggie's wishful hoping?

Ms. A maintained her walking and talking, continuously gesturing with her hands. She didn't mince words, was quite sure of herself, holding her head high in a confident posture. "So anyway, as I was saying, you have done well thus far. You have taken your gift as a star and used it to help others. Let's see, just to name a few—you have helped your co-worker Stan with his daughter Grace, flying her out on your private jet. Really cool, by the way, I must say. Did you know that because of your help, Grace may be the recipient of a new treatment that could save her life?

"Also, that little eleven-year-old boy Mitchell Cassidy from New York—you can't forget his email asking you if you really do believe. Of course, you said yes. Did you know that Mitchell was about to join a street gang? He opted to join a church youth group instead because of the inspiration you gave him. Five members of that gang, all under age fifteen, were gunned down the next day." Ms. A paused her fast step as she delivered the saddened news of the murdered teens, then continued to speak on.

"How about the countless breast cancer fighters and survivors you have encouraged? Maggie, you have touched so many. You continue to pass along endless gifts from God to others. This is why you deserve an opportunity from Him yourself, so that you can gain perspective as to why He has placed you on the path He has for your life."

Ms. A looked over to Maggie, seeing her face, she stopped. Sitting completely still, overwhelmed by the news of Grace and Mitchell, rejoicing tears streamed down her cheeks. Praise to the Lord! Blessed news, but how did Ms. A know all this? It was not on the internet. Could it be her so-called "Friends in high places"? Either way, it was truly impressive.

Finally acknowledging Maggie's tears, Ms. A went over to sit with her and hold her hands again. "It's great, Maggie," Ms. A reassured. "What you do with your stardom. You truly are a star in God's eyes. Do you know how easy it is for someone in your position to fall or to lose faith? You are strong.

You have not forsaken your faith in God, no matter what the public says about you, demands from you, or puts on you. No matter how much money you have or what you can buy. Bravo, my dear, Bravo!"

Maggie gathered strength from Ms. A's pep talk, heart sent words delivered with strong conviction. She felt as if Ms. A had known her forever. Made speechless by her emotions, she looked up and nodded in thanks. Gently again laying Maggie's hands down, Ms. A continued to walk and talk.

"Okay, now I am sure you want to know where you will be for almost a month and especially how no one will notice. Well, that's where it gets inventive." Ms. A expressed excitement about this part of the plan.

"Maggie, have you ever heard of a place called Home? Well, I am sure you haven't, it's a small town within an even smaller city, which no one ever comes from or goes to. The population is two-hundred two people. It's very rural.

"The town officials sign a contract, promising not to share your identity. There will be no cell phones, cameras, nor recording devices of any kind allowed. No computers, no internet. No reporters, no tabloids. Honestly, no one who is anyone would be there anyway. A good chunk of the payment for the project goes to the town. In fact, if it weren't for the project and its financial support, the town would be a ghost town, and most of the people there would be without jobs, homes, and food. These are mill workers, farmers, and small business owners. The only mill closed awhile back, so it's in their best interest to keep your best interest. Furthermore, the whole town will be able to regain its strength and continue, just because of you."

Ms. A seated herself again. Leaning on the arm of her chair she declared, "Maggie, I hope you understand. Your privacy is our job. Your anonymity is our purpose. You are the most important thing to anyone in our organization for one whole month.

"We only take one job at a time. And yes, we have done this before. You'd be surprised who has taken advantage of this opportunity. A few blessed who have often said that it saved their lives. We always choose a different town with different circumstances. You see, we don't just pick a town; we pick a town that is perfect for the real you, the person you were before stardom, when you were just a small-town girl yourself.

"Do you remember, Maggie? Remember playing in the fields? Remember acres of land and rows of flowers and small-town picnics? Well, if you don't, you will. We hope you like it. We spent a lot of time setting this up. We are already into this for way more than we are asking from you.

"We spent company funds ahead of time, based on faith alone. We called in favors that we cannot ever get back. We moved on gracious instinct, hoping that you would participate in the project. We believe in you Maggie; we are giving you reinvented precious time."

Maggie was listening intently to every word Ms. A had to say. She felt like this was all a dream. Her mind was spinning.

Had she fallen asleep during her massage? Was this for real? Maggie took a deep breath and looked up at Ms. A, who had finally stopped herself for a breather. Feeling overwhelmed, she couldn't think of what to say. With a million questions going through her head, what ones should she ask? Afraid and guarded, half of her mind considered how insane this was; the other half was saying, if it's real, how amazing.

Obliged to agree, she initiated a handshake with Ms. A, hoping the honesty was mutual. "Thank you, Ms. A. Thank you for this. I guess you know how badly I need it. When do we get started?"

Ms. A smiled fondly, standing to shake hands, while removing her sunglasses.

Maggie saw her clearly now. A beautiful lady, somewhere in her late fifties or early sixties, a little worn around the edges but striking, tidy neat hair, and flawless makeup surrounding strong dark eyes. Maggie felt like she had seen her somewhere before—there was something familiar about those eyes. She didn't have a chance to think it out before Ms. A continued.

"Maggie, it is against protocol for me to reveal myself, for obvious privacy and confidentiality reasons. I have never had a client who has seen me without cover or has been this close to me. There is something about you, Maggie. You were my personal pick for this project. I put my faith in your remarkable kindness, and I know you won't let me down."

Ms. A leaned forward to give Maggie a hug which was welcomed. All of the emotions she had been feeling—fear, excitement, caution, worry—seemed to melt oddly away.

First to interrupt the embrace, Ms. A straightened her hair. "Okay, dear, enough of all this mushy stuff. Time to get to work. First, I have to know if you believe without a doubt in the project and if you think it will help you."

Maggie replied instantly, "Yes, I do."

Ms. A continued. "I will call you tonight from a secure line to your private cell. You must answer it yourself at precisely nine p.m. I know you have a break in your schedule for a few days, and this is when we will move. I will need you to gather a month's worth of clothes from your private clothing line. They will be for the doppelganger to wear to convince others that she is you. Also, choose any jewelry, handbags, or other accessories that are distinctive to you. Don't worry. They will all be returned."

Maggie wondered aloud, "What happens to the doppelganger when the project is finished, and what happens to me?"

Ms. A seemed ready for the question. "Don't worry about her, her original appearance and life will be returned to her. She will be compensated for her time and secrecy. She will get a year's paid rent at a great penthouse in the city, including all bills and expenses paid. If she opts for a new career, then we will offer her schooling or a job in that arena. Otherwise, she will be offered ten auditions for parts in successful productions. Our goal is to help the doppelgangers find their dreams. After the project, they will have a better idea what those are.

"Maggie, you will be returned to your life here as a star. No one will know the difference, other than to think that you were on holiday and now are back."

"What about Syl. If they don't see Syl attending to her, won't they be suspicious? He has been with me for years."

Ms. A smiled. "We got that all worked out. Syl is proposing to his girlfriend this weekend. We have it on good authority she will be saying yes. He will ask you for time off for the first time in years to plan the wedding. They want to get married quickly. I guess he has been stalling for a long time, so he will arrange for a new detail for you.

"You know he won't let them be too cozy with you because he doesn't trust many people with your safety. He is a great guy, Maggie. He really cares about you."

Ms. A sounded if she knew Syl personally. Maybe she did? Maggie didn't see how.

"Anyway, the new detail won't be allowed too close to the doppelganger. We have a voice-enhanced phone system that sounds exactly like you as a backup. Otherwise, the doppelganger won't be talking to anyone. We will have it all planned out through your so-called assistants, which will be those of us involved in the project."

"What about Susan, my manager?" Maggie questioned.

"Susan will be unaware that the doppelganger is not you. You have to convince her that you need this month off. Tell her not to schedule anything, that this vacation is your down time. Even if you get that movie deal you just read for, it won't start shooting for several months. Your doppelganger will be glad to take the vacation to the Bahamas that you had planned on taking a year ago. The paparazzi will hang around for a few hours every day, but she will be doing a lot of yachting. You mentioned how you like yachting to a reporter last month. Being far from shore aiming at a moving target makes the photo ops harder. It's ideal. Can you handle Susan, you think?"

Maggie was quite sure that Susan would welcome a time out. She and Maggie were both on the edge of a breakdown. "Yeah, that should be no problem."

"So that leaves your family. Now, Maggie, I know how close you are to your mom. I don't think it is fair not to allow you to talk to her. We have planned for you to use a special phone line that will make it look like you're calling from the Bahamas. You may talk to your mom, but you must convince her that you're getting some rest. I am sure she would love to see you enjoy yourself. Remember, no one must come in close contact with the doppelganger, so make sure your family doesn't plan any surprise visits to you in the Bahamas."

Maggie laughed. "No worries there; I think Mom and Dad are still getting over our trip to South America. Dad was sick for weeks because of some bad food, and Mom got the itches and swears she still has them. My brother is a doctor and we both know how much time off they get." Ms. A grabbed her briefcase. She put back on her sunglasses and headed for the door. As she reached for the door handle, she stopped and turned back to Maggie.

"Maggie, remember; I wasn't here, and this didn't happen. Your secrecy secures your ticket to the program. I will talk to you at precisely nine p.m. Be ready!"

Maggie thought about the money for a minute. One million dollars. That was a lot of money to some people. Well, it wasn't really the amount that bothered her; she had millions. It was just the thought of transferring a million dollars to what? All she had to go on was what Ms. A had told her. After all, Maggie was entitled to doubt. She had just met this lady, and her protective shield was still intact. A person didn't get to where she was without a few rakes over the coal.

A few seconds went by as Maggie went aloft in a daze; her eyes crunched up and her mouth grew taunt over her mind's anarchy. Ms. A snapped at her, noticing "Maggie! Don't get weak-kneed now young lady. Is it the money? Remember, it goes for a good cause. You have to trust me, just as I trust you. You will be delivered exactly what I have promised."

"Okay, Ms. A, I understand; thank you," Maggie replied, seemingly grateful but still on the fence.

Smiling one last time, Ms. A added, "Don't thank me, Maggie. Thank Him." She looked up and then closed the door behind her softly.

Maggie sat quietly thinking. God had reached out to her before through music, lines of scripts, and even through bumper stickers. But this time, had He reached out a bit more directly? Did He send Ms. A? Is this all real? Is this going to happen? Would she be able to be plain old Maggie again, even for a short time?

Maggie felt excited and nauseated at the same time. If this were a hoax, it would be the last straw. To fathom a wacko lady using God and spy moves to pull a fast one was too much to handle. The sensible side of her brain argued logically, but her heart felt something different. It urged her to find her faith. This could be a project from the Lord.

Maggie didn't know what to do next. Should she call for Syl or Danielle? She looked up at the clock. Almost an hour had gone by, but it had seemed like only minutes, since there was so much to absorb. Ms. A was quite a whirlwind to gather.

Sitting perfectly still, Maggie looked around the room. *Oh yeah, cookies.* The delectable answer to her overloaded mind.

Maggie picked up the bowl of cookies and started snacking away. Millions of ideas passed through her head about what her life was going to be like for the next month. The funny thing was, currently, all she really cared about were those cookies. She was glad that Ms. A had not spotted them. Otherwise, she would have had to share. Maggie was generous, but not with Danielle's grandmama's homemade lemon butter cookies. This had to be why Danielle gave Syl his own Maggie humorously mused. She hugged the bowl of cookies she had all to herself.

Flaky lemon treats of sugary goodness, deliciously full of calories, were precisely what she needed right that minute. She felt like celebrating Ms. A's visit, throwing caution to the wind, encouraging her heart's grounded faith in the project, through each little lemony, buttery sweet bite.

CHAPTER NINE
SYL'S NEWS

MAGGIE KNEW SYL WOULD BE knocking anytime to check on her. Not more than a minute went by, and sure enough the knock came.

"Mags, how are you doing? Just about finished?"

Maggie wiped the cookie crumbs off the corner of her mouth and went for the door. She answered it with a smile, greeting. "Hey, big guy, all ready. Shall we go then?"

Syl created a strange questioning look on his face. "Wow, you look chipper, Mags. Must have been a good one, are you feeling better?"

She felt oddly refreshed, even without the massage she had desperately needed. "Yep, all good here. Let's roll," she chirped as she walked out of the room.

Syl and Maggie were on their way home quickly. Syl kept looking in the rearview mirror at Maggie. He still seemed puzzled, as if carrying a sneaking suspicion that he had missed something.

Boy, if he only knew about Ms. A. Maggie smirked. *How did he miss her?* She wouldn't press him; the entire incident was supposed to be a secret. Besides, it was very apparent, Ms. A was good at her job.

"Hey, Mags, it was very quiet in there? How was Danielle? Did she chat your ear off?" Syl did press it, he wasn't about to overlook his instincts. "I stepped up to the juice bar for a minute, but I was keeping an eye out. I feel kind of guilty leaving the door for even a second."

"No worries; it was quiet. I can't blame you for wanting to visit their juice bar; it is really tempting. How was it? Did you get mango strawberry as usual?" Maggie continued before Syl could answer any of the questions. "Oh yeah, Syl, can you drive home the long way? I want to catch a bit of scenery. I love to see the people going about their day. People sometimes surprise you."

Syl seemed thrown by Maggie's behavior. It was odd for her to request the long way home, especially after all the public run-ins she had experienced lately. "Hey, Mags, are you sure? We have been on red alert. You want to risk the long way home?"

Maggie was certain. "Yes, Syl, let's do it. Sometimes you just have to throw out caution and try to live a little. Don't forget to turn up there."

Syl nodded and went back to driving. He may have felt compelled to argue, but he played along with Maggie's happy disposition, put on the jazz, and kept a sharp eye out.

Maggie sat back filling her mind with visions of people and cars as they moved about. Syl paused at a red light near a park. A father and daughter were playing catch while the mom set up a picnic. Joggers were running, some with dogs in tow. Children were swinging and sliding on the playground, a few digging in the sand. The park was thriving with everyday life.

At the next stop, Maggie zeroed in on a couple holding hands, arms outstretched swaying as they happily talked and walked. The couple stopped, and the man put his arms around his lady, giving her a big hug. He reached down to her face gently pulling her closer for a kiss.

Maggie wondered how that would feel—not the kiss, but the love surrounding it. As the car passed the park, she continued to think about the couple. *To be loved—in love—to be kissed like you can feel how much that person loves you.* The last time she had felt some semblance of love was two years ago.

Mark Marsh had been an "up-and-comer" in Hollywood. Maggie had fallen in love with his old-fashioned, down-to-earth charm. Mark and Maggie had something real, like sharing long talks about their goals while lying on a blanket watching the stars. He had promised that he would not allow the Hollywood lifestyle to change him, and together their life would be wonderful. They planned to weather the storm of fame through love, hiding at home coupled in solitude.

Mark liked to sketch, and Maggie would sit for hours and just watch. She could feel his passion for the simple things in life pass onto the paper with each pencil wisp.

Sadly, love had a short life with Mark once he had landed his first big release. All of a sudden, he was too good for her. The simple things weren't enough for him; he pushed them all away to become a limelight junky.

In many ways, Maggie had given up on love after Mark. Based on her schedule and location, she knew the men she would encounter were all show business monkeys. No real prospects among the leading men she starred opposite of. They were all harsh, conceited, and promiscuous. Maggie was regularly turning away advances. She valued herself more than that, no matter how lonely she could be. Occasionally she entertained with a few nice guys in supporting roles, but they were in relationships or on their way to a Hollywood crash. Drugs, drinking, too many women, whatever—a crash was a crash.

In lieu of dating, she found herself enjoying friendships with stagehands and production people. She preferred the working class of Hollywood over the stars. They led normal lives. They were up early and in bed on time. They had wives, kids, and normal family routines. They worked around the fame without becoming famous. They had a job to do, and they took it seriously. Hanging around people like that had an advantage, keeping her as close to normal as possible.

Maggie's chaste lifestyle gave her a bit of questionable press, which Susan wasn't glad about. Reporters in the close Hollywood circles labeled her "Ice Queen" and accused her of being a prude. How wrong they were! Careful with her heart, yes, but not a prude. She simply would rather accompany loneliness over a stand in prop of a companion. She would avoid floating a relationship based on how good it looked to everyone else. She would wait for a man with genuine qualities who was true to himself, not a Hollywood show piece. Authenticity was hard to find in the Hollywood circle, but she kept hopeful prayer, someday perhaps, she would find him.

When Syl turned into the driveway, it was quiet out front. Perhaps the paparazzi had fallen for the diversion of the day. Either way, Maggie was glad to be home.

Syl got out, opened her door, welcoming. "Here you are, my lady; your digs await." He bowed his head and circled his hand in gesture as he bowed.

Maggie smiled and played along, giving her hand to him as she exited the car. "Why, thank you, kind sir; I don't mind if I do." Time spent goofing off was the levity they often invited to make an intense stardom atmosphere, creatively smoother.

She called out to Syl as she ran in. "Thanks, Syl; take it easy the rest of the night. I won't be going out. I am waiting for an important call."

Syl replied, "Okay, Mags will do. I will be around if you need me; then I am going to take off later. Derek will be here to look out after you. He's my best guy."

Maggie didn't reply after hearing Syl, she just kept proceeding into her house. She wondered if Syl was going to see his girl. Was he going to tell Maggie the news about the engagement soon? Maggie didn't let it worry her. She knew he would.

Maggie was starved. The first order of business was to eat. The cookies had taken the edge off her hunger pangs at first, but the sugar had eventually made her hungrier. Starch seeped its way into her mind. Checking the fridge, well knowing, she wouldn't find any in there. It was all low- or no-carb in the abandoned chilled dwelling.

Pasta, more specific, was the focus of her cravings. She missed the food she had grown up on—homemade macaroni and cheese, fried chicken, yeast rolls, and green beans made with bacon fat. A meal like that would be beyond amazing but would blow her calorie count out for a month.

Maggie decided to give in to her cravings. Time to attempt to make homemade mac and cheese, the kind Mom had made—baked in the oven, cheesy, gooey golden yellow love. She called Syl and begged him to send someone for the ingredients, which he was to say were for him. She was just being cautious; modesty was the issue more than privacy this time. Syl came to the door not long after.

"Here you go, Mags—everything on the list. Seems like you're in a mood for something delicious. Can I guess by your ingredients you're attempting Mom's homemade mac and cheese?" Syl laughed, eager to hear her reply.

Maggie gave him an agreeable wink and a nod. She grabbed the bags, and off to the kitchen she went. Syl followed her with his hand hiding something behind his back. Maggie noticed, questioning him with her eyebrows.

"Say, fella, what do you have there? Are you holding out on me?" Syl brought his arm around, holding a dozen white roses. Maggie cried out, surprised with joy. "Syl, what have you done. They are beautiful!"

Syl smiled and welcomed the hug that Maggie jumped up to give him. "Maggie, these are for you because you are a special lady, boss. You have been the amazing grand adventure that is my life."

Maggie stepped back a bit, holding the flowers close, wearing a puzzled look across her face. "Where are you going with all this?"

Syl looked away, rolling his eyes around in hesitation.

"Syl, what are you talking about? Where are you going?" Maggie pressed again.

Syl happily fessed up to ease Maggie's mind. "Nowhere, Mags. I am not leaving you. I have something important to share with you. You are the first person to hear this news. I haven't even told my family yet. I have proposed to Sharee, and she has accepted."

Maggie smiled and hugged Syl again. Overwhelmed in excitement for them, she settled on a quick witty response to celebrate. "Well, it's about time, you big silly. I am so glad for you and Sharee, Syl. You both deserve every happiness."

Syl became stern for a minute and loudly cleared his throat. Maggie ignored his quick jump back to serious from joyous, responding playfully. "Oh, now what? Can't we just be happy for you for a minute?"

Syl replied soberly, "Mags, I will need some time off—probably about three weeks or so. I know that is a long time, and I promise to hurry but . . . "

Maggie would never dream of letting Syl stress or fuss over her now, this was his time. He had done so much for her, for so long. She quickly interrupted his speech. "Syl, you don't have to explain to me. You have always been there for me. Always. What kind of a person would I be if I wasn't there for you? Of course, you can have as much time off as you need. I was just thinking to myself that I need some time off, too. I am finally going to take that trip to the Bahamas that I have been wanting."

Syl, taken aback by her news, became immediately concerned; he spoke up. "Oh, Mags, now? Really? I should be with you for travel. Travel complicates everything: so many places, entrances, and aggressive photographers out there. I wish you would wait on this a bit."

Maggie knew she couldn't wait, nor could Ms. A and the project. She hated lying to Syl, but it was a key stipulation. Time to say something reassuring to Syl, putting her arm up to his shoulder, she coaxed, "Don't worry, dear heart, I will be covered by Derek. You said yourself, he is your best guy. I know he doesn't know me too well, but it will only be light land and sea detail. I will be yachting almost the whole time."

Syl agreed reluctantly. His strong concern for her was priority one. "I hope Derek doesn't get seasick." Syl laughed. His lightened whimsical comment finally shared how happy he was for her break and his engagement.

"Yeah, you're right about that. Hope not. Get him ready!" Maggie agreed. She knew that Syl would drill sergeant instruct Derek on every little step for her safety.

Syl left the house and went off to start training Derek before he left for the night. Maggie went to the kitchen, eager to jump into mac and cheese mode.

CHAPTER TEN

LET THE ADVENTURE BEGIN

IT HAD BEEN AWHILE SINCE Maggie had put her heart into anything related to cooking. Face it; the empty caloric intake that she had been eating couldn't afford the space for heart.

Maggie worked for at least two hours. She took her time with the grating of the cheese and creating the bread crumb topping from scratch. Cooking seemed to ease her mind and keep it clear from distractions.

She set the dining table for herself with a beautiful china place setting and a glass of white wine. Candlelight and Syl's white roses accompanied her. The timer of the oven bell was like the sound of success to her ears.

She pulled out the mac and cheese. "Come to me, you cheesy pan of wonderful deliciousness. I have been waiting for you forever."

Maggie spooned out the mac and cheese, the strings of cheese making a bridge between her bowl and the pan. She commented on the visual. "Oh, yeah, that is what I am talking about right there."

Cutting the strings of cheese with her finger, Maggie moved her bowl into the dining room. She sat down before the lovely feast resting upon her beautiful table. She picked up the fork and was just about to dig in when something stopped her.

Placing the fork down, she folded her hands together. She lowered her head, praying aloud: "Dear Lord, thank You for this wonderful mac and cheese. Please let it taste like Mom's. Thank You for Syl and his awesome news. Thank You for my family. Thank You for today, for Ms. A. I hope You sent her for me. Amen."

Maggie took her first bite. She closed her eyes and smiled deliciously. She shook her head slightly from side to side. "Amen again!"

That mac and cheese was a reminder of being home with Mom and of all the good things overlooked in her life. Taking her time eating and drinking her wine slowly, she relished in it. It was a shame that she would eat only that one bowl. She would let Syl and the other guys who helped him have the rest. She knew if she ate too much, she would have to punish herself at the gym. She wasn't in the mood for self-punishment. Who was? A bowl of hot popcorn would be her light follow-up snack later.

Maggie cleaned up the dishes and headed to the TV room to review some clips from her past interviews. She was always curious as to what was left after their edits. Truly it was a semi-constructive use of time to keep her busy, still a few more hours before nine p.m.

Of course, she was anxious for Ms. A to call. The project must be real. Praying every minute since she met Ms. A, for a healing chance in life just as herself—without the fame. She wouldn't have designed the project any differently if it was her own. It was perfect, like a blessing sent just for her. She had only to believe.

Remember what Mom asked me earlier? Where is my faith?

Maggie soon lost interest watching the boring interview clips. She couldn't keep her mind off the nine o'clock call. Her eyes stalking the clock on the wall, and her finger wearing down the view button on her cell phone making sure she hadn't missed any calls. She played the same clips over and over, her mind looping in the same fashion, not really taking them in. Even hot inviting popcorn wasn't a distraction, at first.

Occasionally she would see herself mess up responding to a question and comment out loud. "Really, that was an odd thing to say."

Maggie playfully threw popcorn at herself on the screen. Eating popcorn brought to mind her brother Michael, how he loved popcorn when he was young. She started to reminisce about her childhood years—her mom and dad dancing in the kitchen while she and Michael secretly watched and giggled from the steps. Then there was the time, Mom and Dad laughed uproariously as she and Michael chased a rabbit for hours; they knew we would never even get close.

As a child growing up in a small town, the days seemed endless. Moments were made to be remembered. An adventure was always a possibility, even when there was nothing else to do. Maggie could never forget walks downtown on a summer night with her favorite ice cream cone dripping faster than she could eat it. Fourth of July picnics where the whole town would come out and the older men would dress in Civil War outfits and shoot canons. In spring, she remembered perfect weather, clean fresh air, and the smell of flowers all around her. Familiarity and belonging all the time, even if she walked for a mile, she always ran into someone who was glad to see her. Maggie couldn't help but smile as those memories brought her much comfort.

She didn't realize her clips had started over for the fourth time. Her cell phone rang. It startled her out of her journey down memory lane, and she dropped her popcorn bowl. Good thing it was empty; the only kernels that escaped were the ones she hurled at herself on the screen.

She looked at her phone quickly. "Oh, is it . . . ?" There was no way to tell who it was; the screen read "Unknown." She took a deep breath before she answered. "Hello?"

There were a few seconds of silence, a click, and then a voice not familiar. "Maggie Malone, we would like to congratulate you on winning our getaway package. Thank you for entering our contest." Maggie was a bit confused.

What? Is this a joke?

She yelled to the caller, scolding them. "I am not interested in any contests. How did you get this number?"

Was the project a scam? Was Ms. A just a glorified scam artist? Was this her doing or was it someone else?

Maggie stood up, filling with anger. She was about to go all crazy on the person on the other end of the line. The caller remained quiet and refused to answer any of the questions Maggie was hurdling out feverishly.

"I expect an answer, pal. This is really—" Maggie demanded.

Just then a different voice responded. "Relax, Maggie, this is Ms. A. I apologize, but I had to kind of play it on the down-low while we secured the line. I'm sorry to have upset you. This is really me. It is nine p.m. This is the call."

Maggie began to shake off her anger, feeling anxious and excited at the same time. "Ms. A?" Maggie asked with a quivering voice. "Really, is it you?"

"Yes, Maggie, it's me. Are you ready to get started?"

Recognition of the voice on the other end settled in. Realizing the importance of her reply, she answered without hesitation, "Yes."

She sat back down, hoping to calm her whole being as best she could while Ms. A started filling her in on the initial steps of her adventure.

Maggie was to board a private plane later that night. She would be shadowed by a detail of bodyguards that Ms. A would supply. Currently, Derek would think she was still at home "mac and cheesing" and watching interview clips. She was to give Syl a call soon letting him know she would be up late and was not to be disturbed early the next morning. Syl would also be told that her plane—in reality, the doppelganger's plane—would be leaving early tomorrow afternoon. Derek was to take over the reins for the trip.

Maggie had already talked to Susan who was expecting Maggie's vacation request. Their conversation had been pretty plain. Susan encouraged Maggie to enjoy her time away, going on and on about how refreshing it would be for her mind set. After all, Maggie was Susan's biggest client, and Susan had learned by now how to back off enough to survive that role. The one-up diplomacy of handling Maggie wasn't something Susan excelled in often, so pouring on agreeable vacation rhetoric seemed necessary. Maggie recognized her game but was satisfied not to pay any mind to it.

Ms. A urged Maggie not to do anything other than follow the instructions explicitly. Not tipping anyone off in any way about her leaving was essential. Maggie had to keep things business as usual for just a few more hours. She would have to get out unnoticed, and the doppelganger would have to get in the same way.

"Wait a minute, Ms. A. No disrespect, but how will you get me out without Derek knowing? Syl has trained him like a hawk on the cameras and security for me. I don't think he even sleeps without one eye open."

Don't worry; we have the most qualified people on the job, adjusting the surveillance system by showing a time-lapsed feed. He won't see you leave. Maggie, I've got it taken care of."

Maggie's fear of the unknown crept up in her mind, allowing questioning thoughts to linger. *So these people are able to take me without anyone knowing? No one I know will accompany me or know where to find me?*

"Maggie, are you still there? I know this is a bit confusing and scary, but remember, your trust has to be one hundred percent. You could blow our cover and destroy the program. Snap out of it! I insist! There is no room for errors in judgment, Maggie! Agreed?"

Maggie closed her eyes and centered herself. Worry had to wait for now. Time to trust and hope. She had already handed it over to God; He had it.

"Ms. A, I agree." Maggie's statement of affirmation fell off her lips and down to her heart, warming it with the faith she was longing to find.

When Maggie finished up with Ms. A on the phone, she knew what to do and when to do it. She didn't need to pack; everything would be provided. Besides, she couldn't take anything with her that would seem like it was missing. Maggie wrestled her uneasiness of a stranger stepping into her life with the inviting idea of stepping out. She nervously packed the bags for her stand in twin, matching outfits and accessories, trying to remember what Ms. A instructed.

Wait. That's just weird! I've never had two of me before. Lord knows, I have wished I had two of me many times. I hope that the doppelganger will find her way through my life. It can be messy. Poor girl. She felt oddly sorry for her.

Now another pressing matter, what apparel is fitting for a "get out of fame" excursion? Honestly, did it matter? There would be no red-carpet affairs, TV interviews, or special events. She could wear t-shirts and torn jeans every day! She relished the thought as she pictured it in her mind—the freedom to dress down as she pleased. Baggy sweatpants, cut-offs, and easy tees sounded as good as they would feel.

Full of nervous energy, Maggie giggled as she straightened. Standing sprightly in front of her long mirror, taunting humorously as she took a bow before her reflection, "Why, yes, I did just roll out of bed. This is an old t-shirt and a holey pair of jeans. What was that you said? I have bags under my eyes. Yes, I do. Minus one pound of makeup, and I've never felt better."

Maggie blew a kiss with a wink to herself in the mirror and flung herself backward onto her bed. Smiling big, looking up at her bedroom ceiling with admiration she added, "Thank You, Lord."

The chance of any break was wondrous, but random thoughts and questions popped into her mind.

To what kind of place will they take me? A small town unbothered by outsiders? Are the people going to be playing a part like actors, or are they real people? The existence of such a place seems like science fiction. No cameras or cell phones? No reporters? In this day and age? How odd, but it sounds like a little slice of heaven on earth. Only two hundred and two people in the whole town? That will be an adjustment compared to Los Angeles. Two hundred people compile a standard lunch crowd in a small LA restaurant.

Maggie sat up; her mind rambling becoming monotonous. She decided to take a visit to her quiet room. Picking up her daily Bible verse book, she read out loud today's verse. "Trust in the Lord with all thine heart and lean not unto thine own understanding, Proverbs 3:5."

As Maggie closed her book, she took a drink from her glass of lemonade before grabbing her purse. The anxiety about the trip was turning into exhaustion and was starting to wear on her. She swiped the bottles of pills around in her purse, like a kid in a candy bag looking for the perfect piece.

"Where are you?" she spoke out loud stopping to think where she had put the other missing bottles, finally eyeing them across the room. "What are you doing over there?" she asked, not remembering having taken them out.

Maggie didn't get up. Instead, she looked back at her book, reading the text out loud again. *"Trust in the Lord with all thine heart."* She peered again up at the ceiling.

"Okay Lord, this is Your journey for me. I would like to do it the right way, Maggie original. No meds, just blind faith."

Taking all the pills out of her purse, Maggie stopped at the last bottle marked *antacid,* laughing as she put it back in her purse. "This one's coming. I plan to eat."

CHAPTER ELEVEN
THE EXTRACTION

TIME WAS METICULOUSLY SLOWLY CREEPING by. Maggie paced the floor; eventually sitting at the computer to keep her mind occupied. She pulled up interviews of co-stars and other friends.

One interview featured Dave Rabet, a new young actor who was "it" now. During the interview, he clamored on self-bragging extensively about his latest film.

Maggie, disgusted, shouted over his interview. "Blah, blah, blah, you're so young and already you've lost your humility. I've been there. It's easy to get caught up, throw money around, drink it up, drug it up, and think you have a million real personal friends!"

She shook her head slowly, bringing it down to rest in her hands. "If only you knew what I know now, you would approach your fame differently."

Maggie stopped the interview realizing how it tore at her. After all, Dave Rabet was just another aspiring young Hollywood actor biting at the heels of stardom. Feeling empowered, the world at his feet, bated breath from fans on his every step. She had seen dozens like him come and go. Literally go. Burn out; die from drugs, drinking, or both.

Her small dose of self-pride holding, she hadn't reached the point of destruction, but fear loomed over her. Was she fast on her way? The constant pressures building were too much for even her. Only one thing helped her overcome the glamorous temptation of existing as a soulless starlet, her faith, regardless if she knew how strong it was or not.

Stars counted their wealth by their fame, their contract amounts, their flashy clothes, their grand homes, and imported cars. It wasn't that Maggie had every material thing she could ever desire; it was how she stayed grounded in spite of it. The accompanying feeling of power was immense. Money could buy a lot of evil when someone became bored with free-for-all spending. Maggie wasn't perfect—she had succumbed to these evils in the past. She regretted the times when she had stumbled; they were many. Thanks to the Lord, she had always overcome.

Family and faith carried her, no matter what she faced. Two things, that without, she would never have made it. Rich in faith, an attribute far more valuable than anything material. Measured only by God, not by the press, nor the public. While Maggie had been watching the interview with Dave Rabet, she found herself hoping that he would find faith. He would surely need it, even more than most.

Maggie headed to the kitchen to pour some more lemonade. She lifted the glass pitcher from the fridge as an echoing blunt sound triggered her ears—a knock at the back door. Maggie froze for a second. Then her heart began to race. It was time.

She put the lemonade away before her anxiousness dropped it. Walking to the back door seemed like forever, a suspenseful slow motion. Maggie reached her hands up nervously grabbing the lock and the doorknob. *Should I say, "Who is it?" Do I open the door without peeking?*

Just then a voice spoke, "Maggie, let us in. We don't have much time!" Maggie didn't recognize the voice, but the person at the door insisted. "Maggie, we work for Ms. A."

The mention of Ms. A was code word enough to convince her to open the door. Two men dressed in black military-style fatigues with dark sunglasses and black caps stood before her. "Maggie, we must move quickly. Close the door behind you."

The spokesman reported into his walkie-talkie watch as the time flashed 11:11. "We have the package; proceeding with extraction. Over."

Maggie grabbed her small bag and closed the door. The three of them proceeded cautiously down the back steps. They ran through the landscaping on the side of the house to the wall surrounding the property.

The spokesman whispered an update into his mic. "Reached wall on southeast side of property. Scaling wall. Please check on bodyguards and make sure there is no movement around the property. Over."

Maggie was told to keep her head down and wait for clearance. Within seconds, the group continued forward.

"10-4. We will proceed," acknowledged the spokesman. He then informed Maggie on the rope and rappel harness he put around her waist to help her scale the wall. The other man reached the barbed wire atop the wall, burning through it with a small torch, and he cleared their escape.

Maggie reached the other side of the wall without incident just after the first man. The second man welded the barbed wire back together before descending.

Maggie was impressed. These men were good. Once regrouped, they all rushed into a white van with dark windows exhibiting the logo *Moses Repairs*. The van sped off.

"Maggie, are you okay? It's me—Ms. A," came a voice from the back of the van. Maggie was silent as she turned to face Ms. A.

She realized the van was filled with computer and surveillance equipment. Two additional people, wearing headphones, sat at consuls. Everyone was turned toward Maggie, waiting for her response.

Maggie, shaken with nerves still raw, managed a few words. "Yeah, I am okay. Thanks."

"My dear, you will have to be a bit tougher if you're going to make it through this transition. I know you can be tough. I saw your interview with Carly Carlotta." Ms. A smiled at Maggie, and Maggie returned a sly grin affirming her Carly victory. "That's more like it. We will be heading to a small private airfield where you will be taking off. Again, everything you need will be provided for you. Once you are dropped off, I will give you the exact time and day to your flight back. It is vital that you follow my next directions precisely. Clear?"

Ms. A was in back-to-business mode now. Maggie was at attention, so she replied accordingly. "Clear!"

"Okay, Maggie, you're going to be in the town called Home. This is all you need to know. No other postings or references visible otherwise to name where you are. You must for no reason leave the town limits at any time. If you do, you will be out of the range of our protection. I must insist you stay put. Do you understand?"

"Yes, I do," Maggie agreed.

"The townsfolk know they will be getting a famous person, but not which one. They have all been sworn to secrecy under special oaths, and believe me, they won't break for any reason. It would be seriously detrimental for them."

Maggie was taken back by the thought. Were the townsfolk threatened? "Did you threaten them, Ms. A?"

Ms. A took a breath, and then proceeded to answer directly. "It is not our style to threaten anyone. We use this project to improve their lives and their families' lives. Their town relies on this to survive in a tough economy. Truly Maggie, there are some things you need not concern yourself with."

Ms. A didn't speak anymore on the subject; Maggie agreed. One little leak from anyone could destroy the project, and Maggie along with it. So, it was better left alone.

"The townsfolk will treat you like a normal lady. Conduct yourself accordingly. No one will be coming out or going into the town while you are there. They are fully supplied for months.

"Remember, there will be no cameras, no cell phones, no televisions, and no computers. Basically, they live off the grid. Most of them don't have use for these things anyway. The project is certainly not stifling their techno side. I suggest you use the time wisely to find yourself again—the Maggie you were before all the fame. Just be you."

Maggie had a million questions going through her head; one thought for every dollar the project cost her. Ms. A continued to cover the important points. "Once the month goes through without a hitch, and it will, then we will initiate the wire transfer for payment. You will be returned to your real life already in progress. We will brief you on what transpired with the doppelganger so that you can answer questions about her/your vacation.

"You must never speak of the project to anyone, as explained in your contract. The compliance of secrecy from your predecessors allows you this opportunity. Your strict confidentiality is important to future projects.

"Remember, you can only contact your mom. A special phone line installed where you stay will reflect you are calling from the Bahamas. Please make your conversations typical. We don't want to accidentally tip her off. No mention of Home or any of the people there. Having been to the Bahamas before, you can use your prior experiences to chit chat. Do you have any questions so far?"

Strangely, in amidst pertinent instruction, Maggie was thinking about Ms. A's use of the word townsfolk. She hadn't heard that term since she was a little girl in the south. It was oddly familiar.

Maggie had one question to ask. "Ms. A, how do the townsfolk feel about the project other than it helps them financially?"

Ms. A smiled, understanding the concern. She leaned towards Maggie with her hands out, again to console her. Maggie laid her hands in Ms. A's.

Ms. A reassured her with sincerity. "Maggie, they will be glad to have you. You have brought a financially stable future for them as a star, but you will bring so much more as yourself. They will love you, for you."

Inspiration from Ms. A warranted an impromptu hug from Maggie. Ms. A interrupted the show of affection quickly.

"Okay, okay enough of that . . . " Ms. A stated pulling herself away anxiously straightening her suit. Ms. A wasn't the type to show her soft side in front of her team. Maggie couldn't be sure, but maybe she got a glimpse of the real Ms. A, if only for a second "I am ready. Can I reach you, or will you reach me?" Maggie asked, moving on with the details.

"I will call you on your secure line when necessary, but don't expect it. If you have an emergency, I will know. I have a few people in place that will be watching out for you. They will reveal themselves only if needed, by mention of my name"

The project instructions wrapped up just in time for them to reach the plane. The runway was in a private coastal area.

Maggie was surprised by the remoteness; they had driven for about only thirty minutes. *I wish I had known about this place before. It's great for ditching clingy photographers.*

The jet plane was already running. The engine roared intensely, echoing off the shore and cliffs nearby. Ms. A bid Maggie goodbye, loudly getting out one last instruction. "Maggie, take good care. Enjoy yourself, and most of all . . . find you."

Maggie thanked Ms. A and began walking to the plane, accompanied by her escape team. The team scanned the perimeter, night vision goggles at work. *All clear* was radioed to the pilot.

After walking up the stairs to board, she stopped for a second and turned around. Ms. A and her team were already gone. Maggie slowly turned back to enter the plane, feeling uneasy about being alone.

Once inside, she noticed the modern jet was decorated to perfection with an abundance of amenities Soon a lovely young stewardess came to greet Maggie. "Hello, Ms. Malone. Welcome aboard. My name is Sarah. I will be happy to bring you anything you need to drink or eat for your flight. Can I get you anything?"

Maggie kindly thanked Sarah and requested some water, though she wasn't even sure if she was thirsty. Her mind fluttered from her nerves, certainly not flying jitters. She had made numerous flights to set shootings all over the world, but this trip was unique. She was more anxious about getting to this destination than any before. She reflected on the warm descriptions she was given about Home, hoping to create a comfortable feeling.

It had been a long time since Maggie had been around this many salt of the earth people on a regular basis. Hollywood was more like a show, where she met sparkly people and shook their hand in a complimentary glaze. Expressing a convincing gratitude how glad they were to meet, mention each other's latest work, and moving swiftly on to the next "blah blah." Not a lot of honest, worthy conversation could be found there.

Maggie longed dearly for genuine people. Down home folks with real personalities, who were not afraid to be themselves. She wanted to be herself, too, fully, if she could remember who that person was. The thought weighed on her. She had been a part of the cycle so long, what would happen when she changed gears?

Maggie focused on things natural to her true side—her family and her faith in God. The two things that made up her genuine personality.

Maggie's mom proudly described Maggie as "my sunshine," a determined spark of a girl who liked to see good in all things. Her mother loved to tell the story of the calico cat that had been the neighborhood pest when Maggie was young. Mr. Stanley, a neighbor from down the street, used to threaten to shoot the cat because it ran around the neighborhood leaving dead mice on everyone's doorsteps. All the neighbors claimed the unfriendly cat left the mice as a warning for humans to keep away from him.

The cat would sit in the weirdest of places throughout the neighborhood. He especially liked to sit on the shaded garden hose box top at Maggie's house. Maggie's father would put up such a fuss, hot mad, because he would have cat hair all over him when he watered the flowers.

No one in the neighborhood fed the cat, hoping it would go away via denial of kind attention. The adults reminded all the kids to abide by this same policy.

Well, Maggie had been bound and determined, as an all-knowing nine year old, to figure out that cat. So every day before school, she would tuck a little milk and tuna under the garden hose box. After school, she would rush home from school to look under the box. Every day the food would still be there untouched. Finally, Maggie had realized the obvious, what was wrong with that darn animal was his unruly stubbornness! Maggie had angrily wondered how it could pass up something so great.

Finally, after throwing away a half gallon of milk and two cans of tuna, she had decided a confrontation was necessary. She had picked the very day that Mom yelled at her for wasting food on a "hopeless creature," as her mom had labeled the bothersome beast. It took Maggie a while that afternoon to find the cat's preferred place for napping.

When Maggie spotted him, he seemed to be waiting for her. On top of the tarp covered barbecue grill in the backyard, there he sat as if it was his own personal throne. He peered at Maggie like an owl on the hunt, his beady little eyes staring at her, his tail slowly waving.

The look on his face seemed to say, "What do you want?" as Maggie cautiously approached him. Maggie spoke in a quiet addressing tone, "Hi, kitty, how are you today? I just want you to know it was me leaving you the food and milk by the hose box. I don't know why you don't just eat it." The cat sat unchanged, still peering at Maggie without interest.

"Listen!" Maggie had raised her voice to keep the cat's attention as she strutted closer to him. She was truly offended when the cat had not started to love her straight away. After all, she had given him delicious tuna and sweet fresh milk. Looking back, Maggie realized that it was whimsical how naïve a child could be. It all seemed so simple then.

Trying the white flag approach, Maggie had stopped walking towards him now. Instead she began addressing him with a soft voice. "I want you to know you need to stop leaving those dead mice on everyone's steps. It's gross, and you're going to get yourself killed by Mr. Stanley." The cat stood up, scrunched his body back, and let out a hiss. The name *Mr. Stanley* must not have settled well with him. Then he jumped off the barbecue and slowly strutted away, stopping about ten feet ahead, squinting back at Maggie.

Now it was Maggie's last chance to get in a last few impressionable words. "Hey, you can walk away now, but if you don't listen to me, you might as well have stayed on that barbecue and let Dad cook you up for supper!" Still unconcerned, the cat turned away and ran off.

The next day when Maggie woke up for school, she ran outside to see if she could spot the cat. She had decided to call him *Mule* because he was as stubborn as an old mule. She opened the front door and yelled out to him. "Mule, here kitty, where are you?"

The cat was nowhere to be found, but Maggie noticed one thing that always stayed with her. Her front steps were the only ones in the whole neighborhood that had dead mice on them, five dead mice to be exact. One for himself, and one for each member of Maggie's family. A gift from an unlikely friend, marking where he truly belonged.

Before heading out to school, Maggie left Mule the milk and the tuna under his spot on the hose box. That afternoon he ate and drank well.

Mule disappeared a month or two later. No one knew if Mr. Stanley had made good on his promise or if Mule had been hit by a car on the highway. It didn't matter to most people as long as the dead mouse gifts stopped.

Maggie, on the other hand, missed Mule greatly. They had become quite friendly. She had always felt like they had an unspoken connection, and she had prayed that Mule was still out there somewhere. Perhaps he had found a home where someone had learned how to put up with his persistent nature.

As Maggie continued remembering Mule, she mused at how Mom compared them to each other. Just like Mule, she had a kind-natured side with a smidgen of absolute stubbornness.

CHAPTER TWELVE
WELCOME TO HOME

THE FLIGHT CONTINUED TO OFFER a smooth journey allowing Maggie to daydream. Campouts with her family. Fun times at high school football games. Her first job at the print shop back home. The first commercial audition she had after she moved to the big city.

Maggie's acting career, like most aspiring actors, had not been easy-breezy when she first started. She had to rent a room from an odd family in L.A. for two years. The people were nice, but they had been caught up in the alien craze. Either way, living that experience, led her to getting a second job in order to save for her own place. While employed at this job, she had met her manager Susan.

The sun had come up sometime during Maggie's daydreaming and a glimmer off the window caught her eyes. The sun shined brilliantly around the clouds, giving them all silver linings. Maggie smiled. *Does every cloud really have a silver lining?*

Hopefully, these clouds were an indication of how the project would go. If a place with a state of calm was all that she got out of it, so be it. To her, a feeling of true peace would be worth a million dollars. Maggie stretched. Sarah came to check on her. She smiled and reassured Sarah that she was fine.

Since Maggie had no way to tell time—no cell phone—she had no idea how long they had been flying. It had to have been a good while. Sarah gladly informed Maggie that they would land in about an hour and a half.

Maggie didn't mind the length of the travel. She appreciated the quiet time to herself. The whole cloak and dagger escape from Hollywood mixed with the nervousness of getting to Home, had worn her down. She dozed off for a spell, only to be awakened by a small bump of turbulence.

Maggie looked out the window. The clouds started to break away as the jet descended in altitude. She could make out bits and pieces of land. Outlines of crops, farms, and water masses slowly came into clear view. Rolling hills of forests and trees became apparent; nature's needle point laid out in patterns from a sky view, took her breath away.

"Green." Maggie grinned whispering into the air. "Green, it's so beautiful." A blanket of good feeling settled over her as the parade of colorful landscaping whizzed by. Ms. A had certainly done her homework, anticipating Maggie's comfort at this welcoming scenic view.

The green creatively detailed out the surrounding areas just like the land she loved where she grew up. She skimmed her eyes over the tops of several tall trees passing by, bushy and lush with leaves. She mused at the memory of walking along a path amidst hovering hundred-year-old oaks. Tall strong shade makers emitting instant fresh air right out of their leaves and into your lungs. L.A. and Hollywood had choking smog and few palm trees could be found.

Maggie prepared to land.

Sarah came by. "Ms. Malone, I hope you enjoyed your flight. Are you done with your beverage?"

Maggie handed her the cup. "Yes, thank you." Maggie wished she could bombard Sarah with questions; however, she knew that would not be cool. Ms. A explained that everyone had a part to play in the project, but keeping their mouth shut was the one universal rule.

The landing was smooth and steady, great piloting. A small landing strip smack-dab in the middle of a large piece of land surrounded by fields. Nothing around except one old rusty airplane hangar.

Maggie waited for Sarah out of politeness. She picked up her things calmly, genuinely wanting to spring out of her seat and get out of the plane to see where she was.

Once the door was open and the stairs were dropped, Maggie was ready to go. She turned to Sarah before leaving. "Thank you for your kindness, and please thank the captain for me. It was a beautiful landing."

Sarah smiled, shaking Maggie's hand. "You're very welcome, Ms. Malone. Enjoy Home."

Once Maggie's feet hit the ground, an older man approached from the airplane hangar. The airplane crew secured the door as they would be taking off again very soon.

A kind face was the first thing that Maggie noticed about the old man. He wore a plaid shirt, jean overalls, and a worn straw hat. He smiled at her, adding a warm greeting when he got close enough. "Hello, ma'am. Welcome! Maggie it is, isn't it?"

He picked up her bag for her, and before Maggie could say a word, the old man continued to talk on. "Well, my name is Earl James, but folks around here call me EJ." He put out his hand for shaking, and Maggie shook it.

"Thank you for the welcome, EJ, and yes, it is Maggie."

EJ was somewhere around the late sixties or early seventies, Maggie guessed. He had a scruffy beard, big brown eyes under bushy eyebrows, and a big inviting smile. He spoke with a very heavy southern accent.

As they walked together toward the airplane hangar, Maggie noticed that EJ had a limp. She tried to walk along slowly not to rush him, but he was moving at his own pace for sure. EJ noticed her looking.

"Oh, that is just an old war wound; acts up now and then, but I usually get around it when it's not getting around me!"

Maggie just smiled. The accent surely was southern. *Could I be back in the South?* Maggie happily wondered.

Once they reached the hangar, EJ pushed open the rickety door for her. She thanked him as she entered first. It was just big enough for two small personal planes, a couple of old tractors, and one classic blue pick-up truck. An old gray metal desk with scattered papers on top was by the door, along with two fold out metal chairs. EJ pulled out a desk chair for Maggie, then one for himself.

"If you would like to have a seat, Maggie, your ride should be skedaddling over here shortly."

Maggie looked around, growing interested in the old tractors. They reminded her of her uncle's farm. She pointed at them. "Do you mind?"

"No, go right ahead; those old tore up machines aren't worth a hill of beans. I just can't bring myself to part with 'em. One belonged to my daddy, and the other was my first tractor. I guess the memories are their real value."

While EJ stayed behind, rubbing his bad leg and fussing at it, Maggie walked over to the tractors. Now settled in his chair, EJ pulled a soda from the cooler near his desk. He called out, "Maggie, can I interest you in a coke?"

"No, thank you, EJ," Maggie graciously replied. She was fascinated with the old tractor that had belonged to EJ's father. It was worn and rusty, still wearing flakes of grain and red mud stuck near the base of the handling gears. She climbed right up on it.

Maggie remembered when her Uncle Frank had let her drive his tractor from his lap for the first time when she was eight. Uncle Frank was Mom's brother, a hard worker and a great family man. Always making time for Maggie, he had no trouble being silly just to make her giggle. He used to tell her, "Maggie, a tractor has a personality like a lady. You have to treat her with respect and take good care of her. She will be temperamental and shifty, but still you have to smile and love her no matter what. That, my little sweet, is how you get the field plowed!"

His advice applied to many things in life, not just tractors. *Good old Uncle Frank. I think he meant to teach me how a lady should be treated. Perhaps so I would know what to expect from a man someday.*

Uncle Frank was not an extraordinarily complex man. He kept life simple, as did most people where Maggie came from. Simple days and simple ways. Maggie had always admired that way of living. Simplicity was one of the things she missed most about where she had grown up. Nothing was simple in Hollywood. Even small decisions came with side effects and ripples. It was all a part of being in the constant public eye.

Maggie sat on the tractor reliving the memory of working the field with Uncle Frank. She smiled, putting her hands on the gears. She could almost hear the motor running and feel the vibrations come up from the tractor base. It was astonishing how something she had done hundreds of times before without thought felt so special to her right now.

Her farm daydreams were stilled by the sound of the rickety door being opened. A man stood in the doorway. He was around fifty years of age, wearing jeans, cowboy boots, and a light blue button up shirt. EJ smiled and got up to greet his friend. "Well, look what the cat dragged in. Cal, how is it going out there today with the new fence? Is it coming along?"

Cal walked to EJ giving him a firm shoulder hug and a handshake then answered. "Hey there, old guy. Fence is coming along fine, just fine." Cal looked over and saw Maggie sitting on the tractor. Then he looked back to EJ with a smirk. "So she's here five minutes, and she's already on your tractor. You don't waste any time for an old man, do you now?"

EJ, embarrassed yet flattered, shook his head back and forth in disconcertment and pointed his index finger at Cal, while his friend laughed uproariously. "You know, you're never too old for a good lickin'. You better mind your p's and q's there, young'un!" he warned.

Cal strolled over to introduce himself to Maggie. On the way, he exclaimed, "I'll mind my p's and q's, but the rest of the alphabet is off limits."

EJ started shaking his head again in dismay and owned the last words on the matter. "Spoken like a true bullheaded donkey, but this here is an airplane hangar, not a barn!"

Cal continued to chuckle at EJ, who was getting all worked up. Maggie joined in with the laughter. The humor wasn't just in the witty conversation; it was the way Cal delivered it. He was looking right at Maggie the whole time. He had a big grin on his face as he waltzed toward her like a kid leaving a candy shop with a pocketful of candy. Cal had dark slicked-back hair and a handsome face with good bone structure. He was very charismatic.

"Calvin Jentry, ma'am." Cal introduced himself properly to Maggie. He reached up his hand to help her down from the tractor. Maggie shook his hand after she was down.

"Maggie, just Maggie," she replied in introduction, flattered by Cal's gentlemanly approach.

"Well, Maggie just Maggie, I will be your transportation and your host. If you will head this way, ma'am, I will scoop your bag up from that old coot over there, and we will take our leave."

EJ grimaced at Cal for the "old coot" remark, while Cal and Maggie made their way to the door. Maggie stopped as EJ held out his hand to shake goodbye, a thought came to her with a smile. Her first acquaintance in home, a sweet old man. She hesitated, inclined to give him a short hug to thank him instead.

After the show of affection, EJ grinned ear to ear, turning red. He could barely squeak out a reply. "Why, thank you, little lady. I hope you enjoy your time with us here in our little town."

Cal only raised his eyebrows at EJ in jest; maybe his earlier comment about her on his tractor was fitting. EJ gave Cal the evil eye and shook a fist at him as Maggie turned away.

Just as the two reached Cal's truck, EJ yelled out as Maggie climbed in, "Now don't go giving her the wrong impression of our townsfolk by acting like a crazy fool. I was the first person she met in this town, and I set a pleasant start!"

Cal grinned. "Wouldn't dream of it, sir."

After closing their truck doors, they were off. Maggie could tell that Cal took great pride in his new, black, shiny pick-up truck. He had wiped a spot off the window as he got in. Riding quietly for a few minutes, Maggie took in the beautiful scenery. There were long green fields with tall oak trees, small farmhouses, crops growing, and grazing horses. She was in awe and overwhelmed with happiness. She felt like a child experiencing Disneyland for the first time. Her window was down, and the cool fresh air streamed through the truck cab. Cal watched as Maggie peered out.

Cal started the conversation. "Well, Maggie, it seems like you haven't seen much of this kind of scenery before. Beautiful, isn't it?"

Maggie turned her head to Cal and smiled. "I have seen it before, but it has been way too long."

Maggie felt so alive, blessed by the landscapes before her: vibrant colors beaming off warm land, blue skies filled with fresh cool air, flowers and animals intertwined throughout the long, grassy fields.

Cal nodded in understanding. "I hear ya, there. This kind of beauty can always make you feel like you're seeing it for the first time. This is truly God's country."

Maneuvering the piece of wheat straw in the band of his hat to the corner of his mouth, Cal kept on driving. Maggie concentrated on what Cal had said. *God's country.* Wow, she had heard that said before in movie lines but never really made the connection—an area of land or place that is so beautiful that you knew God made it and named it after Himself. Yep, she had to agree with Cal. This was God's country.

CHAPTER THIRTEEN
JENTRY FOLK

CAL WAS QUIET FOR THE rest of the drive. He concentrated on the wheat straw in his mouth and the road. Maggie didn't mind. She continued to take in the view.

They soon started up a dirt road. Tall oak trees hovered along the road on both sides, tops bent inward reaching their friends across the road, providing a canopy of ride-in shade. The truck came to a stop at a white wooden farmhouse set in the middle of a few acres of land. It had a matching white picket fence surrounding the yard, a chicken coop, a big red wooden barn, and horses in a fenced pasture. A small separate yellow house sat about a hundred yards behind the main house.

Cal stopped the truck and came around to open the door for Maggie. He started to fill her in on details. "Maggie, welcome to our home. We have a small, fully furnished house out back that will be your place. You will be our company for the duration of your stay."

Cal was retrieving Maggie's bag from the truck when a little girl rushed out of the house.

"Daddy, is this her? Is this her?" The child ran to Cal, throwing her arms around him, nearly knocking him over. Cal steadied himself, scooping her up in his arms with a warm embrace.

"Whoa, little girl. Take it easy there. Yes, this is Maggie, our guest."

The little girl released her dad and marched over to stand straight in front of Maggie. She announced, "My name is Ruby Louise Elizabeth Jentry. It is very nice to make your acquaintance, ma'am, Ms. Maggie."

Ruby Louise had long red hair that was braided into two perfect ponytails. She was only around six, but she didn't miss a beat when it came to proper manners. She offered her hand out to Maggie for a courteous handshaking. Maggie giggled at such an entrance, reaching down to shake Ruby Louise's hand.

"It's nice to meet you, Ruby Louise. Thank you for the kind greeting. You are very polite for such a young lady."

Looking up at Maggie, Ruby Louise tilted her head, wagging her finger with sass. "Well, we are in the south, and Southerners have the best manners. At least, that's what Pops always says."

Maggie agreed with a laugh and a pleasant nod before Cal interrupted their acquaintance.

"Maggie, let's go in." Cal winked at Ruby Louise and she ran off and started chasing a chicken.

Maggie and Cal walked toward the main house. A wooden swing graced the large front porch and black shutters trimmed the windows. The house was not fancy, just a farmhouse decorated with delicate wood trimming. Inside, little knickknacks of chickens and cows rested on multiple shelves. An old, cozy, brown couch draped with a homemade red-and-yellow-checkered box quilt sat against the wall. The entrance room smelled like cinnamon and apples, with a hint of old wood dust.

Cal set down Maggie's bag and yelled down the hall. "Hun, Maggie's here." Then he turned to Maggie.

"Maggie, make yourself at home; she'll be out in a minute." Maggie took a seat on a small lounge chair that matched the sofa, perusing everything around her.

Hand-crocheted doilies dressed each of the oak end tables, while home and garden magazines sat on the wooden coffee table. All around, the walls were covered with pictures of the family: Ruby Louise and perhaps an older brother, along with Cal and his wife. The pictures included camping and fishing excursions, dances, and rodeo events featuring the kids in full rodeo gear.

One really amusing picture caught Maggie's eye. In this black and white picture, the entire family was wearing western clothes and standing on a stagecoach. The photo was probably one of those antique cowboy photos that people have made at the fair. Cal and his wife were standing tall with shotguns in tow. The kids stood back to back in front, holding six shooters and wearing ten-gallon hats. Maggie laughed as she touched the picture, perhaps just to be close to that moment for a minute.

Suddenly, Maggie was startled by a loud voice in the room. "Oh, isn't that a hoot? We took that at the summer fair last year. We about near died of heatstroke in that get-up."

When Maggie turned around, she was met by a smiling face and an outstretched hand. "Hi, I'm Lynn, Cal's wife. It is such a pleasure to meet you and have you in our home."

Maggie already found herself tickled by the warm, outgoing nature of Lynn's personality. She appeared to be in her mid-forties, with striking hazel eyes and a bright, friendly smile. She wore her long brown hair in a messy bun with little pieces falling all around her neck.

"Hi, it's a pleasure to meet you. I am Maggie. Thank you for having me here."

Lynn, still holding Maggie's hand, continued talking. "We were just tickled pink when we found out that you would be staying here with us. We are the envy of the whole town. I hope you don't mind me saying, but you're sure prettier in person than in the movies." Maggie looked down at her tightly grasped hand before Lynn finally let go.

"Goodness, I'm sorry," she apologized. "I just can't seem to act normal. I guess I am too excited."

Maggie responded awkwardly. "It's okay. I appreciate your kindness."

Lynn stared and smiled profusely at Maggie. The excited housewife finally moved on with the conversation just before Maggie became really uncomfortable. "So, Maggie, let me show you around a bit. Cal is out tending to the animals. It's feeding and watering all day long around here. If it's not the animals, it's the kids!"

Just then a fifteen-year-old boy, wearing earbuds, a faded black t-shirt, jeans, and raggedy tennis shoes, barreled through the back door singing loudly along with his mp3 player. He stopped dead in his tracks when he saw Maggie, and his jaw dropped almost clean to the floor. In a daze, he slowly pulled out his earbuds. Lynn put her arm around his shoulder, and gently but slyly pushed his jaw up to the closed position with the free hand. "This is our son, Cal Jr. or CJ as we call him. CJ, now be polite and introduce yourself to Maggie."

CJ tried to regain his composure as he put out his shaky hand. He mumbled nervously, "Haa . . . haaa . . . how do you do, ma'am?"

Maggie was amused by his response. She reached out and shook his hand, smiling as she replied, "How do you do, CJ?"

Hearing Maggie say his name, CJ stood frozen just staring at Maggie with an open grin on his face. Lynn interceded.

"CJ, go out now and help your dad tend to the animals. Turn that music down long enough to hear what he is telling you to do." CJ snapped out of his trance and ran out the door.

Lynn tried to apologize. "Sorry about that. You know teenagers—all hormones and no brains, especially those of the male gender. His father was the same way when we met. Oh, but I won't bore you with that story."

Maggie smiled. Lynn's sparkle came out when she was around her family. She might complain about her family's idiosyncrasies, but there was no doubt she loved them. Anyone could tell that right off the bat.

Other than exhaustion, Maggie felt perfectly at ease with everything. Her nerves were calm, what a change. Lynn escorted her to the small yellow house in the back.

Lynn was a talker. Her monologue was still going when they reached the house. "So that was the whole family, outside of the animals; the dog is Pete, and the cat, Meow. Of course, Ruby Louise named the cat. We are a pretty normal family, as much as we can tell anyway. We spend a lot of time together. The kids homeschool half the time and attend class the other half. It's a nice balance, and it helps with farm chores. CJ is really good at math, and Ruby Louise is a good reader. They both do great in school. We are just busting with pride over them two. CJ is hoping to get on the football team next year. He is all uppity about it. So long as his daddy don't put too much pressure on him, as most southern fathers do about football. Well, here we are." Lynn opened the door for Maggie.

"Now, it's not much, but at least you have a full kitchen and a bath with a shower. We kept it up pretty well. We used to have Cal's grandma here, but she passed away a couple of years ago." Maggie's face fell upon hearing that news. Lynn noticed. "Don't worry. She wasn't here when God took her home. She was at the hospital."

Looking around, Maggie made herself familiar with her new home. She had a hard time keeping up with Lynn's overload of family information. Yep, it sure was the good old South. A person could hear the whole family story in the first ten minutes within meeting them. Southerners just had a lot to say, and they said it all.

Maggie finally was able to get a word in. "Thanks, Lynn. This will be fine. You have a very nice family. I—"

Lynn didn't let her finish. She cut right back in as she shook and re-folded a blanket lying on the couch. "Okay, great. Well, I will give you a chance to settle in, rest, and wash up. Supper is at seven sharp. I hope you eat meat because we are meat people. Come on over if you need anything, but I think we have this place fully stocked. I will drive you into town to fill your pantry with anything else you need in the morning. See ya at seven, dear." Lynn left in a whirl just like she had come in.

Maggie walked over to the couch and practically fell onto it. She was exhausted. It was a lot to take in. She had a new built-in family, a farm with animals just outside, and a whole town to see tomorrow. She couldn't wait. Wondering what the town would be like, she drifted off to sleep. She really needed the rest, waking up with just enough time to unpack and get washed up for dinner.

Not knowing what to wear to dinner, Maggie opened the closet and found an assortment of sensible country farm styles inside. She especially adored the summer dresses. They were typical of what a country girl would wear to church. Cotton and linen adorned with bright summer colors and wildflower patterns, knee length, with a flared-out bottom. The other options included jeans, t-shirts, and an assortment of blouses with various spring colors. The simplicity of the clothing made her choices a non-issue. It was just as well that Maggie was confident and comfortable with her wardrobe. "This must be what Ms. A meant by 'The things you need will be provided.' I will definitely fit right in." Maggie chuckled. After she dressed, she went off to the house for dinner.

Maggie didn't know whether to knock on the door or walk in. She hesitated, observing the family scurrying around the dinner table. She could hear their conversation.

Cal Sr. was speaking. "Well, I think she is a fine young lady. You can't believe what they say in those trash magazines. Judge and ye shall be judged, right?"

Lynn agreed. "That's right, Hun. She seems sweet. We will have to make her feel right at home, everyone."

Maggie was glad to hear the words of affirmation; it made her feel a fast comfort with the family. She decided to go ahead and knock to stop being a nosy eavesdropper.

Ruby Louise let Maggie in. "Hello again, Ms. Maggie; won't you please come in? Mama has made my favorite meal tonight—mac and cheese."

Maggie put her arm around Ruby Louise. It felt like a natural gesture of affection. "Thank you, Ruby Louise. It smells wonderful. I can't wait to try it."

A Southern home-cooked meal wasn't just good. It was like a magical plate of great taste married warm filling happiness. It didn't matter if the meal was pork, beef, or grits. It was all delicious.

Maggie hadn't had a home cooked meal like that in a long time. It had been months since she was last home. Even when she had visited her family, she didn't eat much of Mom's cooking. She was always worried about getting out of shape.

Lynn fixed Maggie a plate with smoked barbecue beef brisket, homemade macaroni and cheese, and green beans. *Oh my!* Southern style mac and cheese, containing mounds of real cheddar cheese kissed by cream, oozing hot with pasta. Not to mention the green beans, prepared to the extreme degree of total deliciousness in the South. Bacon grease is the name of the game there! Slowly smoked barbecue beef brisket smothered in homemade sweet barbecue sauce, enough said.

Maggie couldn't believe what she was about to eat. Goodbye, Hollywood diet; hello, Southern comfort! Grateful that Lynn didn't put too much food on her plate, Maggie thanked her as she received it. She noticed that no one had started to eat yet, so she waited patiently for everyone to be served.

Cal reached over and took the hand of his daughter and his wife, who were sitting on either side of him. In turn, they took the hand of the person seated next to them at the table. Ruby Louise had insisted on sitting next to Maggie, so she took Maggie's hand. CJ, very red in the face, stretched out his hand to Maggie on her other side. *Grace.* Maggie finally realized. They were going to say grace. Maggie picked up CJ's shaky sweaty hand.

"Maggie, since you're our guest, would you mind honoring us by saying grace?" Cal requested.

Maggie was flattered, but she wasn't sure she was the right candidate for the job. Her prayers were always private. Obviously, she faced outside pressures to keep them that way. She hadn't shared a prayer with a family like this since she had been home. She felt unsure but answered right away. "I would love to. Thank you."

Maggie considered taking the safe route, with a standard prayer from Bible school for the blessing of the meal. It would be easy, and she still knew them by heart. No one ever forgets those prayers from Bible school. After all, they were recited every day of childhood. On second thought, though, she decided it might be better to go with something special and more personal. The family was deserving of a personal touch for opening their home to her. So, without delaying too long, Maggie bowed her head and began: "Dear Lord, thank You for this wonderful meal and the blessing of the family I am sharing it with. Amen."

Everyone nodded after the prayer, giving Maggie the sense of having done well. CJ smiled at Maggie, not in a hurry to let go of her hand, but he did. The meal was just as imagined, beyond a delicacy. Maggie couldn't help eating too much. It was the one negative of Southern comfort food: it is hard to stop eating, making someone go right past feeling full. After dinner, Ruby Louise and Lynn rose to clear the table and do the dishes. The men headed out to get the animals ready to settle in for the night.

Maggie helped the ladies bring in dishes from the table to the kitchen. Lynn scolded her for doing so.

"Maggie, honey, you shouldn't be doing that. You're our guest. Please put those dishes down and stop messing. I am sure you're exhausted from the long day. Go on home and get some rest. We do breakfast at six a.m., but you're welcome to come over later, and I will fix you something."

Maggie loved the natural mothering instinct that Lynn revealed to her. It was the coating around the "right at home" feeling.

"Thank you so much for dinner; it was amazing."

Lynn was not only a talker, but also a hugger. She threw her arms around Maggie and gave her a great big squeeze. It was natural for sweet, Southern people to shake hands the first time meeting someone but then hug every time thereafter. This family was that kind of family, full of Southern kind goodness.

Maggie enjoyed her hug, startled at first but soon growing a smile and saying, "Good night."

Then she was off to the little house. As nightfall approached, the sound of bugs and toads becoming boisterous surrounded the farm. A cool breeze mixed with humid damp air created a refreshing peaceful feeling. Maggie couldn't help but close her eyes and take a deep breath. She stood there with a grin on her face, and her arms outstretched over the field. This was the first real sensation of total peace she had experienced in a long time. A God-sent heart-alive again feeling.

CHAPTER FOURTEEN

FARM FRESH

MAGGIE COULD HAVE STOOD THERE in that field forever. The only thing deterring her was the cold chill she felt creeping across her arm. No wait, it's a mosquito! She soon remembered those summer night pests of the South, as she swatted her arm. Her mom used to tell her they were drawn to her natural sweetness. How cute, the way moms can make up such corky things on the spot, just to create a smile on their daughter's face. A mother's knowledge came through her kind meaningful words, creating the greatest communication of her love.

Finally, Maggie reached the little house and sprung open the squeaky wooden door. As she walked to the bedroom, the floor creaked as the heat of the day met the cool night. The entire house had a unique smell about it. It was a cozy quaint smell, a mix of aged cedar and dried wildflowers. The history of the home displayed on several pictures lining the walls. Maggie zeroed in on a picture of Cal's grandma. She was sitting on a rocking chair, with CJ and Ruby Louise hugging her.

Maggie looked over to the corner of the room; the rocking chair was still there. Golden stained oak, etched flowers adorning the head-board, and worn soft spots in the wood on the arm rests. A beautiful baby blue and princess pink handmade quilt strewn over the back of the chair.

Drawn to it, Maggie walked over and picked up the quilt, instantly feeling the soft patterned cotton fabric squares illustrated with children's drawings. She threw the quilt around her before she sat down in the chair. The cushioned cloth hugged Maggie like a warm, swaddled child. She sat quietly and rocked, reflecting on how Cal's grandma felt in that chair. How sweet to end each day rocking, wrapped up in this quilt, with your loving family just steps away.

Considering her elderly days ahead, Maggie's mind wandered quickly from sweet old comfort to the physical appearance of age. If Susan had her way, Maggie would never get old. She planned on preserving Maggie, using surgery and any other means necessary, like a million-dollar mummy.

Getting old, having a family—what was the future for Maggie going to look like? Maggie's mother regularly asked, "Mags, when are you going to find a special someone, settle down and raise a family? You can't lose sight of your own life while you're acting out everyone else's."

Maggie thought about what a wonderful grandma her mother would make. Michael had focused on his college, career, and opening his own practice. He had just married the preceding year and was planning kids soon. He was sure to have kids before Maggie. Without question, Michael would be an awesome father. After all, he had many years of patient practice as the older brother to a bratty little sister.

As she continued rocking, Maggie smiled at the thought of Michael and Theresa, his wife, as they walked hand in hand. *Will I ever meet that someone special? It would be a miracle in my line of work.*

Being a movie star in Hollywood was equivalent to the odds of winning the lottery.

Few and far between were the men in Maggie's life. There were minor relationships over the years with co-stars. However, the double limelight drama always got in the way.

As a result, Maggie was sure no man could survive a true relationship with her under the scrutiny of Hollywood. The list of requirements focused on patient and forgiving qualities would be endless, who could ever measure up?

First item on the list, typed in bold, "willing to sacrifice all privacy." As a star, she had been given no choice; she knew a lack of privacy came with the territory, even if she didn't agree with it. No man in his right mind could want that for himself or his family. A relationship with a movie star was a huge gamble. What if it didn't work out, what if it did? How long could anyone withstand it? How did someone ask that of anyone she loved? Sure, other stars in Hollywood had tried to keep their private lives private. They had tried, but most of them failed. The public and the press were relentless, never giving up, crossing boundaries daily.

Technology quickly advanced, so ensued the creepy creative ways to use it. Digital photography molded in new invasive ways of catching private moments meant for a husband and a wife or a mom and a baby. They left nothing sacred when it came to celebrities. Nothing.

Maggie had zero private previous dates. Every movement was on display: dinner, shows, and even just a walk down the street. She always had to stop to wonder—was this guy really with her or just after the bragging rights? She had finally stepped away from it all, strict dating freeze for over two years.

Because of the self-standoff from dating, the press had to swing it some way. They were always demanding some type of explanation from Maggie. They expected answers. If they didn't get answers, they simply made up their own.

"Maggie Malone is Practicing a New Religion of Celebrity Celibacy," tabloid headlines read. The hurtful things they could come up with just to sell a story were unreal.

All the negative future instances Maggie braced for every time she met someone were too much to handle. So she built a cardiac brick wall, brick after brick, keeping her heart protected, but also empty and dormant.

As soon as Maggie quieted her thoughts, she stopped rocking and changed for bed. She hit the pillow, gave God thanks for the moments of received peace, then fell quickly asleep.

A rooster crowed. Mornings came early on the farm.

Maggie sat straight up, startled. She was not used to waking up to a rooster crowing at six a.m. Blinking her eyes and rubbing them, she tried to focus. Her hair seemed to stand straight on end, statically sticking out in every direction. Humidity hair-do. The weather in the south had never been kind to her hair.

Looking like a hot mess, but feeling elated recalling where she awoke, she jumped up and dressed for a run. How long had it been since she had a run without strategic planning, back doors, and ten bodyguards? A run free of anxiety; just the entrancing rhythmic sound of her feet hitting the ground? She couldn't remember when; it had been that long.

Maggie hurried across the creaky floor in anxiousness to see the farm in the morning light. She flung open the front door; a welcoming wave of cool fresh air kissed her face. As she proceeded out, she stretched her arms up and her legs out on the edges of the steps.

Maggie noticed that no one was around; the Jentrys must be eating breakfast, so she started out on a run around the property. Quickly, she settled into steady breathing. It was just her, all her. The only audience were goats, sheep, and a few horses, silently encouraging with a look of "You go, girl" as she passed them. Running with steady speed and distance, Maggie enjoyed it immensely. Finally, as she lapped the animals again, she slowed down, making her way back to the house to hit the shower. She had just finished dressing when a knock sounded at the door.

Maggie hollered as she towel dried her hair. "Come in!"

Lynn opened the door ready to talk. "Good morning, Sunshine; how did you sleep?" Lynn continued before Maggie could answer. "I brought you a plate since I knew you were probably tired from yesterday. We have eggs, bacon, grits, and toast."

Maggie became deliciously aware of the plate. The smell of hot, Southern-style breakfast wakes the nose senses fast. The inviting aroma drew a pleasing smile to Maggie's face.

"Oh my, Lynn, you sure have outdone yourself again. This looks and smells so great. Thank you."

Lynn nodded as she headed back to the door. "Well, you are certainly welcome. Enjoy. As soon as you are ready, we can head downtown, I will show you around. You can pick up anything that's not here that you need."

Maggie smiled. "That would be great. Thanks, Lynn. I will catch up to you at the house."

Lynn left, and Maggie savored her breakfast before getting up to get ready. It was time to choose an outfit for the day. Picking an outfit designed purely for comfort and practicality was new. She stepped over to the clothing choices in the closet, reasoning with the selection, talking out loud to herself.

"Okay, well we have skirts, shorts, and dresses. All cute country-girl wear, fitting for a small town. It shouldn't be that hard. Does plaid go with flowers?"

Maggie laughed putting her hands over her mouth, amused a bit by the overwhelming patterns. Finally, she settled on jean shorts and a blue plaid shirt.

"So there we go! Not bad—it's just me, isn't it? Well, it is today!" She smiled to her reflection in the mirror.

Quickly putting her hair up in a ponytail, she made little attempt at any makeup, just a touch or two. She didn't see the need. The point was to get away from all that. However, she still indulged in a spray of her four-hundred-dollar perfume—her necessity.

Maggie and Lynn chatted during the pickup truck ride to town. Lynn informed Maggie of the festival scheduled for that night. It was the entire buzz around town. Lots of preparations and decorations were underway. Food—lots of food—a band, carnival rides, and a bouncy house for the kids. Main Street was the place to be that weekend.

Lynn was eager to stop at the local clothing store, Lander's Laundry. She thought it would be fun to shop together. Maggie agreed. It had been forever since she had shopped with a lady friend.

She was excited but tried not to let on to Lynn. She didn't want to come off like a giggly teenager at the mall.

"Maggie, I hope you don't mind the styles they have at Lander's. It's not too fancy, but I think it's nice enough. You're probably used to a lot nicer things, I'm sure."

Lynn sounded a little jealous, but Maggie didn't take any offense. An awkward silence lurked over the two women for a moment then Lynn comedically added, "I mean it should be fine because . . . girl, you could make a paper bag tied with a rope belt look just fabulous."

They both began laughing out loud together. Maggie knew at that very moment, they became two friends, bonding over a contagious carried away laugh

"Lynn, you're too much. I just don't know about you," Maggie said as she tried to gain some composure, catching her breath.

Now parked, they both got out of the truck. Lynn came over to Maggie's side, putting her arm through Maggie's to accompany her on a stroll.

Lynn still giggling, added to the amusement stating, "Well, honey, like my husband says—the best part of knowing someone is the ride to figuring them out. We'll have a great time."

They both headed toward Lander's Laundry, feeling giddy and ready to shop.

CHAPTER FIFTEEN

TOWN MEET AND GREET

THEY WALKED AROUND THE BLOCK to Main Street, perusing the window displays. Suddenly, the all-too-familiar overwhelming feeling of being watched came over Maggie. She turned to see everyone on Main Street stopped and looking directly at her.

Maggie's excitement about the day quickly turned to fear, so she turned to Lynn for security. Seeing the frightened look on Maggie's face, Lynn put her arm around her shoulder and loudly exclaimed. "What is wrong with y'all? It's just Maggie. Go about your business!"

The shocked townspeople simply nodded. A few of the old men smiled and tipped their cowboy hats. Quickly everyone went back to whatever they had been doing.

No one is going to rush me? Flash me with a camera? Shove a pen and notepad for an autograph in my face? None of that?

This was a first for Maggie. She turned to Lynn and hugged her. Lynn looked confused. "Darling, what was that for?"

Maggie smiled. "Just thanks; you're cool!"

Lynn laughed. "Being cool comes after many years of being a hot mess."

Together the two friends walked into Lander's.

"So, Lynn, what do you think? I think you would look great in a baby blue summer dress with daisies?" Maggie suggested.

"Hmmm, now you're talking! If only they have something like that in my size: rounded minus a few pounds. I haven't lost my entire figure yet."

Maggie shook her head at Lynn, remarking on her comment from earlier. "Girl, you could make a paper bag with a rope belt look fab-u-lous!" They both laughed.

Lander's Laundry was a vintage country clothing store with flair. All the fixtures, including clothing racks and tables, were dated wooden fixtures. The counter even boasted an early 1900's brass cash register. Antique metal signs and posters with pictures of ladies' clothing from the fifties graced the walls. One of the posters read, "Only $3.29. The must-have dress you need to impress your guests at your next dinner party." The sign stuck in Maggie's mind; she thought how practical and stylish women's fashion was in the fifties.

The store smelled of fresh flowers and mothballs. It was like potpourri mixed with a spray of camphor. Tall ceramic and wooden mannequins stood around the inside perimeter. One ceramic statue was a flapper dancer wearing a black dress with a black feather head-band. Across the store was a hand-carved dark brown wooden grizzly bear statue that stood life size. The bear was wearing a hula skirt and a coconut shell bra top. In the middle of the store were lots of old fabric mannequins, sporting various outfits. Maggie adored a few of the square-dancing dresses displayed, with their bright patterns like bandanas. All in all, Lander's was quaint, appealing, and not too big—and it didn't really need to be. The store focused on dresses and other summer wear for ladies.

As Maggie continued to look around the store, an adorable older lady appeared around the corner of one of the racks. She looked to be around seventy years of age, and Maggie immediately fell in love with her smile and the great dimples surrounding it. The pleasant older lady was dressed in tan slacks and a summer country red paisley shirt with a thin white linen scarf tied around her neck. She was about five feet tall, with gray-blue hair. She wore bright red lipstick, and her cheeks were covered with a rosy blush.

Lynn spoke to the lady first. "Good Morning, Fanny. How are you on this fine day? You look like a million dollars. I love your scarf. Is that a new shade of lipstick? It's all wonderful."

Fanny scurried over to Lynn, answering as she scurried.

"Why, thank you, ma'am. I just got in a new batch of scarves. I thought I would take this one for a ride. It's fashionable and keeps me warm. The lipstick is an old one. I just had the nerve to wear it for the first time today."

Lynn turned her attention to Maggie. "This is Maggie; she is the lovely lady staying in Grandmama's old house, visiting with us all for a while." Then the introductions continued.

"Maggie, this here is Fanny Lander. She is the owner of Lander's and a town council member of Home. She is a sweetie with a big heart but tough as nails when it comes to her politics!"

Fanny stuck out her hand to Maggie. "Well, certainly nice to meet you, young lady. Welcome to our little town in the south."

Maggie shook Fanny's hand and thanked her while Lynn moved on to view the merchandise. "So, Maggie," Lynn sassed, "let's see what she has here that will turn us into two hot chicks or at least two medium warm ducks. Shall we?"

Lynn walked over to one particular dress stand, while Maggie went in a different direction. Maggie flipped through the dresses on the rack; many of the styles were similar, but the colors and patterns differed. Maggie felt sure she would find something nice to wear to the festival, so she kept looking until she chose a few to try on.

Maggie's search was interrupted by a distracting clicking sound coming from the corner of the store. She curiously headed in the direction of the *click, click, click* to investigate. When Maggie saw a flash, she finally started to place where she had heard that sound before. It was a camera! Maggie's heart began to race; startled her mind immediately went from calm to angry.

Again, really? A camera? Who is taking pictures of me? Who is in that corner spying? Maggie rushed over and fiercely shoved a small rolling dress rack that was in her way. She was determined to expose the culprit hiding there. She was going to let them have it!

There behind the rack crouched a five-year-old girl who had been frightened by Maggie's foot-pouncing approach.

She was holding a toy camera. She was scared and startled but still managed to speak. "Sorry, ma'am, I . . . I . . . I . . . didn't mean to bother ya. I was just playing fashion show."

Maggie wiped the sweat that had started beading on her forehead and took a deep breath to calm herself. Catching herself just before her anxiety set in, Maggie bent down and put her hand out to the little girl to help her up. "It's okay, sweetie. My name is Maggie. What's yours?"

The little girl was still a bit nervous. "Cindy Trebush, ma'am." Then she curtsied politely.

"Well, Cindy, I am a bit camera shy; how about I take a photo of you on the runway?" Cindy giggled now feeling better and nodded her head playfully yes at Maggie's suggestion. Cindy handed Maggie the camera, and Maggie did just that.

"Wow! You are a natural, Cindy. You would make a great model," complimented Maggie.

Cindy tossed her hair back with a hand flip and spun her skirt around smiling big at the camera. Maggie motioned to Cindy, reminding her to keep her chin up and to bat her eyes. They played on for a few moments before Cindy ran off with her camera to find her mom. She gave Maggie a thank you as she toddled off.

Lynn had been chatting away with Fanny, so she had not even realized that anything had happened until she saw Maggie's face.

"Maggie, what happened to you? Your face is white as a ghost. Are you okay?"

Maggie didn't want to admit that she jumped to conclusions, assuming the camera and all.

"Oh, I am fine. There was a little girl over in the corner, and she just surprised me, I guess."

Fanny raised one eye and leaned over to peer at the corner of her store. "That Cindy, she is always going around getting into something. She is sweet as sugar but as sly as a fox. Her momma works next door at the drugstore. Now and again, she moseys along over to my store."

Maggie assured her new friends that everything was fine before heading to the dressing room and choosing two dresses. Lynn insisted on paying for the dresses, and off they went, bidding Fanny a good day. Lynn and Maggie stopped at a few more shops before continuing their window-shopping. Time went by quickly, and lunchtime arrived.

Lynn suggested they grab a bite to eat at the café at the west end of Main Street. "It's a bit basic," Lynn said, "but you can't get a better plate of chicken and dumplings. They are almost as good as mine."

Lynn had been right. Maggie, once again, was deliciously overwhelmed, although she couldn't eat much. She was still full from Lynn's generous breakfast. After all, she was not used to having that much food in an entire day, let alone each meal.

Before leaving town, Lynn wanted to stop by the hair salon to say hi to her friend, Alice. One side was a beauty parlor for the ladies, and the other side was the barber shop for the men. The layout was nice, making it convenient for everyone to get hair tended in one location.

Lynn introduced Maggie to Alice Whit, the hairdresser, and her husband Johnny Whit who was the barber. They seemed like quite an interesting couple. Maggie was intrigued by the wedding picture hanging in their shop. It looked like Alice and Johnny had been no older than sixteen when they were married.

As Maggie and Lynn took a seat, Lynn was hoping to hear the latest news in town. All the best news i.e. gossip came from the hairdresser. Alice and Johnny were both working on someone's hair, while arguing about their hound dog lying just inside the door to the shop.

"Johnny, you're full of it. Old Judge is about nine years old 'cuz I remember Momma was still alive when he was a pup. He used to chew her best house slippers," Alice scolded.

Alice appeared to be about forty with black hair and pale skin. She wore startling blue eye makeup. Her slim figure was evident since the slightest curve could not have been missed in those tight black spandex half pants she was wearing. She was popping her gum like a firecracker as she yelled across the room at her husband. Her red high heels gave her a self-made soapbox.

Although Johnny was about the same age as his wife, he looked as if life had been much harder on him. Or maybe it was just Alice who had been hard on him? With slicked-back brown hair balding slightly on the top, he wore tan trousers and brown sandals with a green plaid shirt. Johnny grimaced, eager to get his words out.

"Listen here, woman! That is my dog. I know better than anyone that he is only eight years old. He still has lots of good hunting years in him. Ain't that right, Old Judge?"

Johnny stopped cutting the hair of the old man in his chair in order to take a gander at Old Judge. Old Judge returned a questionable stare, sighed, and laid his head back down. Alice and Johnny continued to bicker over the tops of the heads of the two unfortunate souls sitting in their cutting chairs. Their distressed looks of concern towards each other revealed their level of discomfort.

Soon a much-needed interruption brought a pleasant sound catching everyone's attention. The door flung open, causing the chimes on the door to ring. Maggie turned to look as a good-looking man entered. Obviously in his late twenties, he possessed a fit body that was sporting Wrangler jeans and cowboy boots. His tight black t-shirt read "Rodeo Clowns Rock!" and matched his black cowboy hat perfectly. As he entered, he sang out loud what sounded like a country song: "She don't love me anymore. She took my heart and went out the door. Feelings deep inside, I can no longer hide. She don't love me anymore."

Maggie loved his voice. It was both strong and deep, and she was caught up in his performance. Of course, his song was set off by his gorgeous smile.

Her heart skipped a beat as the unassuming man waltzed in paying no mind to who was there. He walked with a comfortable-to-be-himself swagger. After heading directly to the water cooler, he gulped down a drink of water, squashed the paper cup, and tossed it towards the trashcan across the room.

Everyone in the room was still. They were not in a swooning daze like Maggie, but they had simply stopped in anticipation, waiting to see if he would make a basket in the trash from that far away. In it went, without any interference.

He grinned. "Three pointer!"

The crowd cheered and went back to what they had been doing. The shooter seemed impressed with himself, until his eyes met Maggie's.

He tilted his head to the side in kind, removing his hat; he smiled as he walked over to her very slowly. Their eyes never lost their lock the whole time.

"Hello, ma'am, I am Jacob Ryan, but you can call me Jake. You must be Ms. Malone."

She nervously scooted herself back onto her chair and brought her feet in closer to the bottom. Her arms fumbled around in search of the armrests.

His entrance, the bells on the door, the singing, his stopping in front of her, and his whole approach had left her speechless. Furthermore, he was still looking right into her eyes. How could she possibly reply when she was lost at sea peering into what were the bluest eyes she had ever seen?

Maggie had been charismatically addressed by dozens of good-looking men over the years. It was one of the perks of being a beautiful movie star. She knew enough to see through the barrage of fairytale stories that Hollywood personifies. Always expecting, a lot of putting on a show for the sake of show, so to speak.

So when she confidently opened her mouth to reply, she didn't expect to say, "Maggie, that's fine. Maggie. Right."

She sat mortified as the last word tripped out of her mouth, as if her new lips had just arrived. Maggie somehow managed to put her hand out, so he grinned and started to shake it, flattered with her antics. "Well, Ms. Maggie, you have very soft hands."

Maggie found herself in a trance created by her fast-beating heart. *Get it together, girl.* Pulling through, finally, she slipped her hand away from his. She sat up straight and loosened her feet from their stiff position. *Time to stop looking like a drooling teenager!*

"Thank you," Maggie replied, a bit more confident now.

She sat there wondering what was going to happen next. Jake turned and spoke to Johnny.

"Hey, Johnny, I see you're busy now; came for a quick trim but will check with y'all later."

Johnny didn't look up from his cut. "All righty then."

Jake walked toward the door, brushing back his silky waves of dark brown hair with his hand and reapplying his hat. Maggie was watching his every move. All the ladies were. Once Jake got to the door, he turned his back to it as all the ladies quickly turned their peering eyes away.

He looked over at them with an amused expression and tipped his hat, saying sweetly, "Ladies." He pushed the door open with his back and exited the shop, leaving in the cool fashion in which he came. It was like Rhett leaving Scarlet; however, this time there was more than one lady in dismay, and they all were a bit sad to see him go.

CHAPTER SIXTEEN
FESTIVAL, LIKE NO OTHER

JAKE STARTED WALKING DOWN THE road, making sure he was clear of the view from the barber shop. He grabbed off his cowboy hat and hit himself in the head with it. He scolded himself. "Was the staring at her too much? Darn, I bet it was! Great, you fool!"

He shook his head disagreeably and put his hat back on, continuing, "Still, you can't blame a man for being shook up by such a beauty."

Jake noticed Mrs. Dupree out of the corner of his eye. She had been watching him the whole time as she rocked methodically on the front porch of her antique store. Fanning herself feverishly, she worked hard to keep her heavyset body cooler. She didn't seem impressed with Jake's behavior. Jake thought it best to address her politely, and then move along. "Well, hello there, Mrs. Dupree. Nice day."

She shook her head negatively in frustrated wonder, replying smugly, "You're just plain nuts, son. Walking down the street, talking to yourself all crazy, hitting yourself, just plain nuts, I say."

Jake couldn't help but burst out laughing, however Mrs. Dupree was completely serious. Jake cleared his throat. "Well," he smartly whipped with some comic composure, "I thank you, ma'am, and all the same to you."

Mrs. Dupree gasped at his comment. She got up and stomped into her store, slamming the door behind her. Jake laughed at her stubbornness and started back up the road.

Maggie was awash in the adrenaline rush from meeting Jake.

Lynn stepped in to save her. "Maggie, you okay? You look a bit flush. Jake sure does have that effect on women. Great guy, too."

The mention of Jake had Maggie all ears. Lynn was such a talker that in order to survive an afternoon of her constant word flow, one only half listened most the time. It was just hard to keep up. Lynn continued, of course.

"He's not married. I don't think he is seeing anyone either." Lynn raised up her eyebrows. "Hmmm?"

Maggie smiled and gave Lynn a dry answer. "Well, I just met him. He seems like a nice enough guy, but I am on a break with relationships for now"

Lynn shot over a very questioning look, chin down and eyes up, all the while wearing a curious smirk.

"Listen, honey, break or no break, there's not a single lady in this town that wouldn't spend some time with him."

Embarrassment flushed her face while hitting Lynn on the shoulder in jest. But Lynn wasn't done talking, shocker there. "Well, you know the festival is tonight, and I'm sure Jake will be hanging around with the rodeo group. Maybe you just might run into him, unplanned of course."

Lynn was being a sly smarty pants, winking at Maggie as they left the shop. It was the perfect time to go since Alice was trying to talk them into a rock-hard hair sprayed "up do" for the festival tonight.

Once back at the Jentry farm, it was dinner time. Dinner with the entire Jentry family was a time Maggie looked forward to, and it was Ruby Louise's turn to say grace. Maggie was touched when Ruby Louise mentioned her name in the prayer. She ended her grace with an interesting request. "And Lord, please let Maggie consider allowing me to wear some of that fancy perfume she brought from Hollywood."

Lynn scolded Ruby for making a personal request when she was saying grace to the Lord for their meal. Hearing Ruby Louise say the word Hollywood caused Maggie to wonder. She thought about many things: Syl, her unanswered fan mail, and the doppelganger.

As Maggie's thoughts turned to Hollywood, she didn't think of the hustle, the paparazzi, the long days, the traffic, and the unrelenting attention. She didn't miss those things at all. Coming to such a realization made Maggie quite uncomfortable; after all, it was her life. It was taunting how easily she could get used to life in Home. Spending time with the Jentrys made her feel like a real part of their family. Unfortunately, these feelings were out of place and dangerous for everyone involved in the project.

After dinner, Maggie helped clean up against Lynn's wishes. Lynn finally shooed her out of the kitchen to go get ready. They needed to leave for the festival in about an hour.

Maggie walked over to the small house and sat down on the porch swing. The sun had started to hang low in the sky as evening approached. The animals began to quiet down, and the cool night air was creeping in. Closing her eyes as she swung back and forth, Maggie lay her arms across the back of the swing and rested her head back.

She took in a deep breath of fresh clean southern air, like breathing in pure oxygen. Clean air was such a welcome change from the city smog. Pure relaxation for a moment was interrupted by a tiny little noise. Maggie brought her head up and opened her eyes. She had a guest. A tiny hummingbird drank and buzzed around the feeder hanging on the house trellis. Maggie immediately stopped swinging so as not to frighten her small friend. There flew a small white and black majestic body adorning a bright crimson red neck and face with fast moving wings floating against the grace of the pending sunset. So beautiful and amazing, Maggie was taken in with awesome wonder.

Once the hummingbird had its fill of drinking, it flew just over Maggie's head. It seemed to nod then politely fly away. Maggie sat in awe. *Did that hummingbird just nod at me?*

Maggie often had extraordinary signs in her life. Unexplained little things would happen to remind her that God was always with her. This was one of these times. The little visitor made Maggie feel full of joy, and she couldn't wait to tell Lynn about it. *Oh yeah, Lynn. What time was it?*

Maggie jumped out of bird watching mode. She still had to get ready for the festival, so she hurried into the house. Her thoughts wandered to Jake, and she couldn't help but hope she would see him tonight. She promised herself not to get too excited.

"This is the one." She held up a light blue, shoulder-strapped eyelet lace summer dress that would swing gently around her knees. Maggie spoke aloud, trying to calm her nerves.

"Now don't get all excited; it's just a festival, just like the millions you went to as a kid. No big deal. Try to keep your cool. Okay, so this dress with the red cowgirl boots. The dress says country girl, and the boots say kind of sassy lady. Yep, perfect!"

With the wardrobe now chosen, Maggie worked on her hair.

She put on her delicate silver cross necklace. She wore that cross every chance she could, especially on important days like graduations, award ceremonies, and Mom and Dad's anniversary parties. It had been a gift from her dad when she was nine. Dad told her that it would protect her always seeing her through anything life brought. She often wore it underneath her attire at work per Susan's demand to tone down her faith. She was ashamed that she had ever hidden it. She looked into the mirror, placing her hand on her showing cross, and declared; "Now I am ready."

Maggie walked over to the dresser to add a quick spray of "fancy perfume," as Ruby Louise had called it. Speaking of the little miss, she was knocking at the door with Lynn just then. Maggie asked them to come in.

"Hey, Ruby Louise, you look adorable," Maggie complimented.

Ruby Louise was dressed in the cutest little pink and yellow summer dress with matching ribbons in her hair. She sweetly replied, "Why, thank you, Ms. Maggie. You look pretty good yourself."

Maggie shrugged her shoulders and made a sad face. Ruby Louise ran over to her immediately and held her hand in concern asking, "Are you sad? Why are you sad, Ms. Maggie?"

Maggie's face broke into a smile as she knelt to hold Ruby Louise's hand right back. "No, I'm not really sad. I just noticed you're missing something as part of your outfit tonight."

Ruby Louise looked puzzled as she looked over her own clothing, carefully touching the bows in her hair and checking her shoes.

"Come with me," Maggie requested. They walked down the hall hand in hand, followed by Lynn. Maggie asked Ruby Louise to close her eyes as Maggie reached over to the dresser.

"Now keep your eyes closed," Maggie reminded Ruby Louise. Ruby Louise did just as she was told as Maggie sprayed a squirt of the "fancy perfume" over Ruby Louise's head. Lynn and Maggie smiled at each other as the perfume began to fall. It wasn't long until Ruby Louise got a whiff. She broke out in a giggle and a cheer of' "Yes, thank You, Lord!" without even opening her eyes. They all laughed, and out the door they went to the festival.

As they headed to the car with the rest of the family, Ruby Louise was still glowing, enjoying her awesome perfumed-up self. "I bet Joey won't want to chase me tonight. I bet you anything he will want to dance with me. I just know it. Well, he will have to beg I tell you. A girl has to be choosey you know," Ruby Louise announced proudly.

Maggie and Lynn both got a kick out of Ruby Louise's words. For a girl so young, she sure had life all figured out. Cal rolled his eyes. The thought of his daughter and boys was not something he wanted to consider just yet. CJ nudged his little sister playfully.

The ride to the festival went by quickly. Maggie sat back and listened whimsically to the family talking about who was going to be there. It was fun to hear them talk, no matter what they were saying. A Southern accent was like a way of life—a few words full of meaning all delivered with intentional emotion. Simple, sweet, and to the point.

The first steps onto the parking lot came with a wave of festival smells. There were hints of hot buttered popcorn, home-baked cakes and pies, and fresh perfume and cologne. These scents were a gift compared to the downwind of cow and horse aromas that usually blew into town.

Everyone in town was nicely dressed, like a red-carpet walk but hometown style—lots of summer cotton dresses, linen striped men's shirts, and cowboy boots on most everyone. Carnival rides and games, accompanied by music on Main Street, filled the air with entertaining festival sounds. All around, little kids were running with balloons and cotton candy. Maggie watched in awe, taking in the familiarity of it, feeling youthful. Everyone was truly happy to be together enjoying each other's company.

"Maggie," Lynn called her attention away from the ambiance. "Quite a going on, isn't it? Care to head over to the dance tent? Cal and I want to show them how it's done. How 'bout it?"

"Sounds great!" Maggie agreed, and they all headed toward the music barreling from a big white tent set smack dab in the middle of Main Street. The band was playing fast two-step music. Dozens of couples were going at it, 'round and 'round, dancing. A site of whirling and shuffling with each turn and step exactly on the beat. They were all quite good at it and it showed.

Lynn bid Maggie goodbye as her and her beau aimed for the dance floor.

"Well, doll, wish us luck."

Cal chimed in. "By the look of this crowd, we are going to need it." He turned his eyes towards his wife. "Well, my love, shall we?"

Lynn replied, "Why, heck yes." And off they went.

Maggie looked around and saw a familiar face. Fanny motioned her over, so Maggie walked to meet her at the refreshments stand.

"Good evening, Ms. Fanny, good to see you again."

Fanny handed Maggie some lemonade and replied sweetly.

"Well, girl, it's good to be seen. You look pretty, by the way. Are you going to give it a whirl on the dance floor?"

Maggie hadn't thought about dancing until now. She was definitely rusty. She had won a couple of two-step awards in high school, but she wasn't sure she still had it. She replied hesitantly. "Oh, I don't know. I haven't danced like that in a long time."

Fanny wasn't hearing that. "Nonsense, honey! It's just like riding a bike. It will all come back to you."

Maggie smiled and thanked Fanny for the lemonade before she found a seat at an empty table. She searched eagerly around the dance floor for Cal and Lynn. There they were holding tightly to each other, totally trusting as they spun around to the next move; they were in love, and it showed.

Maggie mused in their happiness. She felt such admiration for them and what they had.

Taking her eyes off of them for just a second to grab her lemonade off the table, she looked back up and there he was—Jake, sitting at the table just across from her, talking and laughing with a couple of guys.

Maggie quickly noticed he might have been listening to them, but his eyes were fixed on her. She felt a little nervous and turned away, not wanting to stare. Taking a deep breath, she coached herself, *Okay, be cool; don't look. Just be cool. Is he still looking?*

She checked, and he saw her. Thus, the scolding continued. *Oh, yes, he is still looking. I think he just saw me check to see if he was still looking.*

Looking back over to him again, she noticed he was gone, and her stomach flipped. *Where could he have gone?*

Suddenly she felt a touch on her shoulder, followed by his voice. "Will you do me the honor of a dance, Maggie?"

She turned to see Jake smiling with his hand extended. He was dressed in a white button-up cowboy shirt, blue jeans, black cowboy hat, and black cowboy boots. Perfectly handsome and smelling as good as he looked.

Putting her hand in his, she accepted. "Yes"

The band started playing a song that was a favorite of hers when she had danced the two-step in high school. *Could it be a coincidence?*

She felt witty enough to share the unique turn of events with Jake. "And oh my, they are playing my song."

Jake chuckled at her comment, and they started dancing. Fanny was right. Maggie was instantly stepping right along, remembering her moves. They danced together perfectly without a step out of turn.

Jake looked at her with a bit of surprise. "You've done this before?"

Maggie laughed. "Well, this isn't my first rodeo."

They were lost in each other. Maggie felt as if nothing outside of the music, Jake's smile, and their dance rhythm existed.

CHAPTER SEVENTEEN
JAKE OF ALL TRADES

UNFORTUNATELY, SOON THE SONG ENDED, and so did the dance with Jake. Maggie thanked Jake for the dance and began to walk away. She didn't know what to do or say next, and retreat seemed like the best option. As she turned to go, he grabbed her hand. The band had just started playing a slow song when Maggie looked back to him.

"Don't go and leave me standing here all alone. I'll never live it down."

Maggie felt as though everyone was watching, maybe they were. Did it really matter? Maybe she agreed to another dance because of the longing puppy dog face Jake was giving her or maybe she just felt like dancing again. Either way, she took his hand.

"Okay, I guess I just can't leave you out to dry."

Jake smiled. "You are truly a lady. Thank you kindly."

They danced together; first, hand in hand, and then slowly Maggie found her arm cuddled around Jake's waist with her head lying on his shoulder. Maggie felt strangely protected while in his Jake's arms. She had not let her guard down like that in a long time. Something about him, gave her a secure feeling. Was it a sense of false comfort? After all, did she really know enough about him?

Maggie's anxiety began to build up as her thoughts ran wild. Alarmed at her ease of trust in Jake, she felt a red flag go up in her mind. Her heart beat faster and faster, and she couldn't seem to catch her breath. She stopped dancing and looked at Jake.

He smiled until he noticed her quick breathing and frantic facial expression, and then he grew worried. "Maggie, you okay?"

Maggie just couldn't take it. She had to get out of there. "I'm sorry, Jake. I have to go."

Maggie ran out of the dance tent and down Main Street as fast as she could, dodging a group of children with balloons, several older people, and a few dogs. She didn't stop running even after she passed the crowd. She found herself at the high school football field just past the end of Main Street.

As Maggie sat down on the bleachers, crying into her hands, she wiped her face on the underside of the bottom of her dress. She felt so alone. *Was this all just another stupid game for money, or do they really care about me—the real me? Does Jake really care?*

She sat in the dark, distressed with no meds, and she was ruining her cute dress with makeup-stained tears. There was only one thing to do. Pray.

She knelt on the bleachers, head down and hands clasped. "Dear Lord, please give me the strength to see the truth about the people of Home. I want to believe their care and true goodness can't be bought. I found a haven here. Show me the truth. Help me to open myself to them with full faith through You. That's why You brought me here."

Maggie stopped crying, pulling herself back up onto the bleachers, wiping away her last tears. She started to breathe normal, seeking to calm her anxiety. Finally, she became ready to walk back.

How can she explain why she ran off like that? Would he understand?

It dawned on her that she could be overthinking the people of Home. They had given her no reason to believe they were not genuine. So why assume that Jake would be any different? She had prayed about it. God had it for now, and it was time to move on.

As Maggie started to head back to the festival, there, under a string of lights at the end of Main Street, stood all the Jentrys. Lynn ran up to Maggie.

"Oh, my goodness, Maggie. You gave us all a scare. Are you okay? What did Jake do to make you run off like that? Him and I will have a word, you had us worried sick!" Lynn put her arms around Maggie without hesitation and gave her a good old southern bear hug. Maggie felt it could quite possibly be the best hug she had ever received.

"I'm sorry, Lynn. I didn't mean to worry you all. I just had to have a minute. Jake was a perfect gentlemen. I think I was just a little overwhelmed by the festival"

Lynn scrunched her eyes, confused by Maggie's response. "Is that what it was, honey? I would guess you have been to bigger, crazier parties than our town festival? Well, either way you're okay. That's all that matters. Now come on back, the kids are set to ride the rides. It will be great watching them twirl around."

Maggie agreed.

Ruby Louise, Cal, and CJ caught up to Maggie and Lynn. Ruby Louise reached up to hold Maggie's hand. "Come on, Maggie. We can ride the carousel together."

The little girl had the biggest smile on her face. Maggie liked the feeling of her warm little hand in hers.

"Sounds like fun. I can't wait!" Maggie replied excitedly.

They all walked back to the festival chatting up about the beautiful night's weather. The kids pointed out the fireflies across the lake. Ruby Louise told Maggie all about their grandpa's explanation of fireflies.

"Fireflies are God's summer fairy angels come to play with the children just before bedtime to bring them sweet dreams," she explained.

When the whole family returned to the carnival area, Ruby Louise was eager to get Maggie on the carousel. It was an amazing carousel; hand-carved wooden animals meticulously and colorfully painted, all shining under the glow of hundreds of white bulbs. Maggie rode a white stallion with gold tassels, and Ruby Louise chose a majestic lion wearing a red coat. They giggled as they went around and around. Maggie had never felt a mothering feeling deep down in her heart like that before. A sweet, fun little girl like Ruby Louise would bring that out in any woman.

After the ride, it was time to look for Jake. She really wanted to apologize to him for earlier. She excused herself from the family and headed over to the dance tent. He wasn't there. She checked around the food court and where the rodeo horses were stabled. No sign of Jake. She stopped looking when she reached the elementary school playground just outside the festival. Maggie sat on a swing, kicking the dirt under her feet. She was disappointed not to find Jake, and the swing provided a great distraction. Swinging back and forth led to her remembering how it felt to be a kid.

Oh, to be a child again.

Maggie started to think about her youth, about her older brother when they were little. They would swing on a tire swing from a huge oak tree in their yard. Michael always pushed her too hard. She would get after him for that, but he would laugh and mock, "Oh, stop your bellyaching; you're not going to die, Maggie."

Maggie smiled from the thoughts. How fond she was of that time in her life. Fussing and wiggling in her swing seat a little, it obviously not her size anymore, she mused.

"I don't recall these swings being so small." Maggie looked at each side of her swing.

Almost immediately, a voice replied, "Well, I reckon you were a little bit younger the last time you were on a swing of that size."

Maggie turned her head to see Jake standing behind her. He smiled before giving her a gentle swing push. Maggie smiled back, glad to see him. She stopped the swing as Jake walked around to the front of her.

"Jake, I am really sorry that I was so rude and ran off like that. It was just that . . . "

Jake gently put his finger on his lips to shush her.

"Maggie, it's okay. I realize that Home is a lot to take in. You don't have to explain. It was just you and me enjoying a dance together. That's all."

Maggie felt somewhat reassured.

Jake and Maggie stood smiling at each other awkwardly. They fidgeted like two teenagers. Maggie thought to brush off her dress, trying not to let the makeup stains show. She could not imagine what a mess her face must be. Jake put his hands in his pockets, then took his hands out and straightened his hat. There was no doubt that there was a strong attraction between them.

"So, Maggie, how about more swinging—together this time? Or do you want to take a little walk? I would love to show you something."

Maggie smiled, replying as she looked back at the swing. "Sure. A walk would be nice. I think I had better give up on the swinging. I am sure half my butt is still stuck in that seat."

Jake laughed. He reached for Maggie's hand and she gladly accepted. Their walk took them down a dimly lit dirt road aligned with tall trees. The gentle wind blew among the leaves, making a shuffling sound at their tops. Maggie felt the strength of Jake's hands around hers, a perfect fit, gently connecting them together. Holding hands was new to Maggie, not something she shared with the past men in her life. A simple romantic gesture meant to feel true kindness and connection; this is how it felt with Jake.

Maggie started a conversation to keep her mind off obsessing on their holding hands. "Lynn tells me that you're a Jake of all trades. Rodeo clown? Very interesting."

Jake laughed and replied. "Jake of all trades. That's a way to put it; I like that. I enjoy carpentry, working with my hands. I do the horse wrangling and farm work to pay my way. Rodeo clowning keeps me alive and on my toes. It's a lot of fun."

Jake didn't mention the horse camp he ran during the summer for disabled children. Maggie wondered if he would bring it up, but he didn't. So she decided she would.

"I also heard that you run a summer horse riding camp for disabled children. I really think that is so great Jake." Maggie felt proper kudos were deserved.

"What else did Lynn tell you?" Jake smiled at Maggie. He seemed a bit flattered to be called out on his work with the kids. Not in a showy way, but a proud way.

"Well . . . " Maggie decided to be funny and keep him hanging. They both stopped walking, and Jake looked over to Maggie in eager anticipation. Maggie looked up to the stars playfully twiddling her hair around her index finger. Jake shook his head in witty dismay smirking at her goofing off.

Finally, Maggie stopped fussing and fessed up. "She said that you were a great guy."

Jake disguised his blushing face by looking down at his boots, then up again. "I guess I am nice enough. I am a bit selfish with the kids that come to the horse camp. See, when they get up on that horse and it starts moving, their smiles are so big and bright it just blinds a person. I'm a smile junkie."

Maggie smiled pleasantly amused.

"See there's one I could get easily hooked to," Jake said, noticing Maggie's big smile.

Maggie kept smiling taking a deep swooning breath. "Thank you," she said. Jake nodded to confirm her thanks, and they continued their walk.

CHAPTER EIGHTEEN

A LITTLE STAR AND A BIG FERRIS WHEEL

JAKE AND MAGGIE'S WALK TOOK them through a field to an old barn beside the road. When Jake opened the barn door, the light from inside made them both adjust their eyes. Jake walked Maggie over to one of the stalls.

At first, Maggie didn't see anything, but then as she grew closer, she saw the bent neck and face of a mare standing in the bay. Snuggled next to her was a newborn foal shaking to stand on wobbly new legs. She was such a beautiful site; covered in silky smooth caramel-brown hair with a white mark in the shape of a star on her long sweet face. Maggie put her hands to her mouth, touched by what she was seeing.

"Oh, Jake, she's beautiful!"

"Isn't she though? Little Star was just born about an hour ago. It was actually a good thing you ran off, I decided to come to check on them. Mom was having trouble with the labor. Not sure if the foal would have made it if I hadn't shown up when I did. Do you see the mark on her face? That's how she got her name—Star."

Maggie stopped to realize what Jake said. *Is he saying that because I ran off with a panic attack, this beautiful little creature is alive? Could I be connected to something so precious that way?*

Jake kept talking while Maggie was still running the whole incident through her head.

"See, Maggie, it is true that the Lord works in mysterious ways. I guess all things happen for a reason."

No matter how many dozens of times Maggie's mom told her this, it always made sense and had proven to be true. Tonight, the words touched her strongly. If she had anything to do with the well-being of that sweet little horse, then it was certainly a way of blessing. Of course, she just started the miracle, Jake performed it.

"Thank you for bringing me here, Jake." Maggie uttered, peering into his eyes.

Jake and Maggie stood side by side, gazing at each other. Jake slowly turned his body to face her as she turned to him. He gently reached up to touch her chin. "Maggie, you're so beautiful."

Maggie stood motionless with a small grin on her face, blushing as adrenaline rushed through her body. She broke the connection to turn back to Star. Jake complied, and did as well. Enjoying time with each other was enough for now.

Jake spoke up, clear confidence in tow. "So Maggie, how about a Ferris wheel ride with this horse-delivering rodeo clown?"

Maggie enamoring in the moment agreed. "That sounds great. Bye-bye, sweet little Star. Good luck on your first steps." Maggie blew a kiss to Star, taking Jake's hand reaching to hers as they left the barn.

Maggie and Jake began talking about the town, their friends, and the beauty of the land. Maggie felt as if she were sixteen again, walking hand in hand with a cute boy. They swung their hands back and forth with no worries, their conversation spilling out as a collection of words to connect the smiles they shot to each other.

Maggie could not deny falling again into a certain comfort with Jake. It's the kind of feeling you get from a pair of warm fuzzy slippers you lost years ago, found again, and still fit into perfectly. He made her focus on the simple joys of life, which right now was a companion with strong, soft hands to gently hold onto.

Eyes were all about them when they returned to the festival. Secret whispers and giggles trickled from the women and nodding heads in cowboy hats came by way of the men. No one said a word; Maggie and Jake paid no mind either way, still fixated on each other.

The Ferris wheel ride with Jake was unforgettable. He delivered a pile of witty banter as they rode. "Round and round she goes, where she stops no one knows."

Maggie smiled. "How's about a bet there, cowboy? I bet we get stopped at the top for at least three full minutes?"

Jake thought about it for a few seconds and then replied, "Hmm. Betting lady, huh? Well, I'll have you know that I haven't lost a bet in my entire life. I don't plan to lose tonight either."

So they agreed that the loser would buy dinner, shaking on it to seal the deal. Jake swore that the Ferris wheel may stop for a minute at the top but would not be stopped for as long as three minutes. The ride continued with anticipation as the operator slowed the ride to let people off and on. Jake was gloating, like he knew something that gave him an unfair advantage.

"I must tell you this is not my first time riding this here Ferris wheel. In fact, that operator down there is my cousin. I grew up with him. I know he doesn't play around with getting people on and off this ride. He takes pride in the fact that everyone at the festival who wants to ride the wheel will get to. If you take a good look at that line, you can trust he will keep it safe but real steady moving."

Jake had a sneaky smile on his face as he delivered that information. He folded his arms—sure of himself—and sat back. Maggie laughed. "Is that so? Well, we shall see then. I am pretty good at guessing on these things."

Maggie just about lost it. It took everything she had in her not to burst out—because she, too, had an advantage. Earlier, when Maggie was looking for Jake, she had stopped at the Ferris wheel. She longed to see the dimly lit city from the top. In order to ensure her view, Maggie had given that same Ferris wheel operator a ten-dollar tip to stop at the top for at least three minutes when she came back to ride. She knew it would be dark and peaceful up there, three minutes well worth it. Of course, now that the time had come, she couldn't wait to see if the operator would make good on his pay. Or would this cousin stick to his ride regiment regardless? Jake might lose the first bet of his life to her. Maggie was looking forward to just that.

Jake looked down at his cousin and yelled a bit of encouragement. "Charlie, that's a long line. Is everyone going to get to ride this year?"

Maggie jabbed Jake's arm and scolded him.

"No fair. You can't do that; that's cheating. There's no side coaching in this bet."

Jake laughed, took up his hit arm, and rubbed it in jest. "Whoa, little lady. Okay, let's keep this fair then. No coaching."

They both waited eagerly as people started to get off. They were about four chairs from the top. The first chair moved and went down quickly, sitting only about thirty seconds at the top; the second went a bit faster. Jake started to celebrate early. "You know I will still respect you in the morning, Maggie."

Maggie lashed back. "Oh my, you are sure of yourself. Don't count your chickens . . ."

The third chair went a bit slower. It took about a minute before it moved from its topmost position. The kids that had ridden in that chair were not too happy about getting off, so Charlie needed time to convince them. Maggie and Jake looked down at what was going on below.

Jake was worried. He said under his breath, "Come on, Charlie!"

Their chair was next. The time seemed to stand still. Jake looked at Maggie, who was smiling right back at him. A little betting rivalry was brewing, but they really were truly enjoying each other. Jake laid his hand over hers. It was a small reassurance that the bet was all in good fun. Maggie enjoyed the way he was considerate of her feelings.

Finally, they were at the top. They both took a quick look at Jake's watch and started timing. One minute flew by; Jake looked down at Charlie to see what was going on. Charlie was just about to close the door on the chair he had just emptied. Jake sat back and waited for the wheel to move forward, but it didn't move. Maggie had her arms up relaxed at the top of her head, looking over the city with a smile stretched from ear to ear. Jake looked down—anxious again. There was Charlie looking up at Jake. Charlie pointed to his watch, smiled, and waved at Jake.

"What?" Jake said, puzzled. By the time Maggie broke out in hysterical laughter, it had already been more than three minutes. She had won the bet.

He grinned. "Should have known I would lose my first bet to a smart city girl, but why was Charlie pointing to his watch? What was that about?"

Maggie reached over and gave Jake a sweet kiss on the cheek. She didn't want to rub it in; after all she should feel a little bad the bet was fixed.

Jake smiled. "Well, that was definitely worth it."

Jake didn't question any further. Would Maggie ever tell Jake that she had paid Charlie? Maybe, but not right then. She wondered if Charlie would fess up before too long. No concern either way, as the moment was perfect. Being sly and sweet brought out the best in them both.

The night could have gone on forever; together time was of no consequence. In fact, Maggie and Jake were the last two attendees to leave the festival. Jake offered to take Maggie home, and Maggie gladly accepted.

On the way home, Maggie sat close to Jake as he drove his truck. They sat back listening to Elvis Presley on the radio. Ironically playing, "It's Now or Never."

When they reached the Jentry farm, Jake jumped out of the truck and walked around to open Maggie's door. He reached out for her hand and helped her out.

He slowly placed a small kiss on her hand. Maggie's heart floating, she walked off just after. He called out to her, "Maggie, have a sweet good night."

Maggie stopped and looked back to Jake. She smiled and winked at him. "You, too, cowboy." He saw the wink and flirtatiously tipped his hat to her in thanks.

She ran the last few steps into the little house, rushing to the window. She was eager to see if Jake had watched her go all the way in. Sure enough, once she had closed the door, he jumped in the truck and rode off. *How sweet of him to make sure I got in.* Jake seemed to have it all. Sunday morning came early, but it brought the most beautiful sunrise: gold beams of warmth coming up over the fields with all the flowers slowly waking to reach up towards the light. The farm began to awaken.

Maggie sat on the swing on her porch, sipping her coffee and listening to the sounds that morning brought on the farm. Animals moving about; hens fleeing the hen house, horses stretching their legs trotting about after being let out in the field, and the cows beginning their songs of the day. Her thoughts were happily filled with the festival; time with Jake, the new foal Star, carousel with Ruby Louise, and the best Ferris wheel ride she ever had.

It was so sweet of the whole Jentry family to come look for her when she ran off from the dance. It was refreshing of Jake to allow her to come back and say she was sorry without any argument. It's like they all have known her for a million years—the real Maggie—the one she hadn't seen herself for a long time.

Maggie continued to stare off into the distance. Thoughts of how precious this project had turned out enlightened her mind. She had found such peace, a blessing she would never forget—no matter what.

"Good morning, Sunshine," Lynn called out as she was heading toward Maggie. "How 'bout coming with us to services this morning? It's not fancy, just a small country church. Everyone is warm and sweet."

A church service! Maggie hadn't been to church in a long time. She last attended with Mom back home after she became famous. There everyone had known her since she was born, so they were kind in respecting her privacy. It was the last place she shared worship with a group. There was no chance she could go to church in Hollywood, such a gathering of peace and praise was sacred. Church was the one place Maggie didn't want to turn into a circus.

Maggie stopped thinking and replied to Lynn, "Sure, that would be great. I just need a few minutes to get ready."

"So . . . " Lynn started out nonchalantly, "did you have a nice time with Jake last night? I couldn't help hearing his truck door close around midnight or so, or somewhere around there, wasn't really minding the clock."

Maggie smiled at Lynn. She loved Lynn's way of being nosy, sly and curious, but not rude. Yes, Lynn had a gift.

"Yes, we had a great time last night." Maggie offered a little something to still Lynn's curiosity, as she popped up from the swing and ran inside the house, letting out, "I best get ready for church."

Maggie knew Lynn would be after her for more information later. However, Lynn was a lady, and all ladies must put prying aside when it's time for church. That is how Maggie saw it anyway.

CHAPTER NINETEEN
SOUTHERN CHURCH SUNDAY

THE QUAINT OLD SOUTHERN CHURCH with brown, once red bricking, sat just so. It held high a painted white antique steeple adorned with a black spire and a white rustic metal cross. Just a few gray cement steps welcomed the parishioners inside. Surrounded by green grass and a few shade trees, the setting was perfectly inviting.

Once inside the building, anyone could choose to sit in any of the ten glossy wooden pews on either side of the church. The pulpit platform was slightly elevated, with a choir loft towards the back. A large wooden cross hung on the wall behind the choir, lifted high above them, and two spring flower bouquet baskets flanked either side.

The sunlight streamed in gently through the windows on both sides of the small cozy sanctuary. The windows were neatly arrayed with tan swags boasting gold tassels on the ropes that tied them back. The air inside the church smelled of old wood, fresh flowers, and the subtle hint of warm glazed donuts.

Maggie's dress wasn't fancy but was fitting for a church service in Home. She barely made it to the first step when she was greeted with hearty welcomes. All the church members introduced themselves with handshakes. She was overwhelmed with the pleasant comments and polite gestures. Lynn had been right—the crowd was composed of almost everyone from Home.

Lynn swept Maggie over to the welcome table where refreshments were provided. Maggie was taking her first sip of ice-cold lemonade when Pastor James approached. He was a sweet gentleman in his mid-sixties wearing an old-fashioned gray suit and retro black-rimmed glasses.

"Well, here is the beautiful young lady I have heard so much about," Pastor James commented as he shook Maggie's hand.

"Thank you," Maggie replied.

Pastor James continued. "Welcome, Maggie; we are glad to have you with us. I hope you will enjoy the service. It's not too exciting, but we aim to please just the same."

Maggie smiled as she graciously repeated her "thank you." The choir, a small group made up of nine women and five men kicked off the beginning of the service. Their voices were angelic. One of the older ladies led the next number with a strong solo, singing about the greatness of the Lord. Soon the entire church joined in. The song was incredibly moving, and the soloist sang confidently, with such expression in her eyes.

"*Do you know how great the Lord is?*" the soloist asked through the medium of music. Maggie knew God was great and was being reminded while in church with the people of Home. That warm moment took her mind back to church days when she was a child.

She used to make fun of the people who held their arms to the ceiling of the church, closing their eyes as they swayed back and forth singing loudly. They looked so odd. It had taken her whole life to finally realize what it truly meant. They were feeling the Spirit in the form of God's blessings, enjoying the glory of praising God, and reveling in the love of God—all those things—or most of those things. Raising their arms was the most precious, the most loving way they could show God and their church family how thankful they were. It brought them just a little bit closer to Him by reaching to Heaven.

Maggie's realization gave her mind peace as she sang along with the congregation. She didn't realize that tears were pouring down her face until the song was finished. She quickly wiped away her tears, somewhat embarrassed. Lynn saw Maggie's tears and didn't miss a beat. She put an arm around Maggie's shoulder, giving her a squeeze and handing her a tissue.

The church service continued with an extended meet and greet interlude. Maggie singled out the lady from the choir who had moved her to joyous tears earlier. She approached the lady with a gentle touch on her shoulder and an outstretched hand.

"Thank you very much for your beautiful song. I was really touched. My name is Maggie."

"Well, hello there, dear. Thank you. I am really glad you enjoyed it," she said with gratitude, returning Maggie's handshake. "My name's Betsy Pride Purdue."

Betsy wore a powder blue pantsuit with her golden brown hair piled smoothly up in a neat twist on the top of her head. She must have been to see Alice at the beauty parlor. Her makeup gave her a natural glow, and she smelled like roses.

"You must be a professional singer," Maggie commented. "Do you sing around town or do voice acting? You must be popular and make a great living with your talent."

Betsy looked a little flattered and stunned at the same time, but all the while she was smiling. She replied courteously, "Oh, honey, no, but thank you. I sing for the Lord and for my church family. Praising the Lord with song gives me all the riches I need."

Maggie considered Betsy's response. How simple. Betsy sings for the love of singing. It doesn't matter how good she is or how much it could be worth to her. Maggie had a great deal of respect for Betsy's reasoning. Maggie and Betsy wrapped up their conversation in a hurry as Betsy was swept away by the choir director.

Continuing to say hello to everyone, Maggie greeted some of the same people she had greeted earlier. Since it was the second time seeing them, they were reaching for half arm hugs instead of handshakes. Maggie didn't mind their kindness, she expected as much. After greeting time, the service continued.

Now it was Pastor James' turn to preach. He did a quick loud clear of his voice. That did the trick; the people scurried to their pews like a pack of mice when a cat comes in. All except one short busy body of a woman, who just had to say one last hello. She turned and smiled for forgiveness to the anxiously-awaiting people before she finally took her seat.

Pastor James' sermon couldn't have been more appropriate for Maggie. It sounded like it was meant personally for her, as great sermons are often known to do. He talked about choices in life, how God would allow a person to choose his or her path each day. "Would you choose the path of goodness and follow in the steps that Jesus had laid out for you? Some paths lead to good days and good choices, while other paths lead to bad days and bad choices," he said.

Pastor James was convincing when he delivered the sermon. His words were strong, but he had a smile on his face at the appropriate times to make sure his care was evident.

"The question I ask you today, church family, is: Would you choose the path that had only easy, certain-to-be-good days even if it led to a bad ending, or would you choose a path that you knew would end wonderfully but was filled with hard spots, uncertainty, and trying and downright tough times? Would you put all your trust in the Lord then? I pray so, good people, because the Lord puts all His trust in you every day. He is with you on each path, no matter which one you choose. He will be there to cheer you on at the end of a great path choice. He will be there to carry you if you choose otherwise. If the Lord leads you to it, He will lead you through it. He is truly great, trust in Him. A . . . men."

Pastor James always ended with an "A," then a pause, then a "men"—so Maggie had been told. It may have been a standard prayer ending, but not the way Pastor James delivered it. His amen was like an "A" that stood alone—strong, hanging out loud for a few seconds— then a "Men" that came along just after, like a whisper completed with an agreeable head tilt forward of an emotional nature. It was especially curious and convincing.

Before the service was complete, there was an offering and a closing song from the choir. During that last song, Maggie's eyes wandered taking a glance around at all the people attending service. Her eyes didn't roam very far before she caught the eyes that were looking right back at her. There, seated a few pews back on the other side of the church, was Jake.

Where did he come from? He wasn't here at greeting time. He looked very handsome in his Sunday best. His attire was accompanied with a smile so mischievous that Maggie thought everyone in the church would see right through it. She felt the warmth of her cheeks; she must be blushing something awful. She had hoped she could be more mature; they were in church after all. Maggie giggled discreetly. If her mom were there, she would give her a hidden foot kick for making eyes at a guy in church.

Maggie decided it was best to turn around, face forward, and sing. Lynn sensed the go-ing's on and gave her a nudge, chuckling under her breath. Maggie started giggling hard in return. She had to cough to try to cover up the giggles. It was a good thing the service ended and they both could compose themselves.

What was it about getting the giggles in church? Thinking back, Maggie remembered when she and Michael would start it up when they were visiting from college and were sleep deprived from staying out all night the night before. Mom would just give them a gentle kick. Goodness knows, if one of them started nodding off during sermon, they were in for much worse scolding later. It didn't matter what started the giggles. It could have been that she was just plain overtired. It could have been because it was hilarious how the old men would fall asleep and their wives would give them a kick. Or sometimes right in the middle of the pastor's sermon, she could hear a little kid in the pew behind her say to his mom, "Momma, is he done yet?"

Service completed, the line to shake Pastor James's hand was long. Maggie reached him and received a half hug and a handshake. He was curious about her thoughts on the service.

"Well, young lady, did you approve of our service today?"

Maggie smiled. "I certainly did. The choir sang beautifully, the people are all so friendly, and your sermon was inspiring. Thank you so much."

"Great! You're very welcome. We hope to see you next Sunday as well. You have a blessed week." Pastor James kept it short.

His line was endless, and not everyone in it had the gift of patience. Pastors have to learn to talk quickly but meaningfully. Maggie wondered if they taught them that at seminary.

Maggie waited outside the church since the Jentrys were trailing a bit behind in the line. The line had come to a full stop as Pastor James held a baby in his arms while two old ladies were nudging at each elbow for his attention. Jake showed up right on cue. He walked up to Maggie with his hands behind his back, charming approach, just like a schoolboy.

"Good morning, Maggie. You look pretty as ever." Jake handed her a single daisy.

"Why, thank you. This was sweet of you," Maggie replied kindly as she breathed in the smell of her flower.

Jake and Maggie stood in awkward silence, happy to be near each other, before Jake rekindled the conversation.

"So how did you like our little church? It's not too shabby." Jake turned around to look up at the church building.

Maggie looked around, too. "I really do like it. It's very warm and familiar, full of kind people."

"Familiar? Hmm, do I detect a bit of the South in you, Maggie? I wondered about that."

"Yes, I admit it," Maggie gave in. "I was raised in a small southern town similar to this one. I forgot how much I missed it 'til very recently."

"Well, the thing about small southern towns is, they are all about the same, I suppose."

Maggie decided to move the conversation up a notch. "So, about that dinner you owe me for the Ferris wheel bet, how about tonight?"

Jake's eyes widened. "Tonight is family night. Church will transition itself into a buffet of sorts at dinnertime, and everyone pulls up a picnic table. This goes on for a while, and everyone heads home afterwards. So, if you want to have a bite here at church tonight, maybe we can go for a walk after to see Star? I will make that dinner up to you tomorrow night if you're free."

Maggie agreed. "That sounds good. I was thinking of Star earlier; so, how is she?"

Maggie and Jake talked about Star for a while until the Jentrys finally caught up, and then everyone headed home. Maggie planned to get a run in and a shower before church dinner, but first she had promised Ruby Louise and Lynn prompt attendance to their tea party. It was a family ritual for Ruby Louise and her mom. They had tea after church on Sundays while the boys tossed the ball around out back.

Ruby Louise had all her chairs set up with her special friends attending. There was a fuzzy panda bear, a white and pink bunny, a rainbow-colored bear, and a black puppy dog with brown patched eyes—all wearing tea party dresses. Maggie was very cordial.

She sipped her tea with her pinky up and said things like, "I say, are those crumpets?" in her best English accent. Ruby Louise and Lynn laughed at her antics. Maggie relied on her expertise on the subject from her work on the movie *English Ladies*. She quite impressed Ruby Louise and Lynn. She was completely convinced if the rest of the tea party attendees could acknowledge, they would have been equally impressed.

Maggie enjoyed spending the afternoon with Lynn and Ruby Louise. It produced a heartfelt emotion in her to see a mom and daughter bond as they did. Maggie couldn't help but think that someday perhaps she would be the mom having tea parties with her little girl.

Ruby Louise seemed to read Maggie's mind, and she suddenly blurted out, "Maggie, are you married, and do you have any kids?"

Maggie was surprised by the question but not the delivery of it from Ruby Louise. Lynn scolded Ruby Louise. "Give poor Maggie a break. She gets enough inquisitions from your dear old momma."

Chuckling at that comment, Maggie went ahead and answered. "No sweetie, I am not married, nor do I have any children."

Ruby Louise's eyes rose questioningly. "Why not? Aren't you worried that you will get old and become an old maid?"

Lynn scolded Ruby Louise again. "Oh my heavens, child, you shouldn't be so mean. Of course, she isn't going to become an old maid. She will find the right man. She might have already."

Maggie looked up at Lynn in jest. Lynn had her eyebrows raised just above a smirky grin. It was time for Maggie to say something in her own defense. They were both tossing her love life around the room like an old sock, but Maggie decided to go back into English mode. The talk and the questions were getting too serious for a Sunday afternoon tea party.

"Ladies, ladies, gossip and tea are not considered accompanying tastes. You will make yourselves belch and get gas. Unacceptable!" Maggie said, with her nose held as high as the pinky finger holding her teacup. They all began bursting into laughter. It was the sweetest way to end their afternoon together.

Maggie took off to change for her run and her shower. She couldn't wait to get to the church dinner. More food? Oh, my. Maggie loved it but she would have to punish herself later to keep it off her hips. Tonight, she looked forward to visiting with the church family and seeing Jake.

Jake represented thus far the perfect man for Maggie.

He was strong, sensitive, and he made her laugh. But would he fit into her real life back in Hollywood? She knew he wouldn't. He would be swallowed up by it all in no time. The press would have them both for a morning snack. Maggie just couldn't destroy such a great man that way. Besides, she had no way of knowing of how Jake felt.

It was possible he didn't feel anything more than a friendship wrapped up in the joy of having a good time. Or worse, maybe he just wanted the bragging rights to dating a famous movie star?

Maggie prayed Jake wasn't that shallow. Was what she saw in him only a mirage? She would be leaving Home before she knew it. Letting her hair down, being her true self, and embracing simple life were of vital importance. Meeting special people, having some laughs and tender moments, realizing precious things that she wouldn't have otherwise thought of—these were extra added benefits. Her mind was set. No matter what happened, she was blessed to have had the opportunity to experience the project.

Maggie had just finished getting ready when it was time to leave for dinner. She met up with the rest of the Jentrys at the truck, and off they went. Of course, Ruby Louise wanted to sit next to Maggie on the ride. She talked Maggie's ear off the entire way to church. Maggie really loved the perfect balance of spunk and innocence that was Ruby Louise. She was certain to be an amazing handful of a lady someday.

CHAPTER TWENTY

SUPPER, THE PAST, AND SADNESS

THE DINNER SPREAD WAS A mouthwatering, tastebud-enticing buffet! Every delicious Southern recipe all in one place. Homemade, fried, baked, and buttered-up love spread out for everyone to share.

Despite the feast, Maggie did control herself. She limited her plate to bite sizes this time. The trick to eating only a bite was to keep the people who made those dishes from noticing. Offending Southerners was easily accomplished when it came to food. If you weren't eating their food, they were wondering why. They had a lot of pride tied up in those recipes.

Lynn created a moist-awesome pound cake which Maggie swore was entrancingly delicious. Lynn loved the flattery but insisted it was nothing special, saying, "Maggie, that's just my grandmama's recipe, same as most I expect. It is funny how pound cake originally got its name . . . a pound of sugar, a pound of flour, a pound of eggs, and a pound of butter. Isn't that something?"

When everyone had their dinner in their hands, Pastor James settled in for the blessing of the food. "Dearest Lord, we ask that You bless and nourish our meal together tonight—sharing food, praising You as a family and giving thanks. A . . . men."

The room echoed with *amens.*

Maggie opened her eyes to see Jake coming up to get his plate. Sitting across from her at the picnic table, he apologized. "Hi. Sorry I am a bit late. I had something I was working on and just had to finish." Maggie didn't care why he was late. She was just glad to see him. She did, however, want to give him a hard time as usual. "Well, what could have been more important than missing Pastor James' blessing and that A . . . men?"

Jake laughed, shaking his head at her. He became still, softly reaching to hold her hand from across the table. "You're truly something else, Maggie." He delivered his words affectionately while looking with steady admiration straight into her eyes. Maggie didn't know how to take it. After all the kind comments he had showered her with, this one felt intentionally strong. Maggie broke their eye lock by momentarily looking away. Regardless, Jake kept his focus on her waiting patiently for her response to his flattery.

"Thank you, Jake." She gave his hand a little squeeze.

Maggie and Jake stayed with a few older ladies to help clean up after dinner. Those ladies were sweet on Jake. He would flirt with them just a little to make them feel good and giddy, but his intentions were kind. He helped them down the stairs and walked them to their cars schlepping their belongings including their huge handbags. Everyone loved Jake.

Maggie couldn't blame them at all. He was quite a gentleman— and so handsome. Besides, he sure gave off a good persona. At this moment, he was helping Mrs. Hanson and her poodle, Dolly, who was not cooperating with her leash. Jake ended up with that leash twisted all around his leg—what a sight! Dolly hollering like a banshee running around in circles wrapping that leash repeatedly around Jake's leg. He nearly fell over and took Mrs. Hanson with him. Maggie laughed hysterically at the sight of it all. She was so taken with the antics that she overlooked the young lady approaching her.

The woman looked like a twenty-five-year-old bombshell with beautiful long auburn hair, blue eyes, and a perfectly toned body. She could easily have been a Victoria's Secrets supermodel. Her approach was just like her attitude, uppity. "Hello there, Maggie. I am Sally Ashton." Sally had her hand outstretched, and Maggie cheerfully gave it a shake.

"Nice to meet you, Sally."

Sally continued talking, disconcerted with Maggie's greeting. "I just wanted to give you a bit of a heads up on the whole Jake thing. See, Jake is big to this town, as you can see." They both watched as Jake finally was free of leash and was hugging Mrs. Henson goodbye. "He was born here, grew up here, and probably will take his last breath here. He loves Home, and we all love him. I am especially fond of him. He might have told you that we dated through high school and some in college. We are still very close. Like two peas in a pod."

Maggie took note of Sally trying to mark her territory. She was going to play the high road on this one. "Is that so? Well, he sure is very likable. I can see how much he is loved here."

Sally shifted one hand to her hip, nodding in agreement with attitude. Jake finally saw the last church lady off and hurried over to them, worry etching itself across his face.

"Maggie, I see you have met Sally, and vice versa I suppose."

Sally put her hand up motioning to Jake to stop talking, flung her hair with a disagreeable head shake, and walked away. Maggie was gone just as quick. Her mind was starting to jump to conclusions, triggering her anxiety. Jake called after Maggie, but she just kept walking. He finally ran up to her and asked her to stop. "Maggie, please give me a minute to explain. Sally is history. We haven't been together in a long time. She still goes into these jealous rages, even though I have made it clear to her that we can only be friends."

Jake would have continued, but Maggie didn't allow it. She was clearly upset, choosing to allow her anxiety and anger to start speaking before she thought out things clearly. "Oh really, Jake?"

Jake was taken aback by Maggie's mistrust. "Wait a minute, are you jealously judging me? Come on, Maggie. I have not let on one bit about how I feel just thinking about all the handsome male movie stars you have spent time with. That's a tall order for a guy, Maggie. Feeling like he must pale in comparison to what you must be used to."

Maggie, allowing her anger to block out truly hearing Jake, continued to lash out. "Oh, sure! You get a chance with the star! So now you are the special one, and I am just the one that does this all the time like it doesn't matter!"

Tears streamed down Maggie's face as she felt the pressure cooker of anxiety building in her chest. Maggie and Jake stepped away from each other, arms flailing as they spoke loudly in angry tones. Finally, they both stopped. Regaining control, Jake calmed himself with a deep breath, putting his head down into his hands pushing back his hair. He walked slowly over to Maggie, put his hands gently on her shoulders, and looked down at her. She turned away at first but then drew her attention up to him. Angry tears streamed down her face as she returned his gaze.

He spoke softly. "Maggie, please listen to me. This is my home. I grew up here. These people are a part of me, and I am a part of them. I had a great childhood, and yes, I had girlfriends. Don't we all when we are growing up? I have never lied to you and will not lie to you. I wasn't after you for a shot at the movie star. I don't even know you as that person. I know you as Maggie, the woman who can out-dance, out-bet, and probably out-eat me if given a chance. That's who I like spending time with."

Maggie pulled away from Jake, attempting to inconspicuously wipe her face. Jake pulled out a hanky from his pocket and handed it to her. She took the hanky from him, dried her tears, and blew her nose.

She took a calming breath while her head was still bent down to his hanky. Breathing control was the first step to calm her anxiety, and she knew her next words were crucial. Gathering her thoughts before she spoke, she raised Jake's hanky up towards him with two fingers, the pointer and her thumb. Jake gave her a puzzled expression.

Maggie questioned, "Aren't you a little young to be carrying a hanky in your pocket? I thought that was for old men."

Jake smiled shaking his head at Maggie. He swept her off her feet with a big bear hug swinging her around in a spin saying with half breath, "Maggie, again—you are something else. I mean that in a crazy way, not a sweet way this time."

He put Maggie down and they continued to walk together. Jake added, "By the way, I don't want that hanky back until it has been properly sanitized."

Maggie smacked him on the arm; then she put the hanky right near his face and playfully threatened him while shaking it. "You mean this hanky?"

Jake jolted his head back alerted, pretending to be grossed out that the hanky was so close to his face, and then he ran. Maggie chased him shaking the hanky held high towards his direction.

"You aren't going to outrun me, too!" he yelled back to her. After a few minutes of chasing, Maggie caught up to Jake. Actually, Jake let her catch up. They were almost to the barn where Star was stabled when they heard a horse screeching and thrashing around inside.

They rushed in to find Camille, Star's mom, lurching, kicking, and stomping, trying to nudge her foal. Star was lying motionless on the hay. Maggie gasped and clasped her hands together over her mouth in urgent concern, while Jake hurried to the rescue. He unlocked the latch to the stall quickly calming Camille with soothing words before leading her into another stall. He then hurried back to the motionless foal to see if she was still breathing.

He yelled to Maggie, who was standing motionless in shock, overwhelmed by what she had seen. "Maggie." Jake spoke forcefully. "Maggie!" Finally, she looked at him. "I need you to run to fetch Doc Buford. He lives in the yellow house with the blue picket fence in front. It's about half a mile down the road. Please go, Maggie. Go now."

Maggie ran out the door of the barn without as much as a blink of the eye back to Jake. Every step that slammed down to the ground was made with pure concentration. The pattern of one foot in front of the other was replaced with a stride unlike any she has ever achieved. Her mind focused on keeping her speed and balance, but her heart was focused on Star. When she finally made it to the house that Jake had described, she started to bang on the door aggressively, yelling, "Doc Buford, Doc Buford!"

Doc Buford came rushing to the door. He didn't even get a chance to open his mouth before Maggie started to ramble on. She hadn't taken time to catch her breath.

"Star . . . come . . . quick . . . something's . . . wrong . . . please!" Doc Buford seemed to struggle to understand what Maggie was squeaking out but made out enough of it.

Maggie's heart palpated aggressively as a result of the adrenaline rush from her spontaneous run.

Doc Buford, reminiscent of Santa with a long white beard, gestured toward his steps. "There, there. You just sit here and catch your breath, and I'll drive up there."

He grabbed his vet bag and jumped in his car, tearing off down the road as promised.

Maggie sat breathing heavy, alone in the dark on his stoop. The sounds of the woods called loudly; noises of the Southern jungle—frogs, crickets, owls, and wood critters—all talking at the same time.

She pulled the hanky that Jake gave her out of her pocket to wipe away the mixture of sweat and tears. Once she felt like her breathing was somewhat back to normal, she started back towards the barn. When she arrived at the barn door, she didn't go in. She couldn't bear to see Star lying so still, she stood listening intently to the conversation between Jake and Doc Buford.

Doc Buford mumbled in hushed tones, "Jake, there was nothing you could do. She was just born with a bad ticker. She didn't feel any pain; her heart just stopped."

Maggie could not believe what she had just heard. *Star is dead? How could it be?*

Maggie began to cry hard. She had felt so connected to that little foal. It didn't matter that they'd only just met.

Maggie slowly opened the barn door, not revealing to Jake and Doc Buford that she was there. Jake, filled with angry grief, walked over to the side of the stall and kicked it hard five times. Then he broke down, placing his head against the top of the wood railing of the stall. He was breathing heavily and standing completely still. Maggie went over to Doc Buford, and he put his hand on Maggie's shoulder, lowering his head and shaking it in sadness as he walked away.

Maggie moved closer to Jake, but she didn't know how to approach him. He was silent, and she knew he was hurting. He had not lifted his head or acknowledged her presence. Maggie softly rested her hand on his back and spoke quietly. "Jake, I am so sorry."

Jake raised his head, looking away from Maggie as he ran his sleeve over his face to hide a few tears. He then turned to Maggie and looked directly at her. They moved toward each other for a hug—a long hug where neither spoke—one of those hugs where the tips of their fingers crunch down on the other person's shirt as they reach around, hugging tightly.

Finally, Maggie pulled away to wipe tears from her eyes. She walked slowly over to Star, now covered with a blanket, except for her sweet little head. Kneeling down beside the lifeless foal, stroking her softly, Maggie called for Jake to come over. He came over and knelt next to her.

Maggie looked over to Jake and requested, "Let's pray."

Jake nodded his head in agreement. Jake and Maggie bowed their heads as Maggie prayed. "Dear Lord, thank You for the joy of little Star if only for a moment. Please heal Camille and all our hearts at the loss of Star. May she forever shine. Amen."

After the prayer, Jake and Maggie walked over to Camille who was watching for eager news. Maggie stroked her hair compassionately and kissed her on her head. Jake looked into Camille's eyes, putting his hand gently on her nose and tenderly petting her.

Camille looked to them both, seeming to understand what was said. She blinked her eyes, neighed sadly, lowered her head, and then walked over to the other side of the stall, where she could see her baby lying on the hay. Maggie and Jake walked out of the barn hand in hand. It was time to let Camille say goodbye to her little baby.

Jake and Maggie walked all the way back to his truck at the church. Neither of them wanted to talk after what had happened, so he dropped her off at the Jentrys. No extended goodbye, just a small kiss on the cheek. The mood was too somber for them both.

Maggie lay in bed for at least an hour wondering if she could have run faster or done something more to help. Would it have made a difference? She had heard Doc Buford say that nothing could have been done; nevertheless, Maggie had a hard time believing it.

Star's death frustrated her; she couldn't rest. She tried everything to get to sleep. She rearranged the pillows twice. She changed her pajamas to try to get more comfortable. She even made herself a warm cup of milk and listened to soft music. Nothing worked. Back in Hollywood, she would have taken a sleeping pill or two to get to sleep. Not this time, she was pill free. This was the first time since arriving in Home she felt she might need one, doing well so far without them.

Maggie decided to try one last thing. She sat in the old rocking chair and pulled the quilt up around her neck, folding her legs under her. She swayed her body back and forth to start the chair rocking. She eventually settled and calm came over her, shortly followed by sleep.

CHAPTER TWENTY-ONE
KNOWING JAKE

THE NEXT WEEK WENT BY fast. Maggie helped Lynn tend the garden and learned how to milk a goat. She had milked a cow before, but milking a goat was a new trick for sure. They were sure smaller and feistier.

More often than usual, the afternoon rolled in dark clouds abruptly pouring down buckets of rain. Southern style, even the rainstorms, everything was generous. Maggie and Ruby Louise spent the rainy day together in the sunroom, a simple room enclosed only with screen and wood framing. The thin metal sheath was all that stood between the friends and the flood coming down. The dampness of the mist humidifying all around them made Maggie's hair begin to frizz. She kept fluffing it out of her eyes, swatting it away like a fly. Ruby Louise began to laugh at Maggie's mischief. Her infectious giggles treated their ears away from the steadfast rain pounding on the sides of the house.

Ruby Louise told Maggie that her grandma had loved the sunroom. She recalled her grandma saying that the sunroom was God's blessing for this house. Grandma had called it the "Sit a Spell Sunroom" because of the glorious scenic view of the whole farm one could see from there. So there sat the two friends, rocking in rocking chairs and watching the raindrops fall over the land.

Occasionally they would share a smile, and then go back to watching and rocking.

Over the next few days, Maggie didn't do much other than running. She embraced the freedom she felt when running, especially in Home. She hadn't heard from Jake since the night Star died. His absence during this time was honored, as she herself struggled with Star's death. Raising animals on farms one was supposed to just get over such things, but Maggie's heart was still sore; Star was different. Maggie had only a week and a half left before the project was over. Will he ever come back to the house? Should she go look for him? Maggie decided to wait it out.

One early afternoon towards the end of the week, Maggie walked along the stream down from the farm. The sun sparkled across the water enchanting the dragonflies buzzing over with warm invites. A toad somewhere nearby croaked loudly to announce his presence. He seemed to be taunting those dragonflies.

Maggie took a seat in the shade of a weeping willow tree, lush with green, gracefully hugging towards the area below it. She closed her eyes listening to the sound of nothing but nature surrounding her. In the midst of croaking, buzzing, and the running of the stream, she found clarity and peace. It wasn't long before she heard the crunching of leaves and sticks not too far behind her. She opened her eyes and turned to see Jake. He approached her with a smile on his face and a picnic basket in his hand. Maggie smiled back and jumped up to greet him.

"Hello, stranger. I wondered if I had scared you off or something."

Jake smiled, setting down the basket. He approached Maggie and gently put his arms around her for a hug.

"I am sorry about the past few days. I guess I just had some thinking to do. I missed you"

Maggie considered his words, what thinking did he do? She was so glad to see him it didn't matter. She ignored the impulse to start firing out an inquisition, small talk seemed just fine.

"Well, I have been having tea parties and makeovers with Ruby Louise, and I just don't think my schedule would have allowed much more anyway," Maggie joked in a matter-of-fact fashion.

Jake laughed as she had hoped he would. He reached down to grab the picnic basket. "I know this is not a formal dinner, but I do owe you a meal. What do you say?"

Maggie smiled and nodded her head. They laid out the blanket and started to set out the food: cheese, bread, grapes, assorted crackers, and other picnic treats. He also brought two bottles of old-fashioned strawberry soda. Although impressed, Maggie wondered one thing.

"So, tell me, how is it that you were able to get a great aged Parmesan cheese in Home? I know that is something that can't be a regular grocery item here." Maggie couldn't wait to hear his explanation.

"Well, little lady, you don't have to trouble yourself with that. I have my ways. Plus, it helps to have worked your heinie off for Jim the grocer for two summers, rebuilding his shelves. He keeps the good stuff for special occasions."

Maggie chuckled. "Well, I truly appreciate your hard work. And special thanks to Jim!"

Maggie wasn't surprised that everyone in Home loved Jake. He was truly full of charisma, and eager to share kindness with all. She became lost in the moment; Jake, the picnic, and the warmth of a beautiful day by the stream accompanied with the music of nature. It entranced her heart; a true feeling of happiness overcame her.

Jake and Maggie talked and watched the stream. They finished their picnic, sitting on the blanket leaned up against each other. Jake became quiet and moved the picnic basket to the side before reaching for Maggie's soda and putting it down next to his.

Jake lay back on the blanket watching the clouds dance and stamp the sky with puffy patterns. Maggie lay next to him. They held hands and pointed out the images they could make out in the clouds, mostly farm animals for some odd reason.

Without warning, Maggie pulled away and sat up. Jake looked over to her, confusion filling his features.

"Maggie, is something wrong?"

Maggie took a breath and drew a serious expression across her face while peering deeply into Jake's eyes. "Jake, I really care about you. I enjoy being with you. I just don't know where all this is going. I am leaving in a little over a week."

Instantly, Jake sat up. Maggie began straightening her hair as a nervous reaction. Jake looked across the stream gathering what to say. He turned to Maggie, painstakingly giving voice to his thoughts. "Maggie, I know your life is complicated. I know you have to leave. I also know that I have never felt this way about any woman in my life—ever. I've thought a lot about this over the past few days. The way I see it, we owe it to ourselves to spend what time you are here together. We can let our hearts guide us the rest of the way. What do you say, Maggie?"

Maggie hung her head in dismay, closing her eyes. She did not like feeling put on the spot, nor did she like the carefree avoidance Jake believed in. Looking back up at Jake, she said, "It's not that easy, Jake.

We are prolonging the obvious. We can't just hope that it all works out. We need to plan what we are going to do." Maggie's voice was tense.

Jake reacted quickly to her words, scooting back a bit from her. "Maggie, don't you ever give yourself a chance to live? To toss out reason, planning, and logic for just one second? To enjoy life at that moment? Sure, we can't know if things will work out, but we can do ourselves a favor, trying our best. Without complicating it, just have some faith?"

Jake's last words struck Maggie's heart like lightning. Wasn't that the same thing she had decided to put into practice? What her mom begged of her and what Ms. A expected of her? Having faith. It seemed to be directed repeatedly towards her, longing for a straight follow through. Somehow Maggie, through all her experienced blessings, hadn't taken the time to truly comply with anyone—including herself, to acknowledge that she had faith and it was growing strong. She owed it to the people who meant so much to her, didn't she? Most of all, she owed her growing faith to God.

Maggie stopped overthinking everything, cutting it down to microscopic dissected parts. Overthinking things was one of her biggest struggles; it had led her to miss out on some amazing joys in her life.

Maggie put her arms around Jake, hugging him hard as tears rolled down her eyes. "Okay, Jake, you're right. We're happy. That is what I will think about for now."

Jake clung to Maggie; he kissed her head gently once as she buried it under his chin. Holding tightly to each other, she never wanted to let go. A simple picnic by the stream turned priceless, frozen in their hearts forever, no matter what.

After asking Maggie if she wanted to see his place, Jake led the way to his house located about a half mile from the Jentrys.' Jake's house was a small, maroon-and-white ranch-style farmhouse centered on a neat little patch of land. A friendly brown-and-white Basset Hound with a fat, frumpy disposition, floppy ears, and big dark brown eyes trotted up to them. Jake grinned. "That is Hoss. He's my roommate."

Jake glowed with warmth as Hoss approached; he scooped him up and gave him a big cuddle. Jake was an animal lover for sure. Maggie had figured that out already from the way he had handled the death of little Star.

Maggie's curiosity got the best of her. "Hoss. That's a special name. How did he get that name?"

Jake laughed a bit. "On account of him loving old Bonanza reruns. I have had to leave the TV on for him when I am gone ever since he was a pup. If I don't leave on Bonanza, he howls at me. I had to order the episodes on DVD and everything."

"A dog that's a true fan, now that's cool." Maggie appreciated Hoss' show loyalty.

Looking around Jake's house, Maggie found it quite the bachelor pad. Jake had pretty much the basics: a cozy couch, an old lounge chair, and an end table with newspapers sporting a dirty coffee cup on top of them.

When Jake saw that Maggie noticed the messy newspapers and coffee cup, he swiped them off to the kitchen. She could tell that he had not expected for her to visit. It made her feel more at ease about being there.

"I know it's not much, but it's home."

Maggie reassured him. "Oh, no, it's great. It's perfect. It is amazingly comfortable, homey and sweet. It fits you." Maggie continued to look around. The best part about the first room was the many framed photos adorning every available part of the walls. Tons of pictures of

Jake's family, of his events including rodeo clowning; and of disabled kids on horses, and more. It was an overview of his entire life.

Maggie really appreciated that Jake adored being surrounded by memories of his family. He gladly shared some information about a few of the photos, pointing people out. "That's my family—Mom and Pop and my little sister, Cassidy. They all live about an hour from here. I go up to see them at least once a month. Cassidy just graduated college. I am so proud of her." Maggie could tell that Jake beamed when he talked about his little sister.

She felt comfortable enough to share a bit about Michael. "I have an older brother. He is the best. He's a doctor. He puts up with his little sister pretty well."

As the two stood smiling at each other with thoughts of their siblings musing on, Jake reached for Maggie's hand. "I want to show you something. Will you come with me?"

Maggie nodded, and they went to the barn behind his house. Jake had turned part of his barn into a work shed. It was full of the most beautiful pieces of hand-worked wood furniture: tables and chairs all made of natural wood carved with waves of swirls, flowers, and designs. Maggie was in awe. She ran her hands over the carving on the chairs to feel the smooth grooves that made the artwork come alive. The wood was clear stained with the most beautiful natural tone highlights showing through.

"Oh, Jake, these pieces are so beautiful. You made all these? The woodwork is so amazing. Truly!"

Jake was pleased that his woodworking impressed Maggie. "Thank you," Jake replied. "It's my sort of hobby, I suppose—kind of like crocheting for old ladies, I guess."

Maggie refused to let Jake make light of his talents. "Don't even. You've really outdone yourself here. You are very talented," she insisted. Jake smiled. He studied the way Maggie glued her eyes on his work, continuing to admire it. He observed she gave off a spark when she was inspired.

"Maggie, come over here; I have something for you."

Feeling giddy, Maggie did a little happy dance over to Jake. When it came to presents, Maggie was like a five year old at Christmas. "For me?" Maggie clapped her hands together lightly in front of her face celebrating.

Jake began laughing. "Okay, Maggie, close your eyes," Jake instructed. He pulled off the cloth covering draped over a hand-carved, natural oak wooden rocking chair. Along the top of the chair was engraved "Maggie." Beside the name was a carving of a baby horse with a star on its head. "You can open your eyes now," Jake instructed.

When Maggie opened her eyes, she began to tear up as a smile developed. She walked over without a word to the chair, immediately drawn to touch the carving of the horse. Little baby Star—there she was.

Maggie jumped to Jake and hugged him.

Jake welcomed the hug and replied sweetly, "Lynn told me how much you liked the rocking chair in their grandma's house. I wanted to make sure you always had one for yourself, no matter where you are. It seems fitting that baby Star be with you. She was a bright shining glimpse of love and light that was with us for only a short time and yet touched our hearts forever—just like Home feels about you, Maggie." As their embrace continued, Jake looked into Maggie's teary eyes and spoke softly with full meaning. "Again, you are something special."

Jake closed his eyes and bent his face down to Maggie's to kiss her. The kiss was the kind that only a gentleman would give, sweet and soft. Maggie stood with her eyes closed for a full three seconds after the kiss was over. When she opened them, Jake smiled—amused—watching her blush a little. They walked back to the house from the barn, taking a seat together on the porch swing, cuddled and cozy. Maggie's head nestled perfectly against Jake's shoulder.

She finally spoke. "Jake, thank you so much for the rocking chair. I will cherish it forever."

"You're very welcome, Maggie."

They both comfortably drifted off to sleep listening to the country sounds around them. Maggie had not slept that well in years. She felt so safe and loved.

The first to wake up an hour or so later, Maggie looked lovingly over at sleeping Jake. He was truly a gorgeous man. Jake made all the male movie stars look like pimple faced boy charmers. Amazingly, the inside of this man was just as good-looking as the outside, though she had fallen in love with his inside first.

Jake roused, waking up and looking over at a smiling, staring Maggie. He drew closer to her, his eyes adjusting to the light. He spoke softly. "Hello, beautiful."

Maggie responded with a thankful kiss.

Jake kissed her in return. Maggie went in for a second kiss.

"Whoa girl, give a man a break. I have to breathe." Jake gasped jokingly.

Maggie laughed at his silliness. "What a way to die! Wouldn't it be?"

CHAPTER TWENTY-TWO

WHERE DO WE GO FROM HERE?

TIME FLEW BY; DINNERTIME WAS approaching when Jake drove Maggie back down to the Jentrys. She asked Jake to stay for dinner. Jake eagerly agreed.

At dinner, Ruby Louise just had to ask out loud the question that was running through everyone's minds—as she often did. "So, Maggie, is Jake your boyfriend?"

Lynn scolded her daughter as quickly as the bomb dropped off Ruby Louise's lips. "Ruby Louise, mind your business, little girl."

Maggie smiled at Jake, and Jake returned her smile as he put his hand on hers under the table. Everyone else at the table carried their own expression. Cal wasn't surprised; he was more interested in the dinner he had in front of him. CJ was dismayed as his dreamy chances with Maggie crumbled in front of him. Lynn just wished Maggie had answered the question.

Thankfully, dinner wrapped up after that in quite a hurry. Everyone's conversation grew stale after Ruby Louise's stirring boyfriend inquiry.

Jake walked out to the front yard with Cal to look over a fence that needed mending. As Maggie and Lynn cleaned up the dishes, Lynn just had to get her motherly agenda in: "Hey, Maggie, I know it's not any of my business, but I have to know, will we see you again someday?"

Maggie really didn't know the answer. First of all, she knew the project would not allow her to come back to Home. The real question was, would she come back even if she could?

Maggie choked up a bit as she started to dry the dish in her hands for the second time. Lynn had hit a nerve; all Maggie could conjure up was a few confused, anxious words. "I just don't know, Lynn. I really care about you all, but I just don't know."

Maggie considered excusing herself from the room; the quick-to-flee response was built into her. Lynn stepped toward Maggie taking the dish from her, putting it down gently on the counter. Lynn held Maggie's hand in both of hers.

She consoled Maggie. "Maggie, I'm sorry. I didn't mean to get you all riled up. We have taken a liking to you. We all are so grateful for what you did for our town, but we didn't know what to expect or feel about you as a person. Knowing you like we do now, we feel blessed to have you here. Not just for what you did, but for the person that did it."

Lynn gave Maggie a bear hug before Maggie excused herself back to the little house. Jake was still outside, so he ran over to Maggie. Jake could tell immediately that something was wrong.

"Maggie, are you okay?" Jake questioned.

Maggie looked up at Jake reaching for his hands, holding them in front of her, tears building in her eyes. "Jake, I will miss you all so much. Here in Home I have a made another family who wants to be with me for me. Tomorrow I will be surrounded by a crowd that just wants a piece of me because they think they have a right to one! I do love what I do, but I am really starting to feel hurt by what I am losing in the process. Where do I go from here?" Maggie sighed.

Jake gently held her hands and listened carefully.

Maggie peered up at Jake, waiting for him to reply. He finally did.

"Maggie, you're a very smart, beautiful, strong woman, and you will make the decision that is right for you. Your faith will be there when you need it most, helping you choose, protecting you. No matter what, remember Pastor Jeff's message."

Jake always knew what to say to make Maggie feel better. She loved how he wasn't afraid to show his faith in God. She admired him greatly for this.

After Jake walked Maggie back to the little house, Maggie asked Jake if she could be alone for the rest of the night. She needed to get some rest. Truly, she was exhausted from the roller coaster of emotions. Jake agreed. He didn't mind as he had some work to do anyway. Also, Hoss and the other animals needed tending to.

Maggie changed for bed and made a cup of chamomile tea with honey. She was looking for an extra blanket in the hall closet when she saw a box marked "old movies." She pulled the box off the shelf to find a variety of old VCR movies: some black and white versions and some from the 1960s and 1970s. Maggie remembered a VCR player by the TV in the bedroom.

Maggie rummaged through the movies looking for something interesting. She preferred studying old movies to present films as older films relied heavily on the actor's ability to carry the story. They didn't have all the fancy technical adjustments and special effects like they do now. She found what she thought was a drama, but she didn't recognize any of the names or the title.

Maggie popped the tape into the player before picking up her tea and settling into bed. The voices of the movie started coming through; then Maggie felt the hair stick up on the back of her neck. An overwhelming familiarity of speech overcame her ears. That voice, Ms. A—could it be? Maggie nearly spilled her tea before placing it quickly on the nightstand to hurry closer to the TV. A much younger Ms. A appeared before her on the screen—she was an actress. Maggie sat glued. She watched closely, without taking her eyes off the screen for one second. She could not believe it. Ms. A was right there in front of her. Maggie wanted so badly to internet search the name of the actress, Anna Stack, but alas, there were no computers or internet, town rule for the project.

Ms. A came across flawlessly on screen. She was indulgingly charismatic and well versed, moving across the set with such grace. Had she been famous? This movie was made well before Maggie was born.

Maggie grew up watching old movies with her mom and her Aunt Rose. They encouraged Maggie to have a wide spectrum of education on art, film, music, and literature.

She normally could name and recognize stars from that era of movies. This movie was from a different era—after the golden era but before the new age era. Wait a minute. Is this why she felt like Ms. A looked familiar?

Maggie finished the movie with a new appreciation for Ms. A. No wonder. This is why she is so passionate about the project. It's not just a job to her; it's personal.

Maggie couldn't wait to talk to Ms. A again. She wanted to ask her a million questions; even though there was a good chance that Ms. A wouldn't answer a one of them. Maggie couldn't blame her. Isn't that what she was trying to get away from herself?

Maggie thought back over the entire conversation with Ms. A the first day she met her. Ms. A was extremely convincing on what a total time out could mean to a star of Maggie's caliber. Now she knew why. Lying in bed, the imagery of Ms. A's choosing to leave stardom behind her, Maggie drifted off to sleep.

As morning came fast on the farm, Maggie wasn't awakened by the rooster this time. It was the phone. She jumped up. This phone was only supposed to ring when Ms. A was calling. Maggie answered it, still clearly waking up. "Uh, hello, hello?"

The voice from the movie last night said, "Maggie, it's Ms. A. Good morning. We have to talk." Ms. A carried a demanding tone.

Maggie was fully awake now and sitting up after hearing the urgency in Ms. A's voice. "Yes, Ms. A, I am listening. Is everything okay?"

"Maggie, I have word that you have become really chummy with a certain young man there in Home. Jake Ryan, correct?" Ms. A questioned.

Maggie grew quiet. She knew that Ms. A had spies—also known as protection—everywhere. Maggie was unsure she wanted to hear what Ms. A was going to say next.

Ms. A added impatiently, "Maggie, are you there? Did you hear me?"

Maggie, still hesitant, replied, "Yes, Ms. A, I heard you, and yes, I have been seeing Jake."

"Maggie, you do realize that once you leave Home, you can never go back there. It would jeopardize you, the town, and the whole project. You have to understand the delicate balance created here. You are to drop all communication with everyone from Home going forward once you leave. There must be no ties that link you back to them or vice versa. It's just too dangerous. These rules must be adhered to in order to keep the project running. Please say you understand." Ms. A had been very clear.

There was no room for error, no gray areas. Maggie must accept it. She would never go back to Home. She would never be able to see or speak with anyone from Home again.

Sadly, Maggie dredged from the lowest part of her heart the unavoidable reply to Ms. A. "Yes, I understand."

Then there was a time of silence between the two women, perhaps Ms. A could feel Maggie's heart breaking.

Ms. A finally broke the painful quiet. "Maggie, I understand you have been watching some old movies lately. You may have stumbled on something that you shouldn't have, hmmm?"

That *was* Ms. A in that movie! Maggie smirked; she was right.

"Well, dear, that's another secret you have to keep. In a way, I am glad it was you of all people to be the first project participant to find out. I have no idea how you managed to get your hands on that old heap of dusty film, but you did. Maybe it was divine intervention, who knows? Since you know, let me share a piece of advice, advice that I assure you I am an expert on: Hollywood burnouts are a dime a dozen. Often in the midst of Hollywood's promises, people get lost, setting aside what's real. They push away the people who care most. Even if Hollywood cash pays off for them, they will carry costly regrets that will haunt them forever. Attend carefully to your heart Maggie, but remember you have a responsibility to the project at all costs."

Maggie was beginning to understand. "Thank you, Ms. A. I appreciate your honesty. I understand everything."

Ms. A finished up. "Good. I am glad. Now you have only a few days left in the project. I will contact you the day before your departure date with exit plans. In the meantime, perhaps you should enjoy a little bit more rest and relaxation, ride a horse and tend a garden, do whatever those people do there. And Maggie . . . "

Maggie responded quickly. "Yes, Ms. A?"

Ms. A reiterated one last instruction before she hung up. "Say your goodbyes to the people of Home."

The phone line went dead, and Maggie hung up. Hurtful thoughts jammed her head, banging around back and forth to Ms. A's words "say goodbye, say goodbye" replaying over and over like a skipping record. Maggie broke down. She slid to the floor, face in hands, crying loudly. "Jake, Oh, Jake, how am I supposed to say goodbye. I love you. How do I say goodbye?"

Maggie continued to drown in tears, feeling overcome by loss and sadness. She couldn't imagine not seeing Lynn or Ruby Louise again. They had been so good to her. How could anyone live in a place like Home and not feel as Maggie did about the people here? Leaving Home behind was like leaving her extended family forever.

As Maggie climbed back into bed, she pulled the covers over her head. She craved the numbing effects of her anxiety medicine. Numbness for the pain now and numbness to face the next few days, she longed for it.

Maggie desperately searched all over the house like an addict, just in case there were some old medicines left from grandma's stay here. Once she realized what she was doing, she stopped; disappointed she hit a new low after working so hard.

A knock sounded near the window, so Maggie went to check it out. Who could be at the window? Maggie pulled back the curtain a little hiding her tear-stained red face.

There on the side of the house was a woodpecker. He pecked a bit more, and then turned his head to look straight at her. Maggie forgot all her worries just then as she wiped her flooding eyes and calmed her troubled spirit. She greeted her visitor, "Hello, little friend." The woodpecker nodded at Maggie and flew off.

Closing the curtain, Maggie looked up to the ceiling, gazing toward heaven. "Well, I am out of bed now. You're right; I can't run and hide this time. Can't take a pill and try to ignore it. Time to get on with it . . . having faith."

Maggie was proud of her renewed sense of courage. It was time to face whatever would come her way.

She dressed and headed to the house to see the Jentrys. Cal was already off to work. The kids were off at school for the day, and Lynn was canning fruit in the kitchen.

Lynn welcomed Maggie into the house after recognizing her footsteps on the porch. "Come on in, Maggie. I'm in the kitchen, as usual."

Maggie headed into the kitchen.

"Good morning there. How'd you sleep last night?" Lynn chattered on when she saw Maggie grin. "Good, I hope. Anyway, the whole town is fixin' to give you a proper send off at the end of the week. A town barbecue with all the trimmings and a special impromptu service by Pastor James. A . . . men, right?" Lynn concluded her words with a laugh and a wink before pouring Maggie a fresh glass of lemonade.

Maggie hoped her melancholy mood at saying goodbye wouldn't leak through to Lynn. She tried putting on a good face, but that didn't last for a second and she broke down in tears. The cycle of emotions earlier wouldn't quit. She was a mess.

Lynn held her, saying, "Oh, there, there sweet girl. It's okay. We will miss you something fierce. You know that, but you're meant for so much bigger than Home. Besides if you stayed much longer, you would see that we are all just a bunch of old country bumpkins, boring and tiring you to bits."

Maggie stopped crying to smile at Lynn's self-deprecating comedic comments. Lynn had a strong southern vernacular, and she wielded it well. Tears drew up in Lynn's eyes, laughter from her mouth, overcome with emotion when Maggie's sweet smile finally broke.

There they stood: two lemonade ladies with tears water-falling out of their eyes and laughter belting out of their mouths. Maggie began helping Lynn with canning the peaches. There was nothing like canning fruit as a cure for centering oneself. It wasn't long before they were finishing the job. Just as the last jar lid was being tightened, a knock sounded on the door. Lynn went to see who it was.

Jake stood at the door, asking about Maggie. When Maggie heard his voice, she wasn't sure she could handle talking to him just yet. At Lynn's invitation, Jake walked into the kitchen to find Maggie sitting at the table fixed on her lemonade. She barely lifted her head at his entrance, so he pulled up a chair and sat right next to her.

At first, Jake didn't say anything because Maggie was quiet. He sensed her stressful stillness. Lynn walked in on the silence.

True to her fashion she butted in. "Well, what are you two love-birds up to today then? If you plan on sitting here sulking all day, you can go clean some messes out of the animal pens!"

Maggie thought Lynn was just trying to clear the air, but Lynn was serious. She wanted them out of her way. It was either help with the work in the kitchen or on the farm. Tough—but that's how a farm ran. There was always work to do.

Jake and Maggie walked outside where two horses were saddled and ready to go. Maggie shot a questionable look over at Jake.

"What do you say?" Jake asked.

"Sure, sounds fun." A ride is just what she needed to distract her mind from other things.

Maggie and Jake rode out to the stream. She hadn't been on a horse in a long time. The familiar feel of the warmth of the animal and the stride across the land made her quickly remember her youth. She and Michael used to race their horses, spending hours together on horseback when they were young. Once Jake and Maggie reached the stream, they stopped to give the horses a rest. Jake dismounted before helping Maggie down.

"Well, I now know one more thing about you, Maggie. You were born to ride a horse. Thought I would have at least a small edge over you on this one, but I was wrong. You do have some country girl in you for sure."

Maggie stated simply, "Thanks." She hadn't said much since they left the house.

Jake inquired reluctantly even though his heart was afraid to dig. "Maggie, I can see that your mind is heavy today. I know you will be leaving in a few days. I have only one request."

Maggie was praying he wouldn't ask any promises of her she could not deliver. It would be hard enough to tell him she could never see him again. Maggie stared at Jake with a blank expression on her face.

"Maggie, I only ask that we don't waste any time you're here worrying about when you will be gone. Let's just enjoy ourselves today like we have been for the last several days. No promises, no regrets, no broken hearts. No matter what, we'll be glad that we made the most of our time together, right?" Jake bent down looking at Maggie's drawn face and gave her a sweet, tender kiss.

"You're right; that's what we'll do." Her mind was set. At that moment she decided not to tell Jake. How could she explain such a thing? That once she left Home, she would leave him forever, too. No regrets, just like Jake promised. The project would be protected. Maggie's heart on the other hand, would not be.

The rest of the day, they rode horses and took a walk through the park. As the sun went down, they shared a glass of lemonade together. Maggie remained quiet. Jake was doing enough talking for the both of them. "You know, I found myself wondering about you the other day."

"Oh yeah, what did you wonder?"

Jake smiled. "I wondered how you like your coffee? Do you even drink coffee? What side of the bed do you sleep on? Are you a mustard or mayonnaise gal? Do you snore or drool in your sleep or . . . maybe both?" Jake would have gone on, but Maggie playfully whacked him lightly on the shoulder as punishment for his last comment. Jake responded with a smooth chuckle.

After Maggie stopped giving him the stink eye, he decided to continue, this time a bit more seriously. "I also imagined what kind of mom you would be."

Maggie stopped him there. She put her hand gently over his mouth. She didn't want to hear any more. She couldn't take it to hear more.

Jake's striking blue eyes stared deep into hers. He lowered his head, kissing her hand and moving it away slowly.

"Anyway, how about you come over tonight, and I will fix you the best steak dinner you have ever had? What do you say?"

Maggie couldn't agree more with steak. She would miss the barrage of great food that Home had provided. It was a good thing that she ran consistently to keep fit; otherwise she would be taking a lot more than a rocking chair home with her.

Wanting to freshen up and change, she insisted that Jake go home and come back awhile later. She took the longest shower ever, letting the water run over her. Calming warmth drizzling down her back wrestled most of her anxiousness into submission, giving her a feeling of being absolutely refreshed.

That evening Maggie wore a short dark blue and white gingham dress with a red eyelet edging and red cowgirl boots. She looked stunning. Home had helped heal her inside, which made her outside glow with youth and beauty.

She looked in the mirror. "This is what living a normal country life can do for a girl's complexion. I don't look half bad." She smiled as she sprayed on her perfume. As she finished getting ready, she heard a truck door closing. Maggie's excitement built as Jake stepped to the porch.

When he caught a glimpse of Maggie, he stepped back a bit—chin dropped, stunned by her beauty. "My goodness, you're a vision, Maggie."

Maggie was flattered. Jake was so sincere. Time stood still for a second, as they locked eyes, anticipating time together.

"Oh, how sweet, but . . . really sort of cheesy!" Maggie declared, with a moment breaking wise crack.

Jake, slightly still in trance, wouldn't let her get away with that comment. "Cheesy, geez that was brutal."

Maggie laughed. "Yes sir, a bit cheesy."

Jake slowly walked up the first step of the porch towards her. "Well, you know what I have to say to that?

"What?" Maggie snipped back in fun, curious of his next move.

Now Jake started to advance slowly backwards, blurting out a challenge. "I say, whoever is the last one to the truck is the cheesiest." Maggie tore off the porch after him shouting, "No fair. You had a head start!" She soon caught up to him, a streamline runner even in cowboy boots. Jake was fit, but he was not a runner. Maggie and Jake reached the truck at the same time. They shared a good laugh about their contest.

"I win," he mused, still trying to catch his breath.

Maggie, knowing it was a tie, shook her head in disagreement. "No way, buddy, we were tied. If you didn't have a head start, I would have beaten you."

Deciding to drop the subject, most likely to save face, Jake opened the truck door for her and off they went.

Hoss was eagerly awaiting them by the screen door as they drove up. When Maggie saw him, she gladly greeted him. "Hello, Hoss. How are you, sweet guy?" She reached down to pet him as Jake held the screen door open. Hoss let her get a good ear and neck rubbing in before he retired to his seat.

The house smelled of the spicy aroma of steak cooking, followed by a faint smell of wood and varnish. Jake had moved the new table and chairs that he made into the house. This is where he set out their dinner. The table had been set with beautiful white candles and a colorful arrangement of a variety of flowers. Maggie was touched by his affectionate layout.

"Jake, everything looks so nice. You really didn't have to go to all this trouble for me. You know I don't have to be impressed."

Playing it sly, Jake quipped. "Who's trying to impress? Hoss and I eat dinner like this every night." Jake winked over to Hoss. "Don't we, boy?" Hoss howled on cue, as if to sarcastically reply, "Sure we do!" Maggie and Jake both laughed.

Jake pulled the chair out for Maggie as he noticed her admiring the flowers.

"Of course, these flowers are for you. I didn't know which kind was your favorite so I got one of each . . . a rose, a carnation, a lily, a daisy, and uh . . . well, I forget the names of the rest, but you must know them."

"Thank you, Jake. They are beautiful. I think they are all my favorites now."

Dinner was delicious. Seriously, delicious. Looks, personality, and he can cook, too; Maggie didn't know how she could ever leave.

Jake asked her during the meal, "Maggie, I feel like I know you so well, but tell me something about you that I don't know. Like, what do you like to do when you're not working?"

"Well, I run a lot as you know. I talk to my mom by phone, lay by the pool, watch some TV and I uh, uh . . . "

She couldn't think of another thing. The events and interviews were all work related. She had very few friends that were not from the set. What did she do for her own fun? When did she have time for that?

Jake seemed understanding as she struggled awkwardly with the subject and tried to help her recover. "I know you try to help people regardless of your celebrity status. That is something for sure. It is a part of you."

Maggie was comforted to hear Jake express what he truly saw in her. "Yes, I have been lucky to have helped a few people along the way. This is the real upside to what I do. It gives me the power to help."

Jake picked up his glass of Cheerwine for a toast, and Maggie lifted hers to his. "This is for you, Maggie. May your blessings always be plentiful, may your heart always stay sweet . . . and may God help the man who tries to sweep you off your feet!" Jake toasted.

Making such a suggestive toast, even if he made light of it, appeared hard for Jake. Maggie knew Jake had to be conflicted at the thought of anyone with her other than himself. So, the comedy bit seemed perfect for the occasion. Honestly, she knew it was for her benefit, so she could move on even if he couldn't.

Maggie had no plans to forget Jake. She wanted to make sure he knew it, so she quickly added to the toast, "Especially after a good man set the bar pretty high."

Jake smiled tipping his head in thanks while laying a hand over his heart in gratitude.

After enjoying their dinner, Jake put on some music and asked Maggie for a dance. They danced slowly together, enjoying the closeness. Anne Murray's "Could I Have This Dance?" played in the background. It was a moment that Maggie would never forget. That song, how appropriate and awkward all at the same time.

Unfortunately, the night had to come to an end even though they didn't want it to. Jake drove Maggie home, and it wasn't long after Jake said good night and drove off that Maggie was ready for bed. Before she fell fast asleep, Maggie reveled in the most amazing day and Jake's handsome smiling face fresh on her mind.

CHAPTER TWENTY-THREE

HEARTBURN, IN MORE THAN ONE FORM

MORNINGS CAME MUCH EASIER LATELY. Maggie jumped up and dressed for a run. Her path took her straight to Jake's house. As she ran up on Jake's patio, she noticed a note posted on the door. It read "Coffee and bagels in the kitchen; cheesy guy in the barn!"

She headed out to the barn eager to see Jake at work, passing on the breakfast offer. Almost skipping across the yard, feeling energetic, her delightful disposition came from a good run on her way to a great guy.

Jake was sawing a piece of wood. When he saw her coming, he stopped and smiled.

Maggie went right up to him and gave him a quick kiss. "Good morning, handsome."

Noticing Maggie was in a good mood—joyful and spunky—Jake responded, "Well, someone sure has pep in her step this morning. I trust you had a good rest?"

Maggie smiled. "Yes, very much so. Thank you for the delicious dinner last night."

Jake returned to sawing, explaining he was planning this project for a porch swing to be a gift from Cal to Lynn. Maggie offered to help. First, he showed her how to hold the wood and sand it. Maggie sanded away while Jake stood behind her, distracting her with a kiss on her neck.

"I can't do this right with you doing that. You're going to make me mess it up!"

"Don't worry. I can fix it," he said without stopping for a second.

Maggie pushed him away playfully, and he laughed. She decided she best head back to get some things done. Ruby Louise had a play time arranged for them. Then after, Lynn was taking her to the ladies' quilting meeting.

Jake tried to convince her to stay. Every time she started to head toward the dirt road that led to the Jentrys, he would gently pull her arm back in for a kiss. Maggie did not refuse him. He was very hard to refuse.

She thought she would never be able to leave, so she started to walk backwards really fast. She yelled out to him as her backward fast walk became a forward run. "I'm sorry. I will you see you later, okay? Come over for dinner. I'm cooking tonight. I will try not to poison you. Bye, Hoss!"

Hoss walked up to console Jake, sensing his best friend's feelings of dismay at Maggie leaving. Jake kneeled next to his furry friend to accept his concern. He waved and yelled back to his fleeing lady. "Okay, but I might have to remind you of that later." Neither of them stopped watching, until she was out of sight.

Maggie stepped lightly the rest of the way back to the Jentrys. The soft worn dirt road looked inviting, so off went her shoes and socks. The familiarity of the warm ground powdering under her toes took her back to when she was young. Her dirty bare feet stained red with iron rich southern clay mud had been her only mode of transportation then.

As Maggie walked, she looked over the fields and trees along her path. She felt as if she could walk all day coveted by the sun, the scenery, and her full heart. When the Jentrys' place came in view, Maggie's thoughts centered on a tall, cold glass of Lynn's famous lemonade. She decided to run the rest of the way to hurry it to happen. Once inside, Maggie discovered that Lynn already had a glass poured and waiting for her after catching a glimpse of Maggie coming down the road. Lynn was good like that.

"Good morning there, little lady," Lynn said to Maggie. "I saw you coming up the way. How are things?"

"Fine thanks." Maggie smiled, taking a drink of her lemonade.

Lynn wiped the counter in front of her, and then wiped it again. Maggie guessed by her behavior that something was on Lynn's mind. Finally, she began to speak.

"Maggie, I know I don't have any right to tell you your business, but I hope you will give me a chance to say a few things just the same." There was concern lacing her words.

Maggie nodded, unsure what Lynn was about to say.

Lynn continued. "We are a delicate balance here in Home. We love our families, our lives, and one another with great respect. Our faith is our guide. That is enough for us. I don't want to see you get hurt, but I also don't want to see Home suffer either. I trust you to do the right thing, Maggie."

All this time, Maggie thought about what the project can do for her, or do to her, if it didn't work out. Now being a part of Home, the Jentry family, and being with Jake; Home lay open and helpless if things went public. Lynn really cared about Maggie, but she had to make sure her town was safe. With that said, Maggie comforted Lynn, offering a secure hug to her new friend.

"Lynn, I would never do anything to hurt you all. You have treated me like family, and I will never forget that" reassurance tucked into her words.

Maggie moved forward, changing the subject. "Hey, I hope you don't mind, but I invited Jake to supper tonight. I will do the cooking if that's okay."

Lynn agreed. "Sure, hun, no problem. Let me know what you need, and I will run out and get it for ya." Maggie had secured the chef's approval to use the kitchen.

"Thanks, Lynn. That would be great," Maggie gushed before running off to shower. She had to gather all the things needed for play practice with Ruby Louise. When Ruby Louise got home, they were going to prepare a short, silly version of a southern tragic romance for the family after dinner. They even had a part for CJ. Whether he was going to play along or not was another story. Ruby Louise was a talented actress, which came as no surprise to Maggie. It didn't take much to guess that this little girl would turn heads someday, no matter what she decided to do. Maggie saw a lot of her young self in Ruby Louise.

Once the kids were home, the play practice went smoothly. After practice, Maggie was off to the ladies' quilting meeting with Lynn. Maggie didn't know much about quilting. She would have learned more if her grandma had lived a bit longer. The process slowly started to come back with Lynn's help. Either way, the quilting meeting wasn't just about quilting. It was an outlet to chatty avenue, whereas the women would brew up town gossip.

"Did you hear about George Summers? Oh, I tell you ladies, he is up to no good with that realtor lady from Shady Hills. Hmmm, Shady Hills, that name might just be fittin'. I have it on good authority that he was seen taking her to the movies, and let's just say that neither one of them could tell you what that movie was about," informed Alice Whit, who obviously gathered juicy tidbits while she performed her duties as a hairdresser.

All the ladies replied to that scoop using short exclamations such as "No, he didn't" and "Oh my, that's a shame."

Of course, Lynn added her thoughts. "Well, if I wasn't a lady, I would march right over to his wife and give her an earful. However . . . I don't think I'd be able to find her so easy. She has her hands full with their new field hand, Hank. Tall glass of water about all of twenty-five!"

Everyone burst out in laughter at the mental picture of Lynn confronting the busy wife.

Maggie, amused by all the chatter, soaked it all in. This was the closest she had been to a group of real Southern ladies in a long time. She remained quiet, trying to stay out of the focus of their gossip.

The quilting ladies had one rule, no gossiping about each other. Maggie realized that keeping her out of the local gossip was likely the reason she was invited. Maggie was truly grateful on that account.

The quilting meeting ended when the conversation ran out. Lynn and Maggie headed back to get ready for supper. They drove up to the house to find Cal, CJ, and Ruby Louise feeding a baby goat with a bottle. Cal gave Maggie a turn at it, and she loved it. The baby goat had little wobbly legs and trusting new eyes. As she fed the baby goat, Maggie thought about what Jake had said—about her making a good mom someday. She dearly wanted to have children with the right man at the right time.

Always enjoying cooking, Maggie never had anyone to cook for. Therefore, her skills were lacking. She gave a go at making spaghetti. It was definitely something different, hopefully everyone would like it.

As it turned out, she didn't do too badly, and everyone said they liked it. Maggie wasn't sure if they were being honest or just trying to be nice. Cal had made a face that was a bit unsettling before pounding his chest with his fist. Heartburn must had wrestled him into submission. Lynn covered the whole incident by handing him some antacid before he opened his mouth with an unsettling comment.

"It was like we were all whisked away to some far away region in Italy." Jake gave her a wink and grabbed her hand in support.

After supper was finished, the whole family sat down on the couch to see Maggie, Ruby Louise, and CJ perform their play. Ruby Louise portrayed Dixie, a rich elegant southern heiress to a T, both graceful and stubborn. Maggie played a friend of Dixie's, a simple lady who admired Dixie but was secretly very jealous of her. CJ refused to play Dixie's love interest. He refused to pretend to fall in love with his little sister, so he was thankfully re-cast as the butler. Overall, the play was a success—that was, for a tragic southern romance without a leading man.

Jake and Maggie went for a short walk afterward. They settled on the porch swing when they came back. The thought of being together for only one more night lingered in the unspoken air. Tomorrow night was the big town send-off for Maggie. She would leave right after.

Looking into Maggie's eyes as her head lay gently on his arm, Jake whispered, "Maggie, thank you. The time that I have spent with you has meant the world to me. It goes without saying how much I will miss you. If there is any chance that we could be together again, I hope that we find a way. For now, we will just say 'see ya,' okay?"

Gazing fondly back, Maggie responded, "Thank you, Jake. Because of the man you are, I was reminded of the true me. I could never say goodbye to you. 'See ya' sounds good." Maggie meant every word, and the tears started full stream down her face. Jake wiped away her tears gently with the back of his hand. She could read the difficulty on Jake's face; he was holding something back. Could his thoughts include the word "love"? Jake took a deep breath and held Maggie tight. They sat swinging, holding each other's hands, fingers intertwined with not another word said.

Soon the night air grew cold, Maggie felt ready to go inside. "Good night, Jake," she said, sitting up and turning to him.

Jake's words were punctuated with a sweet hug and kiss. "Good night, Maggie. Until tomorrow then."

Maggie spent the next morning packing and cleaning up the little house she had called home. She sat on the couch, taking into account the joyous events of her time there. On the fridge hung pictures that Ruby Louise had drawn for her. The rocking chair Jake had made for her sat across the room.

Maggie stood up and took down the pictures off the fridge. She looked at each drawing carefully, one at a time. A child's drawing expressed more than a thousand words. One picture showed

Maggie dressed as a queen and Ruby Louise as a little princess holding her hand.

Smiling as she looked down on the picture, Maggie ran her hand across the page, outlining the red wiggly crayoned heart that surrounded both of them. Feeling love, Maggie's eyes began to tear up. It would be so hard to leave Home, but she had no choice. Before Maggie's emotions overwhelmed her, she was greeted with an old-fashioned holler followed by an assertive knock at the door.

"Maggie," Lynn blurted as she stood outside the screen door. "Hey, girl, how about one last girls' day out before you leave. Fanny just got in some new styles!"

Maggie wiped her eyes and smiled. "Sure thing. Let me get dressed quickly." An excursion with Lynn would be a fun distraction, and fun was just what she needed. Maggie ran off to the bedroom to quickly dress.

Soon they were downtown, eagerly scrutinizing and adoring Fanny's new line of clothing. Maggie walked towards the back of the store where Fanny sat in the storeroom with the door open. Maggie spotted multiple male mannequins dressed in full southern military uniforms and historic gentlemen's fine suits accompanied with female mannequins wearing dresses from a bygone era.

"Fanny, Wow! These are great," Maggie exclaimed as she entered the storeroom.

Fanny began showing Maggie around. "Why, thank you. Yep, my husband, Leonard, loved collecting these. In here, you will find Southern dress representing from almost forty years before the Civil War until the late 1870s. These threads could tell tales. Historical tales. The only suit missing would be that of a fine gentleman from around

1830. They only hand-sewed back then. The sewing machine didn't come out till the 1840s, you know."

"Is that right?" Maggie's interest was evident in her voice. "So, are you still looking for the suit that is missing? The men's suit from 1830? Perhaps I can try to . . . " Maggie was eager to help Fanny, even though she knew good and well that Ms. A wouldn't be happy about it. No matter, it would be gratifying to see Fanny's collection complete.

"Oh dear, no. It's okay. We aren't missing that suit; it's just being used. Don't trouble yourself, fussing with all that on my account," Fanny sputtered, wanting to move on. "Come on; let's get back to the store before Lynn gets into some mischief."

Fanny exited the storeroom, and Maggie followed her to the cash register. Both shopping ladies found some lovely additions to their wardrobe, so they paid Fanny and gave her a hug goodbye before they were off.

Maggie was curious about Fanny's husband, so she asked Lynn. "Lynn, where is Fanny's husband? I don't recall meeting him. Leonard, I believe it was."

"Leonard—oh, he has been gone for about five years now. What a great guy! You would have liked him." Lynn filled Maggie in on the details of Leonard's passing.

"Oh, I'm sorry to hear that, Fanny didn't tell me. I am sure I would have liked him. I just love Fanny. She showed me her Southern costume collection, and I offered to help her find the suit she was missing, but she said it was being used."

Lynn smiled, putting her arm around Maggie as they walked up the road. "Oh, sweetie, you are just so cute, aren't you? That suit is being used all right; Fanny buried Leonard in it."

Maggie gawked at Lynn with her eyebrows raised in surprise. "Really?"

Lynn burst out into laughter at the priceless look on Maggie's face. "Honey, you never know what's going to happen in this town. Shoot! Last year someone ran Sheriff Butler's pants up the flagpole!" Lynn turned her focus back to her shopping. "Now girl, how about some shoes?"

Maggie and Lynn continued down the street, laughing as Lynn regaled her with additional fascinating stories of the inhabitants of Home. More shopping, pedicures, and lunch took up the rest of the afternoon before they headed back; ready to sit down for some much needed lemonade.

Maggie realized that it was about time she told Lynn how much she appreciated her. The words tumbled out with kindness and ease. "Lynn, thank you for being so good to me and looking after me. You made me feel like someone who really belongs here."

"Oh, honey, you're so welcome. You're a Jentry now!"

Lynn raised her head up just so, as if making a distinguished pronouncement. They shared a hug.

Lynn was becoming teary-eyed, as Maggie heard a sniffle come out of her, she excused herself to prepare things for the send-off. "Well, I am off to get some things fixed up for tonight."

"Can I do anything to help?" offered Maggie.

"Don't be silly. You're the guest of honor!" Lynn had flat-out refused Maggie's offer.

Maggie had a few hours on her hands before she had to get ready for the evening's festivities. Her packing and cleaning were done, so she decided that she might as well get in a last run.

Sprinting off the porch after a quick change, Maggie began running her usual route past the fields, the animals, and the stream. She inhaled the clean, cool air that was constantly replenished by the hundreds of surrounding trees. Her feet landed in rhythm on the soft ground under her running shoes. In Home, Maggie felt that she could run forever. She wasn't running away from anything here. She was running to everything. Her time in Home had been an encouragement to the faith in her heart. She had laid her future in the hands of God.

Tonight's send-off would be a celebration, not a goodbye. Maggie would be celebrating the peace she had found in Home. It was a surreal place, surrounded by some of the most kind and caring people she had ever met.

Maggie's mind kept pace with her run. She decided that if she just kept running, she wouldn't have to say goodbye. Her thoughts were a far stretch from reality, but Maggie's heart refused to leave this place.

Time raced by as she ran. She stopped on the porch to catch her breath before entering the house. She took a drink from her water bottle and then wiped the sweat from her eyes. There overlooking a clear view of the land that lay in front of her, she made a promise. Determined and fixated she exclaimed out to herself, "Someday I will have a piece of God's country like this—somewhere that I can feel free like I do when I am in Home."

Maggie knew it was time to shower, and she was glad. Now was not the time to wallow, so off she went.

Evening approached rapidly. The sun was diving down kissing the land behind the Jentry farm when Maggie finished up. Maggie settled for jeans and a light blue western button up shirt with her red cowboy boots. She took a good long look at herself in the mirror.

"Well, you look sweet and that's enough," Maggie exclaimed to the mirror. She stepped onto the porch to find Jake sitting there chewing on a piece of hay. "Hey there handsome, why didn't you knock?"

Jake stood up to hug her. "I was just waiting for you. I didn't want to rush you. I can tell by the way you look that I made the right choice."

"Why, Jake Ryan, you are such a sweet talker." Maggie appreciated his tone.

"That I am, now just you don't forget it," he teased as he reached for Maggie's hand. They headed to town together.

CHAPTER TWENTY-FOUR
GOODBYE, HOME

THE ENTIRE TOWN WAS IN attendance. Main Street was covered with sparkling lights tangled in the trees aligning the road. Busy activities including the cornhole competition and the cake walk were surrounded by eager participants. The smell of slow cooked barbecue ribs, sweet cotton candy, and hot buttery popcorn wafted through the air. The stage was lit up with a band performing country two-step tunes for a dance floor full of shuffling cowboy boots. Kids were running about with balloons and snow cones. Everyone in Home was lively and enjoying themselves. Another reason to have a festival was always welcomed.

As soon as Jake and Maggie arrived, they received instant attention. Maggie was receiving hugs and smiles from everyone—the first attention mob scene she actually enjoyed. The atmosphere was considerate and kind, a completely different feeling from the crowds of paparazzi that plagued her invitations in Hollywood.

Once the hoopla of the guest of honor's arrival was over, Jake suggested they have a bite to eat. Maggie filled up on the homemade southern food. After all, it was her last hurrah. Oh, how she wished she could bring the delicious abundance to Hollywood with her. She would really miss it; her hips on the other hand might beg to differ. Even fully stuffed, Maggie still managed to dance with Jake. They danced and danced, wishing it would go on forever. Cal cut in once to share a spin with Maggie.

"Maggie, you are quite a lady. You have been a peach to have 'round that old dusty farm of ours." Because Cal didn't usually say much, his words meant a lot. "Now you just stay well and don't fall for any of that Hollywood hubbub."

Maggie hugged and thanked him before Cal gave her hand graciously back to Jake.

The night was filled with adventure. Maggie bet on a pig race and drove a tractor. She would never have imagined this in her future a month earlier. Regardless, she was now in the heart of Home, knee deep in happy.

Lynn stepped up to the microphone just as the dinner cleanup began. "Hey, y'all listen up. In honor of our visit by Maggie, the quilting ladies and I have a gift for her. Maggie, come up here, darlin'."

Maggie stepped onto the stage as Lynn continued her presentation in a serious, clear voice. "Maggie, you have meant so much to this town. It's not just the overwhelming strength that you have brought to us financially. It's not the opening of our eyes to see that goodness can come from somewhere so unexpected. It isn't even the glam that shines out of you that we all secretly are jealous of, come on admit it ladies." Lynn turned to the crowd, as many women turn their heads to look at each other in denial. "It's because of the person we found in you. The kindness, caring, and love you have showed to us all. Maggie, God brought you to Home for a reason. We needed you just as much as you needed us." Lynn paused, gaining the wholehearted support of the crowd in a cheer. She turned to Maggie, both of them wiping away tears. Lynn needed a handful of tissues before finishing her speech. "Maggie, in appreciation from the quilting ladies here in town, we would like to present you with our recent finished piece. You should know it. You helped create it."

Lynn handed Maggie the magnificent quilt. It was covered with hand-stitched pictures of the town—the front windows of the shops, pictures of animals, the familiar trees on the hillsides, and the clear stream running beside the road. It even had a picture of the little house where Maggie stayed and the Jentry farm and home.

Maggie was overwhelmed as she ran her hand over the quilted masterpiece. She thought of all the hard work and love that had gone into their handmade gift. The crown cheered, "Speech, speech, speech!" Lynn handed Maggie the microphone.

Maggie was put on the spot, but she wasn't worried. She felt very sure of what to say. "Thank you so much, Lynn and all the quilting ladies. I will treasure this forever. I really appreciate you all so much."

Looking over from the quilting ladies—who were a weeping melting hot mess of friends—to the rest of the crowd, she continued, "To the sweet people of Home, these last few weeks have been so special. You have all treated me just like a hometown girl. You have reminded me of true Southern hospitality. Thank you so very much for everything. I will never forget Home or any of you." Maggie tried to smile, wiping away more tears. She kissed her hand and blew the kiss out to the crowd. A few wives threw their husbands evils stares as they reached up to eagerly catch Maggie's invisible kiss as it headed their way. The crowd clapped as Maggie stepped down from the stage. The band began to play, and everyone went back to dancing.

Jake met Maggie as she stepped down from the stage. They walked over to the table to put down her quilt. "Seems to me you will have something nice to keep you warm when you're rocking on your chair. Those two gifts are a perfect fit, aren't they?"

"They are a perfect fit. I like the sound of that." Maggie smiled. She was speaking more about her and Jake than about the quilt and rocker. As they joined the other dancers, the music stopped.

When Betsy took the stage, Maggie became anxiously excited. Betsy's lovely voice could make any event a musical blessing. She sang "Love Will Be Our Home," a song by Steven Curtis Chapman. Each word activated thoughts for Maggie about being in love, the Jentry family, and Home—the huge amount of joy that can come from such a small place.

Maggie stood motionless, listening to Betsy sing every verse, as if it was just for her. Jake stood behind her; his arms wrapped around her. Maggie's heart beat rapidly. The anxiety of leaving Home was causing a tightening in her chest.

Jake noticed Maggie begin to cringe. He spun her around gently, looked into her eyes, and spoke reassuringly. "Maggie, it's okay. Just breathe. It will be okay." He pulled her in close for a comforting hug, while Maggie focused on getting her breathing back to normal.

The security of Jake's soothing words did the trick. "Thanks, Jake. Sometimes my anxiety gets the better of me," she confessed.

"I know. It's okay," Jake countered understandingly. He rubbed her back as they started to walk. Jake handled her anxiety well, like a pro. He was the man Maggie needed in her life. She knew that. It wasn't fair that she had to follow the orders of Ms. A. Hearts don't always like the rules.

The send-off was a hit, and everyone said their last goodbyes to Maggie. The children had each picked a wildflower for Maggie. They presented them to her one by one, and she had quite a bouquet by the time the last child ran off.

Maggie stayed to watch the last family leave. The night became quiet and cold and Jake came over to stand beside her. His face registered anguish, knowing it was time for her to get going. He slowly reached down with his hands and grabbed one of Maggie's, bringing it up to show her palm in the light.

Jake began, "By the way, when I am not horse wrangling or rodeo clowning or . . . "

Maggie interrupted. "Or teaching kids to ride horses or turning wood into art."

Jake smiled, nodding his head before continuing, a twinkle sparkling in his eyes. "Or those things—right. Anyway, I can also read palms. I picked it up one summer as a rodeo clown for a circus. Madame Mystic or Madame Mystify—one of those was her name, I believe—taught me. She taught me all about palm reading."

Maggie smiled, playing along. A "Jake of all trades," blessed with talents. Maggie didn't believe in that stuff, but she just went along with his goofing. "So what do you see in my palm then?"

Jake smiled and looked at Maggie's palm more closely. Peering into her eyes affectionately, he admitted, "I see forever."

Maggie returned his gaze as Jake leaned down and gave her a kiss before she could respond. Bittersweet tenderness. They stood, foreheads touching, for a still moment.

A thousand thoughts seemed to run through Jake's mind, as his face stayed still and his eyes kept closed, but as promised his mouth stayed quiet. He looked down at Maggie's palm again. This time he squinted. He pulled her hand close and then moved it far away and squinted some more, making a silly face. Maggie giggled. Jake knew how to soften the situation. Finally, he explained what he was up to.

"Of course, I could be wrong. I had only one summer to learn the art of palm reading. It could mean . . . forever . . . you will talk, forever . . . you will eat, forever . . . you will run."

Maggie hit his arm as she pulled her hand away. They both laughed as they embraced again. Jake kissed her once more, adding their final, "see ya." Maggie asked Jake not to drive her home. She couldn't stand the thought of a long goodbye. She had planned to catch up with the Jentrys.

Jake agreed reluctantly. Maggie smiled at him from the car as they drove away. He smiled back as best he could.

The Jentrys' car was quiet on the ride home, except for Ruby Louise, who cried all the way. She wasn't much of a crier normally, however losing your own personal movie star now turned dress up best friend was tough to let go of. Maggie reassured Ruby Louise that someday they might meet again. She had to leave her with hope in her heart regardless of what might be an untruth.

Once back on the Jentry farm, Maggie gathered up her last few things. Lynn insisted she take the red cowboy boots with her because no one could ever do them proper Maggie justice. Cal loaded her rocking chair into the truck.

Just then a car drove up to the Jentrys'. It was Pastor James. He got out and greeted everyone, and they did likewise.

"Maggie, do you have a moment before you take off?"

Maggie nodded, so Pastor James and Maggie took a short stroll to talk alone.

"Maggie, I was hoping you would allow me to send you off correctly with a prayer for a safe trip." Pastor James grinned.

"I would like that very much, Pastor James. Thank you."

Maggie was touched by his offer. They stopped and turned towards each other, bowing their heads and holding holds. Pastor James proceeded, "Dear Lord, please travel today with our Maggie as she leaves us. Keep her safe and watch over her with Your angels. Thank You for allowing her to find us and us to have known her. Bless her always with Your love and guide her in the same way You guide us all. A . . . men."

Maggie hugged Pastor James. "Thank you, Pastor James. You have shown me the strength that God can instill in a person through the full-hearted help of others. I pray that I can use that strength wisely."

Pastor James reminded her, "Maggie, Hebrews eleven, one says, 'Now faith is the substance of things hoped for, the evidence of things not seen'. Your faith is your guide. Trust in its honesty." He said goodbye and drove back off.

Time for Maggie to say goodbye to the Jentrys. CJ was first. "Well, CJ, you're growing into a handsome man," Maggie assured him. "I am sure you will make some girl very lucky. Just be yourself, and they will love you." When she hugged CJ, he almost blushed himself into a fever.

Next it was Cal. "Thanks, Cal, for everything. I really think you have quite a remarkable family. I am sorry that I almost killed you with my spaghetti." Cal smirked and nodded his head in agreement. Lynn was standing right next to him, so she gave him an elbow for his agreeable spaghetti death nod.

When the time came for Ruby Louise to say goodbye, she stood sadly looking up at Maggie sniffling with tears rolling down her flush cheeks. Maggie stooped down eye-to-eye with Ruby Louise. She held her little hands in hers, crooning sweetly, "Listen, little girl, you are truly something. A smart, beautiful princess combined with one strong Southern belle. Be yourself, no matter what." Maggie hugged Ruby Louise tightly, tears parading now for them both.

Finally, Maggie turned to Lynn, who tried—and failed—to hide her tears with a hanky from Cal. Maggie was about to say something, but Lynn cut her off as usual. "No more fussing and blubbering. We love you, Maggie. We will miss you somethin' awful. Enough said," Lynn piped out loud and clear as she gave Maggie one of her famous bear hugs. Maggie knew Lynn couldn't take a long goodbye.

"Thank you so much for everything, Lynn," she said quickly, letting her off the hook.

Cal drove Maggie out to the airfield. EJ was there waiting as her plane had already landed. Cal brought Maggie's things to the plane, and EJ gave her a short sweet goodbye. She headed over to the plane and boarded without looking back.

As the plane turned around to get ready for takeoff, Maggie looked out the window. She could barely see EJ and Cal, outlined from the lights surrounding the airfield. They were waving her off in true cowboy fashion, hats back and forth above their heads.

Maggie didn't even realize when takeoff started. She was still trying to focus her eyes to see Home or anything familiar down there, but it was just too dark. Maggie closed her eyes while the tears trickled down her cheek; she fell into a restful sleep, dreaming of all the blessings that Home had brought to her life.

CHAPTER TWENTY-FIVE
BACK TO THE GRIND WITH A TWIST

BACK IN HOLLYWOOD, THINGS WENT back to a breakneck speed. The project staff had Maggie on land and secretly slipped back into her home unnoticed in record time. It was as if nothing had changed.

Maggie sat on her couch, realizing for the first time how lonely and quiet her house was. Although it was fashionably decorated, meticulously neat, and flawlessly clean, it didn't have the earthy smell of a ranch, possessed no cluttered walls filled with old farm artwork and family photos, and lacked the sounds of distant train whistles or cows. Maggie was missing things that she never imagined she would. She closed her eyes and put her head back against the couch. She could hear Ruby Louise giggling. She imagined the cold freshness of Lynn's lemonade, almost tasting it. She felt the soft touch of Jake's hand on the small of her back as he guided her onto the porch.

Maggie sought refuge in her private room. She sat wrapped in her friendship quilt, rocking slowly in the rocker made for her by the man she loved. How she thanked the Lord for the little things—like the ones she had brought with her from Home.

The next morning Maggie was determined to step right back into her star mode. The phone rang to get her started.

"Hello?"

"Maggie, good morning," spoke a crisp voice. "Maggie, this will be our last conversation. I would've much rather met with you in person to see how you felt about the project, but it's too risky. I need to update you on the doppelganger's activity while you were away. It went off smoothly as planned."

"That's good to know. Thank you."

Ms. A continued. "She stayed on board the yacht most of the time, sunning and relaxing. There was an onshore dinner, but it was very remote. It was kind of funny to see the paparazzi scrambling to charter boats in order to get closer. We made sure no boats were available. After two weeks, they got bored just waiting for something to happen and buzzed off. We kept all aerial activity grounded as well. That wasn't easy, but that is why we are the best. Anyway, you shouldn't have any lasting effects of the project on your life."

Maggie responded with a grateful but somber tone. "Okay, that all sounds really good." She thought of Ms. A's statement, "no lasting effects." *What about a broken heart? Does that count?* Her mind was reeling from the loss she was feeling.

"What's wrong, Maggie? Wasn't the project all you had hoped for?" Ms. A tried to keep to business, even if she had a good idea of what Maggie was experiencing.

"Yes, it was. Thank you, Ms. A," Maggie assured her.

They continued their conversation, mostly about the money transfer. Maggie's account would show a charitable contribution to an agricultural reestablishment organization. It would play as good press for her helping rural farm communities get back on their feet after a season of bad crops. It was also tax deductible.

It was clear Ms. A wasn't much for long goodbyes. In a weird way, she was like an older Lynn. She must have a big heart, but it was kept tidy in a suit instead of in a country dress. Ms. A left Maggie with a few last words, before she hung up. "Maggie, I hope that this project served as a way for you to better understand who you are, regardless of how Hollywood defines you."

Maggie appreciated Ms. A's insight. Who Maggie truly was did not completely fit her current life. The project had made that truth a reality. She would just have to deal with it as best she could. For now, she decided to focus one hundred percent on her work.

Minutes after she finished with Ms. A, Susan called. "Well hello, darling, glad to have you back, rested and ready to work. Did you enjoy yourself?"

Maggie smiled. *Boy did she ever!* But she answered, "Yes, I did. Thank you for the break, Susan. It meant the world to me. Where are we on the filming?"

Susan wanted to get right back to business, so she welcomed Maggie's eagerness. "That a girl, back in the saddle, literally. Shooting starts next week. The location is only a few hours outside of the city. Some dude ranch or something or other." Susan finished her instructions; then she and Maggie hung up.

Maggie decided to put off reviewing the script before she left. She had been so concentrated on preparing for the project. Then Maggie remembered. This was a horse and farm movie. How ironic? What timing!

Maggie hoped she could handle the flood of thoughts that filming on location would bring. She had to stay focused on her work. Everything else had to wait.

The following week brought working on the script and remembering lines. Maggie punished herself with extra exercise in an attempt to lose some of those Southern food pounds. Her schedule was extremely busy, easing the project out of her mind little by little.

On Wednesday of that week, she had to sign the paperwork for the money transfer to the charitable organization. She stopped herself, allowing Home to fill her thoughts. One million dollars was certainly a lot of money, but Ms. A had been right: it was worth every dollar. Nothing could replace the time she had spent in Home or the memories that she made there. Finding her true self again and falling in love unconditionally had blessed Maggie, no matter what.

Susan came over to the house that afternoon to update Maggie on a few details concerning the movie, mostly schedules for interviews. "Oh, by the way, this movie is really right up your alley. Did you know that a part of the proceeds go to a foundation for disabled children? It gives them the opportunity to do things on farms and ranches like other kids do: milk cows, watch over animals, ride horses . . . "

Maggie dropped her pen as she was taking notes. She felt the blood leave her face.

"Maggie, are you okay?" Susan asked, concerned.

Trying to stay cool, Maggie nodded her head and picked up her pen, eager to know more. "Yeah, I am fine. I was daydreaming a bit. So that's great about the movie and the charity. Was this the producer's doing?"

"Yes, he's a big fan of ranching and horses. I guess he grew up in Montana or something like that. Anyway, it's a great way to spin the press towards you. After all, you're a charity girl, so let them think that you chose this role for that reason or whatever. It's all win-win either way." Susan continued excitedly. "This is the way to play it up good for the public, right?"

"Yeah, I guess it will make good press. I have even more appreciation for the producer now. What a great cause," Maggie said with secret admiration.

After Susan and Maggie finished up their meeting, Susan took off, smiling big because she knew she would cash in. Maggie would nail this role; Maggie's success was Susan's constant goal.

Maggie sat looking out over her view of the ocean with a glass of lemonade in her hand. Two thoughts rushed through her head. First, she really missed Jake. Starring in a movie that was going to help disabled kids ride horses? This movie was going to affect her in many ways. Second, she missed Lynn's homemade lemonade—this over-priced fancy one from the bottle was no match.

Taking a deep breath, she reminded herself of Pastor James' send-off. "Your faith is your guide. Trust in its honesty," he had told her.

"So, God," Maggie said as she raised her glass to heaven, "I will keep my faith." Maggie took a sip of her glass to seal the deal. She would put aside her emotional rides, anxieties, and panic attacks for a good while. Faith would be her new pill of choice.

The first day on the set came quickly. Outdoor set pieces with cables crisscrossed the scene and lighting equipment was being moved back and forth. Setting up a scene outside was always a huge task. Wrangling with the forces of nature was tough for the crew: bugs, wind, and heat. Thank goodness the weather was cooperating; it gave the crew a chance to set up the equipment more quickly.

The cast spent a few days together running the script. Everyone was eager to put it all together.

Maggie reported to hair, makeup, and wardrobe, following the usual procedure. Her wardrobe was simple: jeans, striped blue western shirt unbuttoned and tied at the waist with a tank top underneath. No surprise for the setting. She did have fun trying to pour herself into those jeans; she hadn't shed every spoonful of her project pounds yet. Trying not to alarm anyone, she just sucked it in. What a long day it was going to be in those jeans.

The next step in the wardrobe process was shoes. "Ms. Malone, have a seat, I have just the thing for you," Charmaine, the wardrobe assistant, instructed.

Maggie sat as requested. In a few minutes, Charmaine came around the corner of the wardrobe trailer carrying a pair of red cowgirl boots. Maggie couldn't believe it. They were exactly like the ones that Lynn had given her. Identical in fact. Maggie was taken back, and it showed.

"I'm so sorry, Ms. Malone; if you don't like these, I will get you another pair. It's just that they went so well with the shirt and . . . " Charmaine quickly apologized, nervous after Maggie's reaction.

"No, no. Charmaine," Maggie interrupted as she reached for the boots with a reassuring smile. "They're great. They will be just fine, and please call me Maggie."

Maggie pulled the boots on, and they fit like a glove. She stood up and closed her eyes for a minute. She could picture herself walking through downtown Home. The memory made her smile.

Charmaine looked relieved at Maggie's smile. "All right, you're all set on our end then, Maggie. Can I get you anything else?"

Maggie thanked Charmaine and headed onto the set. The set was filled with extras for various scenes, makeup people on standby, huge pieces of equipment, and lots of ranch dust.

Warren Blue, the director, walked over to Maggie. An up and coming director with one hit under his belt, Maggie had heard mixed reviews about him.

"Maggie, great to see you. You ready?" Warren moved quickly, walking next to Maggie as he threw his hand over her shoulder to guide her to her spot in the scene. He was a jumpy, high-energy kind of guy, very sure of himself. His personality was infectious, giving full encouragement to the crew while working just as hard himself. Good-looking but not showy about it, Warren knew what sold movies, touching people's hearts. He didn't look a day over twenty-five, but Maggie knew he was over thirty. His dark black hair was slicked back, emphasizing his big brown eyes. He had his quirks as most directors do, but they didn't bother Maggie.

"Yep, ready." Maggie's response was to the point.

"So remember, we are going to start with the first horse scene. Now I was told you are familiar with horses, so I didn't see any reason to have you take lessons like some of the other cast members. We have the greatest horse wrangler guy; he will have you comfortable with your horse in minutes." Warren filled her in as he led her over to her horse. "This is your horse Sweet Pea and . . . " Warren said, as the cowboy boots visible from underneath the horse came walking around to where Maggie was standing. As Maggie shifted her eyes from the horse to the wrangler, Warren continued his introductions, "This is the horse guy, Jake Ryan."

Maggie and Jake locked eyes, and Maggie stopped breathing for at least fifteen seconds. Her heart began to race at the sight. There was Jake standing in front of her. Jake smiled broadly.

"Very pleased to meet you, Ms. Malone," Jake said calmly, playing it cool, putting out his hand to shake hers.

Maggie robotically shook his hand. "It's nice to meet you, too. Maggie is fine." The words were forced out slowly, and Maggie was afraid that they had sounded more like "Blah, blah, Maggie, blah."

Warren seemed to sense something weird, so of course he decided to probe further. "What's wrong, Maggie? You looked flushed, are you okay?" He was extremely nervous by Maggie's behavior and he began chewing the end of his sunglasses.

Maggie had to act quickly; or, her cover would be blown. "Oh, no, I'm fine. Fine . . . uh . . . all is fine. He is all good." Maggie still could not get her words together continuing to sound like a blubbering fool.

Jake just stood smiling at her, shaking her hand. Against her better judgment, Maggie continued to talk. "I mean, this is a fine horse. It will be great working with her." Maggie figured she would switch the attention to Sweet Pea.

Warren looked at her strangely still concerned and turned to Jake. "Jake, please watch over our Maggie, will you? She is precious cargo. A little encouragement is just what she needs. Hopefully she will deliver the script better than she did her last few words." Warren had a lot riding on Maggie—on that horse, so to speak. Warren left Maggie, Jake, and Sweet Pea alone.

People rustled past them, and staging sounds increased in volume around them, but Jake and Maggie didn't notice; they were lost in their own world. Jake only smiled.

Maggie whipped her words out like swords before he had a chance. "Jake, what are you doing here? Why are you here? I can't believe this. We can't be here working together. It's too risky. Why did you do this?" Maggie spoke softly but sternly, not wanting to draw attention but attempting to show Jake that she was furious.

"Well, that is not the welcome I expected. Why do you think I'm here? Maggie, I'm here for you. I still feel the same. I know you do, too. Why are you so angry?" Jake's demeanor had changed as he spoke, showing he was obviously hurt by her response.

Maggie had no answer. Her anxiety was choking her, and her breathing was erratic as she ran off to her trailer. Once inside, she put her head down into her arms on the table, trying to control her breathing.

A flood of thoughts passed through her mind. *He is here. Jake is here. I can't believe it. I should be with him right now, telling him how glad I am to see him. But here I am freaking out, running away as usual. Warren is going to lose it if he sees his star actress in here hyperventilating; he will get rid of me for sure. I must concentrate. I must get it together.*

Maggie'd had only five minutes to calm down before there came a knock on her trailer door. No matter who was out there, Maggie had to let them in. "Come in, come in" Maggie rushed her words, struggling to steady her voice.

Warren entered the room; Maggie took a gulp. But Warren was smiling. "Hey, love, did you get that dust out of your eyes? I'm so sorry about that, but you know the West—it's all dust. We can try to block out some of the edges of the scene with tarps. Don't worry. I will get makeup to touch you up." Warren extended his hand to Maggie to help her up.

"Okay. Thanks so much. Sorry about running off. It was pretty painful; I thought I'd better rinse the dust out right away," Maggie replied, playing along.

Maggie was touched; she knew Jake had covered for her by inventing the story about the dust in her eye. It was an ingenious ruse since he knew she would be crying after running off. He had covered all the bases. Even when he was being dismissed by Maggie, Jake had still watched out for her.

Maggie returned to the set after having her makeup quickly touched up, and Jake helped her up onto the horse. He purposely avoided looking her in the face. They didn't say anything more to each other for the rest of the day. They simply did their jobs.

Shooting ran long, and by the end of the day, Maggie was exhausted. The anxiety attack from earlier hadn't helped, neither did the long day of shooting in tight pants. After obtaining a bite to eat, she returned to her trailer. All she wanted was a cold drink and a hot shower. She was covered in dust and smelled like Sweet Pea.

Maggie's shower was not as relaxing as she had hoped. Her mind worked nonstop on the dilemma of Jake's arrival. If she allowed their relationship to continue, it would go public. Could she be responsible for destroying the future of the project, and directly harming the people of Home? No, she couldn't bear that. But if she didn't pursue Jake, she would lose him forever. Neither choice was an option.

CHAPTER TWENTY-SIX
NO MORE SECRETS

MAGGIE DECIDED TO LET HER heart lead her, toss caution to the wind and live upon faith. Facing the fear of true love lost, she had to risk it. Loosing Jake without a fight was unthinkable; he was the one for her. Furthering her turmoil, another lingering question, what if she lost him anyway? What would the strain of stardom do to their relationship? She prayed right then and there that their faith and love for each other would be strong enough to weather the storm

The first step was to apologize to Jake. Maggie peeked out the doorway of her trailer. The entire cast had retired for the night. Warren was occupied with a few crew members working out some logistics for shooting the next scene. No one noticed Maggie as she headed out to the barn. The barn was not a false front but an actual large, classic wooden red barn. Perhaps this is why they had chosen this property on which to film.

Maggie saw the light on. Hopefully, Jake was alone with the horses. She pushed open the barn door slowly. There stood Jake brushing Sweet Pea. He saw her come in, but he ignored her and continued brushing. Maggie walked over to the stall next to Jake and said simply, "Hi."

"Hi," Jake echoed her greeting with a cold and unfeeling tone. He was obviously still angry with Maggie.

"I'm sorry, Jake. I am truly sorry for how I reacted. It's just that . . . " Maggie said, trying to explain.

Jake stopped brushing and abruptly stated toward her, "Maggie, I am very tolerant of most things, but not too fond of rejection. I can see now that I was a convenience for you while you were in Home, but it's obvious I am not good enough for Hollywood." Jake walked away smoothly with Sweet Pea in tow.

Maggie wanted to call after him, but instead she let him walk away. If only he understood that Maggie was just trying to protect their love. Intrusions and judgments would be flying at them from all sides, and what about Home and her promise to Ms. A? Their relationship could destroy the project if the press got word of where Maggie really was on her vacation.

Maggie stood motionless, disappointed and exhausted. She was halfway tempted to plop down and lay across the hay wishing she could sink in and disappear. Shooting started in a few hours, so instead she went back to her trailer to get some sleep.

The next morning felt like the day before never ended. Maggie was in makeup by four a.m. and on the set by five a.m. Today's highest priority was to conquer the demanding scenes—big, emotional takes that required intense physical drama with anger. She nailed them like a true professional. Perhaps all the awkward stares that she shared with Jake between scenes provided her the fuel. Neither one of them would acknowledge the other.

Jake had his hands full. Managing twenty horses with individual personalities and twenty actors with the same was a tough gig. Good thing Jake had two guys from a nearby ranch working with him; Maggie was glad of that. They were both young—in their late teens.

Jake was great at working with these guys. Maggie enjoyed catching bits of their training. He taught them extensive things about horses that they didn't know: how to read their moods, how to brush their coat to produce more shine, and how to understand their movements. He was a natural teacher, patient with a built-in fathering instinct.

Shooting proceeded, making great strides until a hard rain came in at the end of the week. The rain halted it all for most of the morning. Maggie welcomed the opportunity for more rest. Then she took a long run when the rain slowed.

The desert scenery wasn't as beautiful as the beach. It also didn't have the green-clean air like the South, but it provided for the most amazing sunrises and sunsets.

Maggie finished her run, enjoyed a hot shower, and reported to makeup. Once back on the set, she braced for her riding scene. In this scene, the horse had to stop short and turn back. Maggie insisted she perform the tricky move herself, even though a stunt double was available. She wanted an excuse to be close to Jake.

Jake took his time explaining what to expect from the horse. They ran through the scene together several times for safety precautions. Sweet Pea was a very accommodating participant, true to her name. Maggie paid close attention to every word Jake instructed. The move was dangerous, so they stayed focused.

As a result of the intense practice, the scene went off without a hitch, and Warren loved it. First take and they nailed it! Maggie was frightfully nervous the whole time, but she hid it well from Jake and Sweet Pea.

When they were finished filming the open ride scenes everyone rode back to the barn in the studio van. Jake rode on horseback, leading a few horses behind him. Maggie chose to ride Sweet Pea back hoping to talk to Jake alone. After the others left, she caught up and rode alongside him.

"Hello there. Thanks so much for the great help with Sweet Pea, Jake. You're a phenomenal trainer," Maggie praised as she smiled over at Jake, hoping to spur conversation.

Jake brought out barely a smirk before he replied to her. "You are very welcome."

Since Maggie felt she had broken the ice, she ventured further conversation. "Jake, I really am sorry. I didn't mean to hurt you. I guess I wasn't ready for your surprise appearance. I know I reacted badly. I was just so afraid. I don't blame you for being upset with me. Is there a way that we can start over? I would love a try," Maggie pleaded, pouring out her feelings of hope.

Jake stopped his horse and slowly allowed the other horses to do the same. He looked to her; confusion showed across his handsome rugged face. "Then what, Maggie? At what point will you want to dismiss me again? I can't keep my feelings for you hidden all the time, just letting them show when no one's around. Don't you realize that I know what I am getting into? It's an arena full of running bulls, and this fool is wearing red pajamas. I know it's a huge deal for us to go public. I am willing to do it for you. Can't you see there is nothing I wouldn't do for you, Maggie? I love you; that hasn't changed." Jake delivered his words with strong conviction, expressing off such strength and willingness to work hard unconditionally for Maggie's returned love. Her heart was full, Jake had filled it, what more could she need.

Maggie leaned over and grabbed his hand, with tears of gratefulness streaming down her face. Then she smiled profusely, wiping away the tears, and concluded, "I love you, too."

After shooting a few more scenes, the rain came back hard so their work finished up for the day. Jake and Maggie agreed to meet up later—though discreetly for now. They knew it would be better to rebuild their relationship slowly, naturally seeming to pretend that they had met on set. Maggie hoped that this plan would protect Home and the project. This was of the utmost importance to them both.

Maggie helped Jake walk the horses so they could all stretch their legs. It was a perfect way for them to take their walks alone. Once they were out of sight at the edge of the ranch, Jake led Maggie behind one of the horses. He gently laid a kiss on her, showing her how much he had missed her. She welcomed his kiss—no holding back.

"I missed you," Jake added sweetly.

"Likewise, cowboy; likewise," Maggie replied, winking at Jake. Jake laughed in response.

Every day the sneaking away continued. Sometimes it was only for a moment, but it was something. Two months had gone by; shooting was about to wrap up on location.

Maggie and Jake had another goodbye looming over them. However, this time it would be easier. They knew they would be together again soon.

Before they left the ranch, Maggie was scheduled for an on-set interview. Nothing that warranted any concern for her. All just standard protocol: questions about the movie and an explanation of the program for the children with the horses.

The host was a younger guy named Harry Harriet—an odd name, but he had a great smile. He was a sharp dresser, wearing a navy blue suit and pin-stripped tie. Dark brown hair with highlighted blond locks coifed neatly in waves topped off his look.

Maggie flowed through the interview with witty banter balanced nicely with her serious responses. Harry had a sweet way to interview, coaxing with honey, instead of vinegar. He made her feel comfortable with his approach.

"I have one last question, Maggie?"

Maggie responded coolly. "Sure, shoot."

Harry smirked and leaned forward. He put his hand to the side of his face and whispered, "So tell us about your relationship with the horse wrangler on the set, Jake Ryan. What are you two up to? Maybe snuggling around the campfire, hmmm?"

What did he ask? Maggie didn't see it coming. Staying cool, she tried to stall by smiling, crossing her legs, sitting back, and tossing her hair. However, time did not stand still as she had hoped.

Harry continued. "Well . . . we have it on good authority that you two are spending a lot of time together, perhaps even holding hands? So come on, you can share with us. We're all friends here." Harry really knew how to deliver the pokes—like sugar-coated lollipops. Kind and soft, which made one want to answer as not to be rude.

Maggie took a deep breath; this was not her first time in this spot. She looked to Jake, who was standing fairly close in her sight line. Smiling at Maggie, he ran the pointer finger of his left hand down the palm of his right hand. He smiled softly, mouthing the word "forever" to remind Maggie of the palm reading he had given her.

Maggie looked back to Harry and finally replied. "Well, Jake is a great horse wrangler. He has such a way with the horses. He has even trained me how to do my own horse stunts."

Maggie paused, but Harry wasn't finished. He wanted more. He motioned with his hand for her to keep her words coming. "And . . . go ahead is there more, friend?" he asked.

With a huge smile, Maggie answered, "And . . . he wrangled my heart as well, we are together."

Harry's mouth dropped open, as did everyone's on set. No one had expected Maggie to announce it publicly. Half of the people present had no idea they were dating. Lots of little whispers grew amongst the film team.

Harry sat silently stunned as his producer waved for him to wrap it up. Finally snapping out of his daze, Harry spoke to his viewers. "O . . . kay, there you have it. Maggie Malone possibly has a new love in her life. We are certainly excited for her. Eat your heart out, guys! What a scoop! Good night!"

Maggie and Jake locked eyes, fixated on the happiness evident on each other's face.

The cast and crew buzzed around Maggie and Jake, taking down the interview set. Equipment and lighting moved past inches from their faces, but all Maggie and Jake could do was stare at each other, undisturbed by anyone or anything.

Jake took off his cowboy hat, nodded at Maggie, and then put his hat back on. Maggie's heart began to beat fast. She jumped up quickly, pushing through the crowd, and leaped into Jake's arms. If this instance never ended; Maggie and Jake would have been fine with that.

Moving his arms from hugging her, Jake freed his hands to hold her face gently. He looked at her fondly, saying, "Maggie, I know that took a lot. Thank you. You're so sweet. I promise we will be happy" Maggie smiled in answer, and they hugged again.

Later that evening, everyone on the set was all packed. Maggie was hanging out in her trailer, getting her things together. Jake was busily preparing the horses to return to their owners. He took his time saying goodbye to his two young horse helpers. He offered them jobs working on his ranch for the summer.

Maggie was just about finished packing when a knock sounded at the door. It was Susan. Maggie prepared uncomfortably for Susan's reaction to her interview announcement.

Susan entered Maggie's trailer, dusting off her pants. Her face flushed and a bit worn for wear, she targeted her eyes towards Maggie. "Well, Mags, another fine mess you've gotten us into!" Susan delivered her pronouncement in her usual irritated, condescending voice.

Maggie wasn't going to have it this time. "Stop right there, Susan. You're not going to lecture me or tell me how to fix it, ignore it, or lie about it. This is my life, and Jake is a part of my real life, no matter what. I really don't care what anyone thinks!" Maggie gave it to Susan straight.

Susan took a deep breath, feeling the anger in Maggie's sheer honesty. "Good for you, dear; you just let me have it. You are right. You've gotten to where you are, Maggie, by standing your ground lots of times—against my better judgment. I do want to see you happy though, no matter what! You deserve happiness."

The words burst forth from Susan's mouth, and amazingly she meant every word. She had finally put Maggie first. Maggie threw her arms around Susan in a good ol' Lynn bear hug, showing how pleased she was with Susan's surprising reaction.

"Thank you, Susan, so much. You have been so good to me. I know I pull you towards my own direction making your job pretty difficult at times."

Maggie and Susan enjoyed the moment of bonding. It was the first time Susan had revealed her emotions to Maggie, and they were surely welcomed. Susan's portrayal as a hard woman was part of a tough image she put out, not the real her. Managers and agents are actors reinvented after all.

Susan was glad shooting had wrapped up earlier than expected. Tomorrow was going to be especially busy. A standard press conference about the movie was scheduled. The stars, producer, and director would answer questions from TV reporters and movie reviewers. Normally the event was boring. However, the buzz was building about Jake and Maggie. It was going to be a circus.

Susan went ahead of Maggie to prepare for the conference. Syl brought around the limo to take Maggie back to Hollywood. He had shown up just in time to hear the big announcement.

Syl entered Maggie's trailer as Susan was leaving. "Susan, as always, good to see you. You're looking lovely," Syl managed to blend sarcasm and charisma resourcefully in the same sentence.

Susan echoed Syl's tone. "Syl, same to you. Take good care of her."

Maggie approached Syl with her arms out and hugs ready, happy to see him. "Boy, I am glad you're here," she confessed.

"Yes, I can imagine. You have had quite a day, little lady. So, do you want to fill me in? I would like to meet Jake the old-fashioned way, please—in person." Syl was cool but anxious.

"Of course, you can meet Jake. I am sorry that, out of all people, I didn't give you a heads up. It all just happened so quickly," Maggie apologized.

"It's okay, doll. I am just glad to see you found someone that brings your real fire out. By the way, I think Harry is still in shock. After years of his silly zingers, I think you out zinged him. Too funny."

As Syl and Maggie shared a laugh, another knock sounded on the door. Maggie opened the door to find no one standing there. She started to turn around and close the door behind her but decided to look back once more. Stepping around the corner of the door was Jake. He was in a fitted suit, holding a dozen long stem roses, and smiling with his arms held open.

"Well, what do you think? Do I clean up good . . . for Holly . . . wood?" Jake teased.

Maggie flushed in acknowledgment of Jake's amazing handsome looks. "Oh my yes, please come in, sir."

Jake stepped right in, not noticing Syl's presence. He scooped Maggie up and tilted her backwards for a dance dip and a quick kiss. Maggie giggled shyly upon being lifted back up on her feet from Syl's presence. Jake followed Maggie's gaze to the uncomfortable peering, arms-crossed Syl.

"Oh, sorry, I didn't know you had company," Jake said, embarrassed as he walked over with his hand extended to Syl.

"Jake Ryan." He blushed as he introduced himself.

Syl shook Jake's hand with a firm grip. "Sylvester, but everyone calls me Syl. So you're Jake, Maggie's Jake. It is great to meet you. You certainly have put the smile back in her heart. I take her happiness seriously, if you know what I mean." Syl pulled Jake closer with a strong arm still shaking hands.

Pausing to look sternly at Jake, now mere inches from his face, Syl meant every word. Finally, after he had tortured Jake long enough with targeted silence and the accompanied stare down, Syl continued, "Be sure to keep her that way!" Syl loved Maggie.

Jake welcomed Syl's honesty, respecting greatly his job of protecting Maggie. "Syl, Maggie has told me a lot about you. I should be thanking *you* for always keeping her safe. You mean the world to her," he said with all seriousness.

Syl looked over at Maggie and smiled. "Thanks man." And then he excused himself outside saying, "Maggie, see you in a few. Jake, mighty good to meet you. Be sweet to my Maggie now, you hear." Syl closed the trailer door on his way out.

"Yes, sir," Jake replied hoping Syl heard him.

Jake and Maggie had a few minutes together before they both had to leave. They sat in her trailer next to each other, holding hands. Jake lifted Maggie's left hand up above them examining it.

"What are you looking at?" Maggie asked.

"Just looking; you do have beautiful hands," Jake commented, admiring her hands.

"Well, mister, thank you for the compliment, but they are about worn out after I went cowgirl for a few months. I am sure they would have been worse if I didn't have such a good trainer," Maggie complimented, though her hands were a total mess.

Jake smiled as he looked over to Maggie. While he still had her hand raised slightly, he brought his right hand over to her left hand

and slid the most beautiful antique oval shaped diamond ring on her ring finger. Maggie turned to him quickly.

Jake smiled and asked, "Forever?"

"Yes, forever," Maggie said without hesitation. Maggie kissed Jake, celebrating their engagement.

"Perfect fit!" Maggie said, holding Jake close while admiring her ring as a happiness tears rounded her cheeks.

"Just like us, Maggie," Jake agreed.

"Thank you, Jake. You have made me so happy," Maggie expressed her joy filled with love.

"Right here, right now, together being silly, being in love. Nothing outside that door is going to change that, Maggie." Jake assured Maggie of his love for her.

"Yes, nothing will ever get in the way again. I promise," Maggie declared.

They hugged each other tightly and kissed softly. Together in that trailer, Jake and Maggie set an unbreakable testament to a new beginning that belonged to them.

CHAPTER TWENTY-SEVEN
FAMILY AND LOVE, THAT'S A WRAP!

JAKE HAD RESPONSIBILITIES TO GET back to at the ranch, while Maggie went on promoting the movie. They felt together they could take on the world. Good thing, with that press conference coming up, that is exactly what they would need to do.

She could hear the questions now. All about her relationship with Jake—their past, present, and future—as she now sported an engagement ring.

Maggie didn't mind. She loved Jake, and she wasn't thinking about her career first this time. All those years, she worked endless hours, pouring her blood, sweat, and tears into roles to get recognition. This time, she would shine from the inside out.

Maggie gave a strong performance in this movie, her best work yet. She felt more like the character than ever. Her passion for ranch farming had come alive again in Home. The countryside was a place she truly belonged—the way she had felt when she was a young girl. The project had been a beneficial, soul-refreshing investment in realizing her true self. All the while, giving her hands-on recollection of country living to perform an exact role. It was amazing how God works. He works when He was ready, in His own time, at His right time.

Maggie's ride back to the city was a chance for her to catch a nap. Syl didn't disturb her. She awoke just before they arrived at her house.

In light of recent events, Maggie's mind was on her family. What are they thinking by now? Surely they saw the interview about Jake. Why wasn't Mom ringing her phone repeatedly? Maggie tried calling but couldn't reach her mom, her dad, or her brother Michael. She thought maybe Mom and Dad were out for dinner. Michael probably was on call. Certainly, she would catch up with them by tomorrow. She couldn't wait to tell them herself all about Jake.

Spent and glad to be home, Maggie looked forward to sleeping in her own bed. Syl took Maggie's bags upstairs and came back to see if she needed anything else.

"Mags, that's everything. Is there anything else I can get you?"

"No. Thanks, Syl. I'm good. It's good to be home," Maggie replied as she headed up the stairs, finding it odd now to call her house, home.

"Hey, Mags, don't be startled, but a surprise arrived for you today. It's in the kitchen," Syl shouted up to Maggie just as she was about to open the door. His words were accented with a wide smile and a wink.

When Maggie opened the door, the most intoxicating welcoming smell of home cooking wafted over her. Maggie stepped around the corner to find Mom, Dad, and Michael all in the kitchen. She ran quickly over to them, hugging them all at once. Tears of excitement to see her family began to well up in her eyes.

"Mom, guys, I am so glad to see you. I was just thinking about you all. I tried calling, but this is such a great surprise!" Maggie burst out. Mom didn't want to stop hugging as she began to reply.

"Oh, honey, we are so glad to see you. We had to come with so much exciting news. Tell us all about Jake. When can we meet him? Does he love you, Maggie? Really love you, like we do?" Mom shot out questions one after another; she couldn't wait any longer. Maggie smiled and held out her ring finger shining the news of the engagement. Mom gasped with joy, Dad and brother smiled. They all hugged again.

Maggie spoke, still excited. "Mom, don't worry. I will tell you all about Jake. Yes, you will meet him. Yes, we are in love," Maggie answered as quickly as Mom tossed out the questions. "First though, how are you all? Michael, how did you ever get the time off? I know you have been so busy." Maggie focused on her family. It had been awhile since all of them had been together.

"Well, Sis, once I knew Mom and Dad were coming, I wanted to be here, too. It's true, my schedule has been crazy, but Mom didn't have to twist my arm. She told me it was for you. You look great. Love agrees with you, Mags." Michael delivered his speech as he gave his sister another hug.

Maggie had never been more thrilled to have her family with her. The fatigue of spending months in the hot desert sun battling dirt was soon forgotten. Seeing them gave her such positive energy that she couldn't imagine resting right now.

Mom set before her family a delicious meal. When they sat down to eat, Michael was just about to plunge his fork in for that first satisfying bite, but Maggie reached over to stop him.

"Michael, could you please say the prayer first?" she requested.

Michael had a blank look on his face. He looked at his parents. They both looked at each other and smiled. Everyone could tell it had been a while since Michael had said grace before a meal. Doctors may have only a few minutes to grab a bite, but there were no excuses now. The whole family bowed their heads and joined hands. Michael began. "Dear Lord,

thank You for this meal You have set before us. Thank You for the blessing of being together and having each other. Please forgive me for not
thanking You at each occasion I should, Lord. Tonight You have brought
my family together through Your love for us and I am thankful. Amen."

Maggie reached over to touch his shoulder with gratitude just as
they dropped their hands to eat.

"Thank you, Michael; that was perfect!" she reassured him.
Michael's face shared a look of appreciation and true thanks for his
family, saying that prayer obviously moved his heart.

In case anyone had noticed that he was tearing up, Michael did
the manly thing: he lied, saying, "I think I picked up an allergy recently," wiping his eyes.

"Well, maybe you should see a doctor about that," whimsically
added Dad. Everyone laughed, and Michael's dignity was saved.

Dinner was perfect; Mom was an amazing cook. All the great food
parading once again, there for the taking, against Maggie's calorie
counts. Fortunately, she couldn't stop talking to really dive in. "So, everyone, how long can you stay?" Usually, they were the ones asking this
question. She always needed to jet off within in hours of arriving.

"Well, dear, your father and I thought we would stay a couple of
days and take in the sights. Michael, I believe you have to leave tomorrow night. Is that right, honey?"

"Sorry, Mags, but I have a patient scheduled for surgery. I need to
be there. He's just eighteen years old and was in a bad car accident. I
called in a favor from a surgeon friend of mine and I will provide full
aftercare. He can't afford any of this with no insurance or medical
coverage. He's the breadwinner for his mom and little sisters, so it's
very important for him to get back to work to provide for his family.

"I'm going to make sure he's well as soon as possible. Mags, when I first met him, I thought of you, your kindness with charity work. Besides, he is a big brother, too, just like me. I felt inspired to help him." Michael explained, looking at his sister with admiration.

Maggie was touched; all she could do was smile with brotherly pride and say, "Thank you, Michael. I think that's great!"

The family spent the rest of the night out on the patio, overlooking the ocean. Maggie filled in her parents on all things Jake. How he was very sweet and fun to be with—and a rodeo clown, of all things. Mom and Dad sat back on the porch swing holding hands. They reveled in comfort to see their daughter so happy. It had been a long time since she carried her true smile.

Michael laughed as his sister gestured excitedly and talked nonstop about her recent movie: the ranch, the horses, and the fact that she had done her own stunts. She was chattering a mile a minute. They all spent a long time catching up until the evening chill off the ocean crept in. Mom and Dad were ready to get inside.

Around midnight, Maggie finally felt her exhaustion taking a toll. She took her shower and hit the bed hard. She was just about to doze off when her mom slowly opened the door to her room.

"Honey, are you sleeping?" Mom asked. Maggie looked up squinting from the light of the open door with a smile of contentment on her face. Mom approached, pleased she was still awake.

"Dad and I are settled for bed, but I wanted to say good night again." Mom sat next to Maggie on her bed.

A feeling of Dejà vu overcame Maggie, remembering how when she was a little girl, Mom would tuck her in every night. "Hey, Mom, could you tuck me in?"

Smiling and placing the covers snuggly around her daughter, Mom bent over and gave her a little kiss on the head. "Good night, sweetheart. I love you. You're the best." Using the exact words she would whisper softly to her sleepy girl every night when she was little. Maggie quickly drifted off. It was the perfect ending to a perfect day.

Morning came in with the sound of Mom humming as she cooked breakfast. Maggie was barely awake but favorably alerted at the smell of bacon cooking.

Today was the day of the press conference to promote the movie, a big day for Maggie. She hopped up, anxious to join her family. Michael was on his computer and his phone at the same time. Mom and Dad were giggling about something in the kitchen.

Maggie stood around the corner, watching her parents' relaxed comradeship and her brother's efficiency. Her joy was complete in having her entire family together. She really missed having everyone all under the same roof. Finally, Mom caught a glimpse of spying eyes and invited them, "Good Morning, Sunshine; breakfast is almost ready."

Running over to her parents first thing in the morning was reminiscent to her childhood, giving Mom and Dad a great big squeeze. "Mom, please don't go through all the trouble. I have to keep tight on my calories. I got a bit out of hand on my vacation."

Mom shrugged her shoulders and shook her head in disagreement. "Well, I am sure I don't know what you're talking. Those pictures of you on that boat made you look like you were skin and bones, little girl! Were those photos altered?"

Maggie couldn't tell her mom that the pictures were actually her doppelganger. "Don't worry, Mom; I am fine. Yes, they were. Besides, with your cooking around, I can't resist."

Hugging Mom with one arm, Maggie reached for a piece of bacon with the other. Mom laughed as she popped the bacon in her mouth, making a yummy face of approval.

After breakfast, Syl took Maggie and her family to the studio for the press conference. It was a full house. There was tons of press—supposedly about the new movie—but, in reality, all were abuzz about Maggie's love life. Maggie took her place next to the movie team.

Jake approached Maggie and her family. He didn't make it far before Maggie's mom threw her arms around him. Jake smiled and laughed with relief, hugging back. "Thank you, Ma'am."

"You're the reason that my Maggie glows." Her mom said gratefully, still hugging Jake. As she let go of the hug, Mom held both Jake's hands in hers. They stood looking towards each other as she added sweet and firm, "Son, you call me Mom. I might lecture you sometimes, but I will feed you, too. From what I gather, she loves you. I just know we will feel the same. See to it that you treat my Maggie as a precious gift always."

Jake didn't hesitate to reply, "Yes, Mom."

They continued to talk as they made their way through the crowd. Maggie felt comforted catching sight of Jake arriving. Seeing him with her family, bonding with her mom, gave her strength and confidence.

Dozens of members of the press crowded the room, holding cameras, microphones, and tablets. Ah, the barrage of tabloids with star reporters, and headline entertainment shows! They were like little mice waiting for a smackerel of cheese to fall out of Maggie's mouth.

The producer began the conference with an overview of the movie. Then Warren took over, stirring the aim of their attention, impressing the masses with anecdotes about the filming of the movie. He made sure to thank his team for enduring long hot days on the set and their professionalism in getting it done.

Once the focus shifted to the actors, Maggie took a deep breath. Her first question shot over from none other than Carly Carlotta. Maggie was surprised to see her there in person; usually she sent one of her lackeys. Carly sharply went after it, wanting to get the first dips at Maggie.

"Ms. Malone, so tell us about the love interest you met on set. Who is this ruggedly handsome young man that swept you off your feet?" Carly smirked over her shoulder tossing her hair up towards the other reporters, all peering at her with evil envious eyes. They were steaming she got the first bite of cheese.

Everyone waited eagerly for Maggie's response. It suddenly grew very quiet, which is hard to imagine at a Hollywood press conference. Maggie began to speak slowly, trying to find her words. Susan had prepared a response which Maggie ditched. She wasn't about to use Susan's sell out words for a fluff approach.

"That would be my fiancé, Jake Ryan. He is a world-class horse wrangler who trained me on the horse stunts I performed in the movie. We fell in love on set." Maggie looked over at Jake. He was smiling. She kept her explanation simple. The press grew anxious expecting more, barraging her with shouted questions.

Warren took over from there. "Ladies and Gentlemen, let's address the movie and the questions related to it for now, please. So much was involved with its production; details on the location and how amazing desert dust can truly be on actors and equipment."

Maggie leaned over to Warren whispering a thank you. The press conference continued with everyone now refocused on the movie. Questions about the setting, the other cast members, and the raising of the charity money became the new topics. Soon the press had their fill and prepared to scurry off in true mouse fashion.

Maggie saw this as her opportunity to calmly step up to the podium. She wanted all attention on her at this time. "Ladies and Gentlemen, I appreciate you all being here." Everyone in the room stopped and reset their focus again towards Maggie.

She cleared her throat and continued, "I know that you will do proper justice on covering this movie. It is a truly inspirational film that will reach people. Everyone that was a part of this movie put great heart and dedication into it. Thank you for giving them the professional attention they do so deserve. I know you still have a lot of personal questions for me, so I am taking this opportunity to give you all the information you so desperately want." Eyes opened wide and fingers began writing and typing, here is the scoop they all craved for.

"As you know, I take my roles very seriously, especially subjects that touch the heart. This role was a test for me. Most of you know I was raised on a ranch in a small town in the South. Being around the horses and the land brought back pieces of me that I forgot existed. Securely hidden away, protected from the public, not to be shared. They didn't fit into Hollywood, according to your standards. Being an accomplished Hollywood star while parading around in jeans and cowboy boots all the time, using Southern slang? Eating fried chicken and drinking gallons of sweet tea? This would have been hard to pull off, even for the best of actresses." Heads in the crowd shook a yes in agreement.

"I know you all have been the key to my career; you have made me a success. This success has brought causes to the public, which in turn have brought help to people in need. Unfortunately, Hollywood success comes at a huge personal price for all stars. Privacy is often an entity that is signed over in your own blood. You are expected to open your life's closet, exposing every detail. Sure, an occasional photograph on a run with no makeup or a picture out on the town having dinner with friends; those things are tolerable. The maliciousness comes when strangers dig through my trash or when people are literally living on my father's lawn, destroying all the flowers that he and my mother worked so hard to plant. That's when getting the scoop exceeds common decency. Let me ask you a question. How would you react if the shoes were on the other feet?" Maggie had the crowd's full attention, and they were feeling her justification finally.

"Tommy . . . " Maggie targeted a tabloid cameraman who had been continuously disregarding her requests to stay back for years. "How would you like to open your door to take your son Bradley to school, to face shouting strangers and cameras scaring him till he shakes? You quickly bring him in feared for his safety because they just won't back off. Bradley should never have to cover his frightened ears while you yell in anger and disappointment at the unrelenting camera crew nearly accosting your family on the front steps of your home. Shouldn't you both just open the door feeling the warmth of the sun on your faces and smelling the morning grass, grateful for another glorious chance of peace?'

Tommy put his camera down and dropped his head in embarrassment. Maggie continued to make her plea moving her attention to another reporter. "What about you, Cindy? What if you got sick?

Would you want to have your family find out from watching TV that you have cancer—before you can tell them yourself? You can't get back that lost moment of sad tenderness needing comfort from each other right then. All because someone sold out your privacy at the medical facility you attended. How would that feel?" Cindy put her hand over her mouth and tears began to build while she considered Maggie's scenario.

Maggie took a deep breath, wiping the tears streaming down her face. She was reliving all the times that she and other stars had been hurt, meticulously poked, and continuously invaded by the press. She continued. "Please take a second and think about each actor, famous person, public official, sports star, etc. you have ever pushed just a bit too far for your personal gain or ratings. Ask for their forgiveness. Show them the same kindness you would expect for your own family. Hollywood will bloom forever, no matter what. But wouldn't it be a much sweeter tiny spot on the world if we had some reciprocal respect between press and stars? Positive attention can be a powerful blessed tool for all involved. Sell positive news about people who use their celebrity status to make a caring difference in the lives of others. Get the story respectfully, work with honor and you will find plenty of stories like this. Those people are everywhere in here, out there, and even in Hollywood."

Maggie stopped for a minute, making eye contact with as many reporters as she could. She really wanted to make sure they were feeling her words. Then she finished up.

"Thank you for hearing me out. I have just one more thing to add . . . " Everyone waited on bated breath; what else could there be? She stood a strong ground, forcing everyone to think and rethink again. She kept them waiting for a few seconds as she wiped away dripping makeup. "Today I announce my resignation from the movie industry. This film was my last. I am going back to being the ranch girl that I have pushed away for so long. I will pursue the happiness, the love, and the future that I want for myself, not the one you want me to share with you. Please respect my decision and give me this. Thank you all for your time."

When Maggie walked away from the press conference, Syl was ready with the limo. Maggie's family and Jake were waiting inside. The limo pulled away as everyone at the press conference stood speechless, trying to pick their jaws up off the ground. They could not believe what had just happened. Maggie Malone, the biggest star in Hollywood, had just retired in her prime. Furthermore, she had stuck it to that entire press corps on her way out.

Susan was fit to be tied at first. If it weren't for the effort Maggie put into Susan as a friend, not just as a manager, Susan would have never let her out of her contract. Thankfully the two had created a bond of compromise through a little hard work of understanding. Maggie brought Susan to a new place, creating a new side of her, a place of grace. Susan decided to take the high road sharing in the pride of what they both had achieved. Besides, Maggie knew that she had landed a new client that would make her even more money. Maggie got a kick out of the fact it was a ten year old with a prickly disposition. Susan's built up patience from Maggie's stubborn ways would surely come in handy. Susan followed Maggie's instruction to decline any further interviews. After a month, the commotion started to die down. Maggie was the happiest she had ever been in her life. She was so ready to move forward in a new direction. She spent a couple of weeks with her mom and dad. Jake came to visit often but had to travel back to Home to work.

Maggie decided to purchase a ranch with an immense spread of land about an hour outside of Home as a surprise for Jake. They decided together to designate the ranch as The Star Horse Ranch for Children with Disabilities. Together they would use their new ranch to continue Jake's work making a difference in the lives of others.

Jake and Maggie were married on their new ranch just a few weeks later in a private ceremony conducted by Pastor James. Everyone from Home attended. Maggie's family, as well as Syl and his new wife Sharee, were also in attendance. The town of Home and the project were safe from discovery. The cover-up was an easy explanation: the Home residents were all friends of the groom.

Maggie expected an unwelcome intrusion by the press. She trusted her invitees to keep her special date, but her name was on the deed to the ranch after all. Surprisingly, not one member of the paparazzi crashed the wedding; not one helicopter, photographer, or reporter obtained a photo or video of their wedding. Perhaps Hollywood had finally started on its road to rediscovering the understanding and meaning of the words "respect for privacy."

CHAPTER TWENTY-EIGHT
CONGRATULATIONS, MAGGIE!

A PERSON TO PERSON TELEGRAM came for Maggie a week after the wedding. *Who uses telegrams anymore?* The telegram was short and to the point. No information about the sender was indicated. It read simply, "Congratulations, Maggie. You shine brighter than any star I've ever known. Project is intact. Your Home is safe. Destroy this telegram as soon as you're finished reading it. Regards, Ms. A."

Maggie's joy was complete to have received such a note. What a feeling of relief that she didn't do anything to damage the project. She wondered what Ms. A thought about her choice to leave Hollywood. It wasn't a surprise to figure out that she was proud of her.

Several months after the wedding, everyone returned for the dedication ceremony of the ranch. Camille, Star's mom, was the first horse on the ranch to give a ride to one of the precious, disabled children. The plaque posted on the front gates to the ranch read: "This ranch is dedicated to the children who may never walk but will always ride."

After the ceremony, everyone headed home except Syl and Sharee. They stayed to visit with Jake and Maggie.

"Mags, I have decided to step away from the whole Hollywood scene after your inspiring exit." Maggie smiled and went over to give Syl a hug.

A thought came to her mind. "Hey, I could really use a great head of security for the ranch. We could build you a house on our property. It would be great. We could hang out and have barbecues and . . . "

Maggie was so excited about the idea that she didn't stop until she saw Syl looking away at Sharee.

"Mags, thank you, but we are going to live near my parents. I need my family around me again. But I will miss you and all your craziness, little lady." Syl gave Maggie another hug.

"Thank you, Syl, for everything, including putting up with my craziness." Maggie choked on her words, tears pooling in her eyes. Jake and Sharee smiled at each other shaking their heads at Syl and Maggie.

Now Maggie's days were filled with giggly, happy smiles from children having their first ride on a horse; long swings on the porch with her best friend Lynn next to her, sipping lemonade; tea parties with Ruby Louise; mornings in church and evenings at church dinners. She loved picnics with Jake by the stream and horse rides where they still raced each other. She often won of course. Maggie's life was truly full, just like her heart.

Jake and Maggie were cleaning out the barn one afternoon when CJ came running from the road. He had their mail in his hand. Out of breath, he yelled to Maggie before he was halfway to the house, "Mrs. Maggie, Glenda at the post office said there was something that looked important in here for you." Maggie looked at Jake, both of them wondering what could possibly be so important.

"Well, I guess small town snooping is our new nemesis. Good thing Glenda is so sweet," Maggie said sarcastically to Jake. They both laughed.

Maggie reached her hand out to CJ as he stopped short before running into her. CJ handed her the mail, and Jake watched Maggie as she opened the letter. She stumbled back, letting out a gasp while grabbing her mouth as the rest of the mail dropped to the ground. Jake ran to her side.

She was startled and shaking, so Jake held her, concern evident in his voice. "Are you okay, honey? What is it?"

Nodding her head, Maggie motioned towards the envelope. Jake put his arms around Maggie and held her tight. The letter was from the Academy of Motion Picture Arts and Sciences. Maggie had been nominated for the Oscar for best actress in a dramatic film for her role in her final movie.

Maggie was overwhelmed. She was already blessed. God had given her a chance to be really happy and to enjoy a normal, full life away from stardom. Now she was being recognized by the same people who knew what it had meant for her to sacrifice that life.

Maggie sat for the rest of the afternoon wondering. How did she get in the running? Was it because of her decision to leave Hollywood at the peak of her career? Or was it because she invested every bit of herself into that role?

"It's just like me to have everything I ever wanted and still over think it." No more thinking. Maggie was done with wasting time. She realized that a nomination was an outstanding honor. She should just be proud and thankful for it.

Keeping up with the ranch and its schedule was the current focus of her energy. Besides, she had no chance of winning; she was up against some real pros that were all seasoned and extremely talented. After all, she was out of the limelight, and they were smack dab still in it. Besides her exit was abrupt and dismissing, according to some press who still missed the chase of her.

Maggie framed her nomination and hung it up in her memory room. She gave one last smile at it as she closed the door behind her. Thoughts of Hollywood showed up less and less in her mind as the month went by.

One afternoon Maggie was playing fetch with Hoss when she heard several cars coming up the driveway. She wondered who might be coming since she wasn't expecting anyone. From a distance, she recognized the dark van as being similar to those often used by the paparazzi.

Maggie's heart started to race. She began to yell Jake's name as she headed toward the house.

Jake was startled by her shouting and ran to her quickly. Then he saw what was coming.

"Why, Jake? Why now?" Maggie asked sadly.

Jake wasn't going to let anyone upset her. "Go inside, Maggie, I will handle this," he instructed her. Jake ran halfway down the drive. He put his hands up to motion for the van to stop. The windows were dark, but Jake could make out a couple of guys inside. He ran aggressively to the window that was opening on the driver's side. "You have no right to be here!" He shouted as he got closer to the van window. "You're trespassing on private property. You have been on my property for the last half mile. Now if you want trouble, you will have it. I suggest you turn this van around and . . . "

The driver finally interrupted him. "Sir, sir, calm down. We were sent by the Academy Awards Committee. Maggie has been nominated for the Oscar. They knew she wouldn't come, so they sent us to video her acceptance speech in case she wins"

Taking a deep breath, Jake changed gears from angry protector to proud husband. "Oh, man, okay! Sorry, guys. It's just . . . " Jake rambled on still getting his head straight.

"It's okay, sir. You don't need to explain. We understand. We're sorry for taking you both by surprise, but we are instructed to be very discreet. We could not tell anyone or call you ahead of time. It's a very secret procedure, so sorry. We took a chance Maggie would be here. Is she home?"

"Yes, yes, she's home. She will be thrilled. Give me some time to tell her and to allow her to freshen up, please. You guys come around to the back. Kindly be careful with that equipment. Don't step on the flowers. We just got those to grow," Jake instructed as he left to go to Maggie. His mind was all over the place in excitement for his wife, thus the last minute anxious instructions about the flowers.

Maggie sat nervously hiding in their bedroom peeking ever so slightly out the window. She had seen the entire interaction and felt her anxiety worsening. *Why is Jake inviting them in? What is going on?*

Jake hurried up the stairs to Maggie. She couldn't hold her curiosity in anymore. "What do they want, Jake? Why did you tell them to come in? Jake, I can't take this now. You know that!" She insisted.

Grabbing Maggie's hand, Jake began to calm her. He spoke to her gently. "Hold on there, sweetie. It's not what you think. They aren't here to bother us. Please sit down and take a deep breath. Please, honey." Jake was quite familiar with Maggie's anxiety attacks by now, although she hadn't had one in a long time since her new life had brought such healing.

Maggie and Jake sat at the foot of the bed until Maggie began breathing evenly. Jake continued once she was calm. "Mags, they are just here to video your acceptance speech in case you win the Oscar. It's standard procedure. Please don't be worried, I will make sure it goes smoothly."

Jake gave Maggie a short supportive hug, while Maggie agreed, "Okay, I understand. Let's do it" They grinned at each other; it was meant to be a celebratory moment. There was a time crunch with the guys already setting up downstairs.

"Honey, go ahead and freshen up. You do have an acceptance speech ready, don't you?" Jake questioned.

Maggie smiled a bit uneasily as she shook her head no.

"It's okay, sweetie. Just thank them from your heart. It will be fine. You'll do great," Jake reassured Maggie.

Maggie cleaned up. It took her longer to find something to wear than it did to do her hair and makeup. She assumed she would have some help if they had a makeup person with them.

Heading downstairs very slowly, Maggie took one step at a time, holding tightly to the banister. She was still a bit shaky from all the wonderful commotion. The crew met her at the bottom of the stairs. They introduced themselves and thanked her for meeting with them on such short notice. Makeup gave her a bit of powder.

Maggie sat down in the rocking chair Jake had made for her with the quilt from the ladies of Home draped on the back. They were all set to start. At first sight of the temporary Oscar, Maggie's eyes glazed over in wonder, holding one for the first time. Her hand started shaking as she accepted it from the crew.

"Whenever you're ready, Ms. Malone," the cameraman informed her.

Moving around in her chair, fidgeting a bit nervously, Maggie finally got comfortable. The red light came on the camera, and the cameraman gave her thumbs up.

"Hi, everyone, I am so honored to have received this Oscar. My love and gratitude goes out to the ladies who were nominated right next to me. Thank you all for paving the way for women like me by setting an outstanding example for us to follow. I want to thank my family, my husband Jake, and our church family. You put the South back into this southern girl, the person I truly am the proudest to be. I also want to thank everyone I worked with in the making of this film. I couldn't have asked for a more hardworking dedicated team of professionals to work with on my last film. Thanks for putting up with the dirt, the hot weather, and my stubbornness. My love and thanks to Syl and Susan. You both are a part of my extended family. Thanks for being there as friends. Truly, my biggest thanks goes to the most important person in my life. He is the reason I am blessed with any ability. Lord, thank You. You are awesome!"

The cameraman stopped the video, commenting that it was perfectly done on the first go round. Maggie looked over to Jake as the camera crew started to pack up, grinning in relief that all went well. She politely handed the Oscar back to the crew. It wasn't hers but it was nice to hold one just the same.

The crew was gone as quickly as they came. Things went back to normal on the ranch and stayed that way for the next month or so. Maggie anticipated the televised event of the Academy Awards but had no intention of attending. She felt comfortable with her decision to let that all go the day she left Hollywood. Besides after a nice long talk with Jake and Susan, she wasn't letting anyone down. Susan agreed with Maggie, her performance was certainly worthy of the award, but Hollywood would probably vote differently. Out of respect for Maggie and all her hard work, Susan told her she would attend in her honor.

On the evening of the awards, Maggie sat in her rocking chair on the patio, wrapped in her quilt. Jake had the television running in the family room, and the front door to the patio was cracked open. Maggie could hear the awards presenters just about to announce the award for best actress in a dramatic film.

Jake called to Maggie, "Hun, they are about to announce it. Are you coming in?"

Maggie just sat still rocking in her chair and replied, "I am fine right here. I can hear it."

She was glued to the rocking chair by a little bit of stubbornness—as if it didn't matter—mixed with determination to be satisfied—no matter the outcome.

Then it came.

"The award for best actress in a dramatic film is . . . " Maggie and Jake both separately had their prayer hands up to their mouths, neither one knowing they were doing this.

As the envelope was being opened, the utter stagnant silence that stretched all the way from Dolby Theatre in Los Angeles, CA, to the Ryan ranch in the southern USA was lingering.

"Maggie Malone in *Her Country Pride*."

Jake stood straight up, in shock, sputtering, "Oh my gosh, oh my gosh, Maggie . . . you did it! You did it!"

He was so taken by the moment that he couldn't stop looking at the television. Finally, he got a hold of himself and rushed to Maggie's side concerned for how excited she would be.

Maggie sat still, her hand gently resting on her stomach. Her eyes filled with proud tears and her heart was overwhelmed with love. She looked fondly down to her very pregnant belly and cooed, "Look, sweetie. Look what Mama has done. Through the blessings of God, you can accomplish anything!"

Jake came over to her in a hurry and knelt to hug and kiss her. His words poured out tenderly, "I am so proud of you, Maggie. I love you so much."

Susan was at the podium, thanking everyone on Maggie's behalf. They played Maggie's videoed acceptance speech. The whole crowd started to applaud and one by one everyone stood up, until all the seats were empty. There weren't just applauding for her win of the Oscar, they were applauding for her win against the paparazzi. What she had done, paving a way for respectful privacy for actors, would never be forgotten.

Maggie closed her eyes as a joyous tear rolled down her cheek, reminding her of Philippians chapter four, verse thirteen she had read earlier that day in her prayer daybook: "I can do all things through Christ which strengtheneth me."

For more information about
Annmarie M. Roberts
and
Hollywood is Not Home: A Novel
please visit:

www.AnnmarieRoberts.com

For more information about
AMBASSADOR INTERNATIONAL
please visit:

www.ambassador-international.com

*Thank you for reading, and please consider leaving us a review
on Amazon, Goodreads, or our websites.*